The enigmatic end to Bethany Reed

THE DEBUT NOVEL BY

ASHLEA STANNARD

THE ENIGMATIC END TO BETHANY REED

For information contact:
ashleastannard.business@gmail.com

Book and Cover design by Ashlea Stannard
ISBN: 9798596356076

First Edition: November 2021

for my mum,

because you're wonderful and i don't say it

enough.

hell is empty
and all the devils are here.

WILLIAM SHAKESPEARE

THE BEGINNING

bethany

SEPTEMBER 21ˢᵗ, 2017, 4:12pm

This town is wretched. It is a grotesque, aching thing burnt to the bone by prejudice and violence and the innate suffering that accompanies infinite dullness. There is nothing but raw pain behind every street and every light and every speeding car.

Eastwood, Maine.

It's a pretty name—promising trees and nature and beauty and Maine's charm. Eastwood, Ashwell County. *Ashwell.* That is a pretty name, too—promising sophistication and nice streets with nice names and close communities and tight-knit families.

Eastwood.

Eastwood, Ashwell County, Maine.

It is as ugly as the thing inside of me you might call a heart.

**

September 21.

I've never particularly enjoyed Thursdays, but I feel as if this one is an emphasis on that. There's this new kid, Nicolas, who hit on me in French. He's kind of cute.

Nevae got turned down by her crush (although I never really thought Elodie was much of a nice girl anyway).

Jackson. Well, Jackson is always okay.

I've just gotten home. My sister, Evie, on the couch opposite me, is sifting through and ripping up sheet music. I watch her sleepily, as she sorts through her perfect life and organises it with the keenest of concentration. I wish I could be more like her.

Fourteen, a freshman, and untouched by many of life's most anguished sides. I've wanted to be like her for as long as I can remember. Excellent grades. Saving up for college. She works part time in the kitchen at Cathy's Diner. She has a very close friend, Mae, and they've known each other and loved each other for twelve years.

Nevae and Jackson might be my friends, but we don't love each other as endlessly and faultlessly as Evie loves Mae and Mae loves Evie.

"What are you looking at?" Evie is talking to me.

I blink. "What?"

"Are you okay?"

"I'm fine."

Evie nods and goes back to what she's doing. Lean, long fingers running over paper as if they are the most delicate thing in the world. In a moment, she will put it all down and set up the music stand that lies on the floor and nestle the honey-coloured cello by her side between her knees and tighten her bow and rosin it and start to play. Mom and Dad will come out of the kitchen and listen to the startling, lengthy measures of Bach and smile at each other in that tight-lipped way they do now that they hate each other.

I will sit there and listen and try not to cry because *why the fuck did I become the messed up one.*

PART 1

EASTWOOD

IS

MY

HOME

EASTWOOD, ASHWELL COUNTY PD
CASE NO. 2018010902
Incident Report
Victim: **BETHANY NICOLE REED**
Manner of death: **SUICIDE**
Date and time of death: **01/09/2018 21:19**
Cause of death: **DROWNING**
Place of death: **EAST BANK OF CLERWOOD RIVER, EASTWOOD FOREST**

Witness statement of individual who discovered the body:

Name: **ARNOLD WINDSOR, 4 FOREST ROAD (WICKSTEED COTTAGE)**

Statement:

I was out late, searching for firewood. I didn't realise our winter store had run out (it's never happened before), but I reached for a log to put on the fire and, alas, there was none there. So instead of bothering the neighbours, since I'm not sure they like us very much anyway, I decided to get some fresh air and took off down to the woods with my axe. I heard the splash: but god, it was quiet. I wasn't too far from Devil's Pathway at the time, and it seemed to come from that kind of direction, so I headed over to take a look, make sure the teenagers weren't messing about and disturbing the wildlife. My own daughter, Hailey, has been brought home in a police cruiser a fair few times. Anyway, I headed on over to the river, and there was some kind of figure lying in the water. Not struggling or anything. I dropped my wood and my axe and leaned over the edge, then pulled her out. I recognised her immediately, but there was nothing I could have done.

She was dead when I pulled her out of the water, and people don't drown that quickly. Call me a cynic, but I don't think she drowned, Sheriff.

1] GOOD DAY TO DIE

JANUARY 9TH, 2021, 1:36 pm

It's almost overwhelming how many trees there are. Tall pines and silver-trunked birches stripped bare of their green by the harsh grips of winter. They're on all sides of the truck, squeezing and covering and suffocating.

I tail Dad's SUV carefully and slowly, trying to take in my surroundings. It's hard to believe this is the place I'm supposed to call home. This place couldn't be more different to the flat, grey landscape we left behind.

The road we're on is long and winding, and we haven't seen another car for ten minutes. It feels like a trap.

"We're almost there, River, just turn left up here and then look for the sign," Dad says through the walkie talkie on my dashboard. I reach up blindly for it, fishing through chip packets and cans.

"Roger that," I say before tucking the radio into the centre console.

The song on the radio fizzles out when I start to turn the corner, and my phone buzzes with a *no signal* warning.

Great. The truck staggers around the corner and the town's name appears on a sign that looks like it's seen better days.

It's battered and weathered and some of the paint is worn down and missing. Yet through all the wear, you can still make out the words painted onto it.

Welcome to Eastwood, where the trees are always green.

I scoff and look around at all the leafless trees, barren by the harshness of the January cold. *Yeah, okay.*

"Almost there, son! Just keep following me," The radio crackles again. The truck's windscreen is suddenly filled with a panoramic view of my new home.

Before he announced we were moving here, Dad never mentioned this place. Not once. But when he came home with the news we were relocating to America, he told us about his hometown. It was green, he said. So green. And there was a river that the children played in, and it was beautiful and fun, and *we would love it.* His stories painted pictures of liveliness and vibrance and his words were bleeding, stuffed full of nostalgia and leaking bright gold into his usually dull eyes.

That is not the Eastwood we see now.

It's pretty dismal, to be honest.

The street we're on is bordered by squat little houses that look like they're made of paper, and they're all spattered with the same amount of dirty paint and overgrown lawns. In its entirety, the town looks like it's in a perpetual state of dismal rain. Everything is wet, soaked through, and I can't help but pick out large areas of rot.

The town's elements all seem to reside in the same shade of grey or beige— from the damp silver of the asphalt on the sidewalk to the sky itself, dark grey and ominous and promising nothing but misery.

"Just like I remember it," Dad says, but there's an edge to his voice. An uncertainty that's rare for him. It's clear that this town aged alongside him. All those years he spent pretending this place never existed, it withered away in the clutches of time. Or maybe it always looked like this, and a child's eye created facades; only choosing to let the good through, and that is the Eastwood he remembers.

We turn down another road, and there's a few shops and a grocery store with a couple of teenagers milling about in front of it. A car zips past us—an ugly purple Volvo Estate looking like it's headed out at inhuman speed. Whoever's driving seems like they hate this place as much as I already do.

**

Our house is on the other side of town.

Northern Eastwood is made up of newer developments organised in neat rows but still managing to portray the town's messy, clumsy essence. This part of Eastwood is just an extension of the other parts—copy and paste. The dull, stumpy structures are all here, but now they are crammed together like an army of overwhelming, suffocating *beige*.

Hastings Road. Number 16. It's pretty small and dank and exaggerates just how different my life in New Brunswick was to the one I am fitting into now. Especially when you compare it to the airy grey stone, five-bedroom colonial in the suburbs that we left behind.

The new house is one story and doesn't look to be much bigger than a trailer home. It looks like all the other ones on the street, and the street next to it, and—well, you get the picture.

"Home sweet home," Dad says with a satisfied huff. He's got Hadley in his arms, and she's asleep. Good. She's been crying since the border, crackled and loud through the radio. I wonder if she'll remember this when she's my age. If she'll remember the heartbreak we left behind or the way that Dad looks now—breathless, exuberant. It could be my hopeful imagination, but I swear there's a whisper of disappointment or something akin to it in the shadows under his eyes.

"Home sweet home," I repeat, quietly, under my breath.

"You like it, son?" Dad claps me on the shoulder and pulls a set of keys out of his pocket. "I love it. It's the house I always wanted."

I nod along, hauling my backpack out of my truck and following him through the front door. The inside is as melancholy and scarred by years of damp and mould as you'd think. Water damage bleeds across the walls, manipulating them into dull shades of yellow. Dad sets the keys down on the wobbling but intact kitchen table, and kisses Hads on the head. "We'll head over to grandma's in a bit, just get your stuff into your room."

Grandma lives a couple blocks away from here, I think. I've only ever seen her in photographs. She never wanted to leave Eastwood and until now, Dad didn't want to come back, so she stayed here, and we stayed in Canada. I wonder again what could possibly have driven Dad away from here and scared him off so badly that he never even came back to visit his own mother.

2] IN MEMORIAM

evelyn

JANUARY 9TH, 2021, 7:42pm

It's late. I didn't mean for the sun to set, but it has.

I didn't mean to spend so long out here, but I have.

The air is cold, and the wind pricks my skin like a thousand tiny needles. I can't see the trees anymore, just a sheet of darkness, broken only by the dull glow of the stars through the thin wisp of clouds. I can't see the river anymore, but I can hear it. The sound of it moving. The rush as it hurries from one place to the next.

Home. It sounds like home.

But everyone is scared of the dark at least a little bit, so the lack of light and the inability to see the path that leads back to the Volvo and, therefore, back home, puts me on edge.

I'm unnerved: hands fidgeting, legs trembling from a mix of fear and the chill getting to me.

January 9th.

Three years ago, probably around this time, the police knocked on the door and asked for my parents, so I called them from the kitchen and Deputies Cabot and Tia told us that they'd found by sister's body in the river, that she'd killed herself, that they're sorry for our loss, that-

Bang.

A sound louder than anything I've ever heard before shatters the forest, splintering it into a thousand pieces. My heart picks up. My feet pick up.

Fear and instinct make my feet kick off the ground and I'm running almost before I've really registered what the sound really is. A gunshot?

No.

The only guns around here are in Loye Valley, used in their hundreds of acres of Eastwood Forest. Hunters aren't allowed in this side of the forest.

Something's wrong.

Maybe you can tell when someone has died nearby.

I swear I can taste it— the salt of blood, the dank air clinging to my skin, fear and exertion tugging sweat from my pores.

And then

I

stumble.

3] FAMILY OF MINE

river

JANUARY 9TH, 2021, 3:38pm

When the heating's on, my bed has sheets on it and I've turned on the lights, my room isn't that bad. It's tiny, with just a double bed pushed into one corner and a desk under the window with drawers across the room. This is all stuff that an old friend had picked up from a Goodwill nearby for us.

Exactly two hours after we arrived, the light through the windows gets weaker. It's nearing four, and Dad's wearing a *tie*. We're going to see Nana— the mother Dad left behind.

At the sight of my father in an actual tie, I'm quite frightened to meet this Nana. If she can get my Dad in a tie (who's literally the most chilled out and disorganised person I've ever met I didn't even know he owns a tie) then she can probably do anything. Dad looks over my

outfit (road trip clothes— wrinkled t-shirt and faded jeans
with rips), and then scrunches his nose.

"I can change if you want?" Into what? I don't own
anything even remotely close to what this Grandma seems
to want to see.

"Don't worry, son, I'm sure you'll be fine."

"I don't want my first impressions to be disastrous," I
counter, taking a step back, towards my room, towards
nicer clothes.

Dad unlocks the door and Hadley squeals. "Don't
worry,"

He's wound up like a spring, and quite frankly, it's
terrifying. I haven't seen him so frowny and odd since
Grace's funeral.

"Nana!" Hadley squeals as I reach down and swoop
her up into my arms. Her hair smells like sweat and greasy
gas station food, and I make a mental note to wash it later.
It's plaited into two uneven pigtails and tied off with
orange ribbon. She's wearing her good dress: the only one
that isn't stained, the one Grace made.

We take Dad's green SUV, and the drive through the
town is nicer now. It's rush hour, so the streets are filled
with cinematic, hazy headlights fighting through the
rapidly dimming light. I can see the stars a little, and only
strips of houses are illuminated by yellow streetlights. It's
beautiful in an eerie, strange kind of way.

Nana lives at the end of Beaumaris Avenue in a house
not unlike ours, just with a bit more life. There are flowers
lining the path up to the porch and a porch swing covered
with cushions with dogs and ducks on them. There are
wellington boots outside the door and a welcome mat.

This is the Grandma house I had always imagined.

I'm surprised at the stark normalcy surrounding this house, since Dad's side of the family has always seemed dysfunctional and mysterious and just as strange as Dad. I guess it's kind of weird to see something so… different from what I imagined.

"Knock knock, Mom!" Dad knocks on the door and grins at us both. There's a strain to it that makes my stomach churn and dread settle in my stomach.

When the door opens, I'm surprised.

Nana is short and thin, with Dad's Hispanic tanned skin and wispy dark hair that falls around her face in thin waves. She's not as old as I imagined a Nana would be. Early sixties, maybe? When I look at her closer, I can see the resemblance between her and the face I see in the mirror every day. She has my round chin—curving like a smile—and my long legs and short torso.

"Oh, Mateo!" She coos, hugging him and patting his back with surprising strength. When they pull apart, she steps out of the door and cups my cheek, dark eyes staring into mine. A tear traces a path down her cheek, and I smile in that tense *I don't know you I'm just being polite* type of way.

"River." She says. She says my name like she's never said it before, like it's a secret she's afraid of telling.

"Hi, Nana," I say.

She moves onto Hadley, who's sitting against my hip. Hadley reaches out for the locket around Nana's neck and smiles without looking her in the eye.

"Hadley." Nana says. "It's wonderful to meet you both. Come on, come inside out of the cold,"

She is not at all what I expected, but what did I really expect?

**

We sit in her little living room and Dad has some beer and Nana gives me orange juice, and Hadley tucks into a plate of chocolate cookies. I tell her about school and how my SATs went, and which colleges I plan to apply to in the spring (Saint John College, my plan is to go back to New Brunswick and pretend Eastwood never happened). She doesn't mention my mom, or any of Dad's other wives. She either doesn't know about them or is wise enough to know they're not really a conversation you have in front of your grandkids.

When we leave it's nearing eight and Hadley is asleep in Dad's arms. "It's been a long day." He says to Nana, who finds Hads a blanket from one of the armchairs in her living room and wraps her in it, cooing over the two-year-old with such motherly instinct that I wonder if she misses having her son around.

She insists we take the blanket home with us and kisses me on the cheek before we leave. Whilst Dad straps Hadley in, she tugs me onto the porch and hugs me tightly. "You look after your old man," she says, "he needs you. You need him."

I nod. "Of course,"

And she gets all teary-eyed. "It was truly wonderful to finally meet you, River. Eighteen years is far too long to not see your grandchildren, or your son. I'm glad he's brought you all back. Eastwood is where you belong,"

I want so badly to ask her what changed; why Dad left the place he loved so much, but I just nod. She sounds so sure of herself, but I really don't believe that I belong here. It's all so foreign and quiet and not seeing the city on the horizon is something I'll probably never get used to. So I smile and step off the porch.

"See you soon, Nana."

"You too, River!"

And for some reason I feel a little bit better about Eastwood after meeting Nana. Is this how people feel about their grandparents?

**

It's whilst we're on the way home that it happens.

The SUV's radio is cranking out shit from some oldie station, and Hadley is asleep in the backseat. Dad is humming along to the song, and I am staring at my phone, plucking up the courage to text Ophelia, a friend from New Brunswick.

The road is dark except for the occasional headlight brightening the rain-soaked roads. It rained whilst we were at Nana's. I'm slightly terrified that we're going to drown in this town.

And then, out of nowhere, a figure staggers into our way.

Dad slams on the breaks so hard and so abruptly that my head flies forward and nails into the dashboard, making stars appear behind my eyes. But there is no impact.

I look up, letting my eyes focus on what the hell just happened. And there she is: a girl, hunched over the front of the car, covered in blood.

4] LOOKING FOR LIGHT

evelyn

JANUARY 9ᵀᴴ, 2021, 7:58pm

The first thing I can discern under the dim glow of the streetlights is the hazy red stuff under my fingernails and on my hands and it's leaking into my clothes and I. Can't. Breathe.

The second thing I can discern through the ringing in my ears is that someone is talking to me. Voice like honey, but a little raw in places. Panicky. Anxious. I know the shaking unsteady edge to the words as well as I know the curves of my own voice. This voice is fucking terrified.

"Where are you hurt?" It's asking me.

I choke. Cough. Splutter a reply. "I'm *not*,"

Because I'm not, am I? There's no pain. Other than the splitting, sharp ache in my chest but I know that's more from shock than anything else. And the skin on my hands is puckering and red from the asphalt and my knees are grazed. But I'm not dead.

A hand. On my elbow, my arm, helping me up, helping me stand but my legs won't hold me, and I stumble.

"River?" Another voice. Louder. Authoritative.

The voice of a father, I think.

"Call an ambulance, Dad."

Dad.

"No!" I say, sudden strength filling me. Our insurance ran out last year. I grapple at this person. *River.* That's his name. *River.* Ironic.

"What?" River asks. I cough again, standing up straighter. Forcing my legs to cooperate and do their effing job.

"I'm not *hurt.* Just take me to the Sheriff's station," I manage.

There's silence.

I clear my throat, letting go of River. "Please." He looks torn and conflicted. I wonder what it means to be a stranger that cares so much about other strangers.

They put me in the front seat, next to River's Dad. River, who I can now see properly in the SUV's bright interior lighting, sits in the back next to a sleeping baby. River is tall and lean (his father is, too) and has skin the colour of milky coffee and toast just the way I like it. His hair is black and curly and messy and as wild as my own. I reach a shaking hand up to my hair, feeling the familiar frizz and suddenly getting the urge to smooth it out as if my appearance can be made bearable.

"Sorry." I say. The engine comes to life and sets off down the road.

River's Dad arches a brow, "For what?"

"For getting blood on your seats,"

He chuckles. "Don't worry. They're leather, it'll just wipe right off."

I wish my own pain could be so impermanent.

****

The building that houses Eastwood Police Department (a branch of Ashwell County Police Force) is a tall, towering thing. Old, one of the oldest buildings of the town. It's leaning to the side now.

The Sheriff's Department insignia is sprawled across the front doors, and the light is on outside. I pray and hope to everything in the sky that Mohamed Whittle is working tonight.

"Thank you," I say to River's Dad and River, and I hope the little girl asleep in the back hears it too, because she's waking up and, well, the bloodied teenager is invading her space as well. River's Dad and River nod and smile like perfectly polite people and I wonder vaguely why I've never seen them before. Eastwood is a very small town.

"Good luck." River says. He waves. I wave back, not really wanting to leave the warm car with the lights and the polite people because that means facing reality, and reality is not a very nice place right now. In this town, it never is.

I heave myself from the front seat and shut the door, waiting on the sidewalk until the SUV drives away, off into the night, and I wonder if I will ever see these people again.

River and River's Dad and River's probably sister. Nice people. Mannerly people.

There's a brutal silence, a stretch of quiet, frozen time where it is just me and the streetlights (one's broken, one by the entrance, and there's a patch of shadow there, waiting) and my dark, gory thoughts. I don't look down. Down at my shoes, which were my sister's, which are probably caked in blood and mud and if I think about the only thing I have left of Bethany then I will cry.

And I don't want to cry, because Mohamed will worry, and he will call my mother and my mother will fuss and see me covered in blood and think of Bethany and-

"Evelyn?"

James Cabot is standing in the doorway of the Sheriff's station, watching me. James Cabot is a good person. Strict, neat and from a fancier town in a fancier place, but he is a good person. Tall and solid and peaceful.

He looks at me.

"Are you okay?" He asks, rushing down the steps. I am confused for a single moment that is broken away from the rest and then I realise that I am, in fact, covered head to toe in blood and mud.

"I'm fine. I promise." I say, waving away his fuss single-handedly. James steps back. He doesn't fuss, he's not that kind of person. Did I hit my head?

Dizziness forces spots and clouds into my eyes and I stumble a bit on the pavement.

"But—"

"The blood isn't mine,"

James stares at me. Really, really stares at me. And then his face falls. Collapses in on itself like a broken building. "Oh, *Evelyn*—" Because somehow it is even worse that the blood is not my own, that I had to experience something that ended with this much blood.

21

My eyes start to sting with the promise of tears, but I tell them off and instead put on my best *I am completely okay but please don't talk to me anymore because I will cry* face.

"I need to talk to Sheriff Whittle, and I need to talk to him now." I am surprised at the tone of my voice; at the way it doesn't break.

James winces and nods and leads me up the steps, and I don't know how I'm following him because I can't feel my legs. Shock. I must be in shock.

Shock.

Yeah, I effing got a bloody shock.

Inside the station is quiet, as is probably usual for the late evening. I recognise Deputy Tia, hovering by the photocopier in reception, and she recognises me. She goes to move, and James gives her a look, which makes her stop. One of Tia's hugs, though, is exactly what I need right now.

We head down the hallway, to the end, where Mohamed's office is. James knocks twice. "Sir, I've got Evelyn here. She needs to talk to you,"

"Two minutes, James! Take her to the waiting area, and I'll be right out."

"No, sir, I mean I think you need to talk to her, like, *now*,"

There's a quiet stretch and I try to stop my hands from shaking.

Then the door opens, and Mohamed is there and he's looking at me and just like that I'm crying and sobbing and shaking and stumbling and coughing and he's holding me, holding me as I fall into him.

"Jackson—" I choke, barely breathing, "Jackson is *dead*."

*****

Jackson is dead. This fact is very, very true. This fact is also very, very painful to think about and to believe.

Mohamed holds me for a bit. James leaves us there in the hallway. And then, a thousand hours later, he steers me into the sterile interview rooms. The harsh scrape of heaving, painful sobs rises up in my throat again, but I push it down with every bit of strength I have left. I don't want to do this right now.

"I don't want to do this right now."

I sit on the plastic chair on one side of the table.

"I know, Evie, I know." But he doesn't get up.

"I can't think straight, Mohamed, I can't—"

"You *can*. You're just blocking it out because it's too painful."

"I don't want to think about what happened." I say. "*Please*. I just want to go home,"

His face is grave. His uniform creased from a hard, long day that I have just made impossibly longer. I wonder if Jackson's parents have been contacted yet, if my sister's best friend is being mourned as much as she was. I wonder if I will ever be able to go back there. To the forest. My favourite place, before Jackson was on the floor and I was tripping over him and falling and

"Would you like to tell me what happened?"

"I—"

The silence.

It's loud.

"I was in the woods."

He waits.

"I was in the woods, and it was getting later and later and then it was dark, I guess."

23

"What time?"

"Like seven? Maybe? I don't know." This is difficult. It makes my heart ache and my breath come to me in short, staccato gasps or, some seconds, not at all. "Anyway, it was late— I must have fallen asleep or something, I remember there was a really loud noise,"

"Like a gunshot?"

Yes.

Like the deafening, deadly, monstrous *crack* of a bullet.

"Yes."

"What did you do then?"

I can see in the deep brown of his eyes the same fatherly kindness that has been there since the day I fell over on the pavement outside my house. Mom was inside, screaming at Bethany and my father and so I sat there, crying silent tears, until Mohamed came out and put a Band-Aid on my bloody knee and took me inside and I met Mae. Her mom, Julie, was pregnant with the twins and it was a wonderful, wonderful beginning.

"I ran."

I did. I ran through the dark woods, like something out of a crappy horror movie. Leaping and ducking and not doing a very good job, because half of me is stinging now, as the adrenaline wears off, as tiny but painful cuts start to announce their presence on my hands and my cheeks.

Mohamed is very quiet and very still. Waiting, again, I realise.

"And then I tripped on something, something hard and solid and… and big." I remember this part clearly. It will probably live at the forefront of my mind for the rest of my life. "I fell. Onto his body."

Mohamed looks like he himself is about to burst into tears. I feel an ache in my chest for him. Because it's him and Julie who are probably going to have to pick up the pieces from this, because God knows my Mom will try but she will not do a very good job.

"Oh, Evie." Tender.

"I tried to stop the bleeding, Mohamed, I swear I did, but it was like just coming and coming and oh, *God*," And I'm crying into his chest and he's holding me, and I can't breathe because

Jackson is dead.

EASTWOOD, ASHWELL COUNTY PD
CASE NO. 2021010901
<u>Incident Report</u>
Victim: **JACKSON MILLER**
Manner of death: **HOMICIDE**
Date and time of death: **01/09/2021 17:19**
Cause of death: **GUNSHOT WOUND TO HEAD**
Place of death: **EAST BANK OF CLERWOOD RIVER, EASTWOOD FOREST**

Witness statement of individual who discovered the body:
Name: **EVELYN REED, 17 HASTINGS ROAD, EASTWOOD**
Written statement:

I spend every year down here, at the bank (my sister's favourite spot in the forest) on the anniversary of her death. So I did this year. I came down early afternoon time and sat by the river and, you know. Time went really fast, I might have fallen asleep at one point, and when I realised how late it had gotten it was dark. It was about half five maybe when I got up to leave. And then I heard a gunshot, and it was really scary, so I ran and I ran and I tripped on something. It was Jackson. I tried to stop the bleeding or something, but I couldn't. So I kept running like an idiot and then there was this really bright light.

5] UGLY

JANUARY 10th, 2021, 9:21am

Day two in Eastwood is a rainy day. This is absolutely
not an exaggeration: it's like the sky is projectile vomiting
icy, grey stuff all over the ground. It's like sleet. Maybe, if it
was colder and we were a bit luckier, it would be perfect
white snow. But no. Instead, it's ugly insipid stuff that slips
down your back and makes you shiver.

I wake up in my new bed, but I don't get that second
of bliss where I think I'm still in New Brunswick, ready for
another day at Saint John Public School where I could
blend into two thousand students. No, I wake up and I'm
immediately in Eastwood, making a mental note to buy
blankets later. Many, many blankets.

I mean, New Brunswick came with its fair share of
cold days and colder nights, but this is jarring. A shock to
the system I only got once before, when we were on

vacation in Vancouver. Further north than the modest city
of Saint John.

Once I've gotten over the fact that I am, in fact, still
in hell and I did, in fact, find a bloody girl in the middle of
the road last night (as far as first impressions go, that was
certainly memorable), I lean over the bed and dig around
on the floor for the socks that came off last night and left
my feet resembling blocks of ice.

I put them back on and climb out from under the
covers. My door is ajar, and I push it further open, already
able to hear the sound of sizzling bacon (oh dear) and the
crashing of plates (double oh dear). Fun fact: Dad can't
cook. Not at all. Not even if there were fifty kids being
held at gunpoint, he would still manage to burn the eggs.

Making my trip to the bathroom as short and efficient
as possible (and discovering that he has not turned on the
hot water this morning), I enter the kitchen. Hadley is sat
on the counter, finding Dad's struggle unbelievably
entertaining. I start the disaster control by removing her
from the danger zone and placing her on the floor, near a
dollhouse that has obviously been haphazardly assembled
this morning.

And then I greet Dad, who looks a bit dazed.

"It's alright, Dad, I'll do it."

He smiles, but there's a reluctance behind him letting
go of the spatulas. I have to dump the bacon in the trash,
because unless he's developed a sudden craving for actual
charcoal, the blackened strips won't be eaten today.

The cooked breakfast, the not minding that I got up
far later than usual; it's all like he's trying really hard to be a
good dad, a good *person*.

"I love you, son." He says.

And he never says that to me anymore. I try not to tear up, and I say, "Love you too, Dad."

And he looks like he's trying not to tear up as well.

"I know you don't like me very much for this move, River, but it'll be good for us, I think."

Good for him, maybe. And then I hate myself for being so impossibly selfish.

"I know, Dad. I believe you."

Dad pulls away from me and goes to play with Hads on the floor, laughing and smiling like I haven't seen him do since Grace was alive. *Grace.* Nope. Not going to think about Grace right now. Instead, I'm going to make pancakes and French toast and prepare for my first day of senior year at a completely new school tomorrow.

I am so tremendously *not* excited.

6] MOTHER

evelyn

JANUARY 10th, 2021, 9:10am

She's tutting at me, clucking her tongue, like I've done something wrong.

"Always getting yourself in trouble, you are." Mom says, stroking my hair and handing me a mug of coffee. My eyes are tired, sore from a night of fitful, fleeting sleep. "Silly girl."

Silly girl. Silly girl, for tripping over a dead body.

"Silly, staying out so late. Calling for trouble,"

I stay silent.

"Silly." She says again, quietly under her breath. "Silly, bothering strangers like that."

I stay silent. I watch as she makes her way around the kitchen table, back to the counter, checking on the bread in the toaster. It's burnt. She butters it anyway and sets it down in front of me. She takes the seat next to mine and watches me with eyes the same pretty hazel as my own. The same pretty hazel that Bethany had.

My lovely girls with lovely eyes. Dad used to say that to us, admiring us like we were expensive art, and he couldn't quite believe that we were his.

I'd give anything for him to admire us all like that now. I'd give anything for us three to be together, a matching set again.

But my mother and Bethany and I will never be together again. And Dad will never admire us again.

"I'm sorry, Mom." I say. My throat is raw from crying.

She sighs, clucks her tongue again, and leans her head into her hand, watching. "Don't be sorry, Evelyn. I'm sorry that you had to find Jackson like that. Poor boy." She takes on a heavy look of sympathy. "Poor Mrs Miller."

She loses herself for a second, zoning out onto a spot above my head. I let her be. Mom knows what it's like to lose a child to that forest— knows the bottomless grief far too well.

"I might make them a casserole later." Mom says. "Poor family."

Poor family. I'm sure they're as broken now as we were three years ago. I'm sure that, three years from now, they'll still be as broken as we are now.

"And you can take some cookies or something to those lovely strangers that pulled you off the road before you ended up like Jackson."

The ruthless, stark property to her words take me by surprise. My mother is usually one to dance around topics like this. The abnormality of her statement is a testament to how much this has rattled her.

"I don't even know where they live."

"Across the road. The Lopez family just moved in across the street. Teenage boy, River, like you described. Man, too, Mateo. Mateo Lopez, River Lopez, and little Hadley. They look like a lovely family."

I'm taken aback. "They moved into number 16?" That house has been emptying since the Islingtons moved out in 2017. Mr and Mrs Islington lost their son, Aiden, to a car accident in the winter and moved out, to one of the neighbouring towns I think.

"Yes. Yes, you'll take them some muffins I think." Mom says, already standing up. She does this when bad things happen— she cooks and she gets things done, focusing on things other than the pain.

6] CONFIDE IN SOMEONE

river

JANUARY 10th, 2021, 12:58pm

Someone knocks on the door at almost exactly one in the afternoon. I'm in the shower, testing the limits of the water pressure (not the same jet wash feel as New Brunswick, but not as horrendous as I thought it would be), and I turn the steaming hot water off just as Dad pushes the door open.

There's muffled conversation, and then, "River! There's someone here to see you!"

I'm epically confused because I haven't lived in this town for quite twenty-four hours and the only person I've met that isn't related to me so far is—

"Hurry up, son, it's the girl from last night!"

And I realise then that she is just "the girl from last night" because we never exchanged names, and I wonder how she knows that we live here, but then again it's a very small town so news like this probably spreads pretty fast. I hurriedly jump out of the shower, towel off, and in five minutes I'm hurrying down the hallway. Only they're not at the door anymore, they're in the kitchen and the girl from last night is standing by the counter, watching Dad make coffee.

I smile, brushing the floppy mess of unstyled hair out of my face.

"It's you." I say.

She turns around, hearing my voice, and smiles back. But it's edged with something. Of course, she must be utterly not okay after last night. I mean, she was covered in blood, and apparently it wasn't hers.

"Are you okay?" I ask.

She nods, tight-lipped. "You're River, right?"

I wonder how she knows this information, since I definitely don't remember telling it to her.

"Yeah," I say.

She sticks out her hand, pale and small and calloused. I don't know what from. "I'm Evelyn."

"Evelyn." I say, as if testing the word out on my tongue. Dad finishes up the coffee, pouring the hot liquid into three mugs.

She winces at her name, "You can call me Evie. Basically everyone does,"

"How did you know I live here?" I ask her because I truly am curious.

"Small world. Smaller town. Besides, I live across the street and recognized the car. No one's lived here in ages, so I noticed. I also didn't recognise you last night, and I know everyone in this town. You just moved here?"

I nod. "From New Brunswick. You live across the street?"

"Number 16, Hastings Road." She nods. She picks up her coffee and takes a big swallow, even though it's piping hot, and I can't even dip my tongue in. Impressive.

"Are you alright, though?" Dad asks.

She nods, and I know by the look in her eye that she's just being polite, that she isn't okay at all, and why should she be?

"I'm good, thank you. I just came by to say thank you properly. I wasn't really with-it last night but what you did for me was really nice and yeah. Thank you,"

"It's no problem, really. We just did what anyone else would have done." Dad says.

I just sort of stare at her, trying to work out what happened. Why she was covered in blood that wasn't hers. Evie takes another big gulp of the coffee and winces as it goes down.

"Not people in Eastwood, really." She says, and her eyes go dark. "I really think you made a mistake moving here,"

Dad shifts, uncomfortable tension leaking into the air. "I grew up here, Evie, we moved back to be closer to family."

"Things have changed in the last few years, and I should probably go now because if people hear you've been talking to me or my family, then you'll never hear the end of it."

Dramatic and mysterious. Evie is quite something.

She sets the mug on the counter and smiles at us as if she didn't just give us such an ominous message and waves awkwardly. "Thanks again. Thanks for the coffee. River, will I see you at Elizabeth Gingham tomorrow?"

Elizabeth Gingham Memorial High School, mightily long-winded, is the only high school for miles. Located on the Southern edge of the town, part of the original Eastwood development, it's the biggest part of the town. More students go to the school than people who live in the town. I nod. "Yeah, yeah you will."

And she waves again and lets herself out, leaving the house in grave silence.

****

Later in the afternoon, I've finally finished unpacking the bulk of my boxes. There isn't enough room in the tiny room for some of my stuff, so I decide to pack it into the back of the truck and take it to the nearest Goodwill. Google Maps lets me know there's one in the next town over, Loye Valley, so I climb into the driver's seat and take my first outing.

The roads here are winding but wide, bordered on all sides by thick trees until you cross the bridge to Loye Valley. Then, they thin out and you can tell that this town is much bigger, vaster, and fuller than Eastwood. The road is littered with various hardware stores, factories, etc. and the further in you go, the more the sidewalks are crowded by bookshops, grocery stores, office stores and a plethora of other classic small-town amenities.

Goodwill is on the other side of town, so there's ten minutes of navigating the road through town before I come to the large building on the side of the road. After dumping the bags I brought into the donation bin around the side, I mooch in and end up buying a nice lamp for my nightstand.

When I'm back in Eastwood, I stop by Cathy's Diner, a little cafe/diner a minute from the house. The building is short and wide, like most in the town, with a neon *OPEN* sign and a few cars parked on the street outside. I push open the door, and immediately the frigid, rainy air outside is dispelled by the full blast of overhead heaters. The surprisingly small interior is littered with burgundy booths and large windows showing the rainy, miserable world. I catch Evie and another girl sat in the corner, drinking coffee, and having what looks to be a very intense discussion. At the counter, I order from a college-age looking girl with red hair and a pretty smile and a face full of freckles like stars. *Hailey*, her name tag reads. I order a large latte, because I need the warmth, and they're surprisingly cheap. She hands the drink over with a smile and I make my way to the exit, before being stopped by a hand on my shoulder.

Spinning around, my eyes land on Evie. Up this close, I can see the freckles on her cheeks. She blinks hazel eyes and smiles tentatively. "Want to sit with us?"

Before I can really say anything, she's dragging me to her table and pulling me into the booth next to her. The other girl looks at me, a sly smile on her face.

"So you're Evie's knight in an SUV?"

"Um—" I start, but Evie speaks up.

"Mae, shut up." She turns to me, "Sorry about her. River, this is my best friend Mae, and Mae, this is my new friend River."

So we're friends. The thought makes my insides go a little warm.

"We were just talking about last night," Evie says.

There's a silence that goes on for centuries.

"I thought maybe I should tell you what happened, since you know, you are the one that miraculously didn't hit me and didn't ask too many questions,"

I nod, because yes, I'm interested and if she wants to tell me then, well, she can.

"Only if you want to tell me, though, it must have been pretty intense." I say.

She picks up her coffee and takes a big gulp. "Yeah, it kind of was. But it's okay— I already told Mae without dying, so I think we'll be good,"

I nod, not really sure what to say to that.

Evie takes a deep breath, another big gulp of coffee, and starts. "Okay, so, if you did any research about this town at all before you moved here, you'll have read about the Bethany Reed case."

I nod, because yes, I did do research and yes, I read the ominous articles about it and yes, I now realise exactly what she's going to say next because the girl in the pictures looks like an older version of Evie and there's suddenly an aching hole in my chest for her and all that pain.

"Yeah, well, Bethany was my sister, and she killed herself three years ago. Yesterday was the third anniversary."

Oh, *god*.

"Every year on her anniversary, I visit the place where she died, which is also the place she spent so much of her time anyway. And as I was going home, I tripped over a body. The body of Jackson Miller, who was her best friend."

7] BONES

evelyn

JANUARY 11th, 2021, 7:14am

I get to school early on Monday. The weekend's rain
has finally stopped, although the sky still promises
something of a shower later in the day. I escape through
the student entrance, into the warmer corridors. This
school is huge, consisting of one massive building with
four wings: Science, English, Maths and
Creatives/Humanities. The cafeteria spills out into the
courtyard in the centre of the building, but it's closed off
today due to the pond flooding with the weekend's rain.

My locker is on the West corridor, near the English
wing. The hallway is completely deserted since most
people show up around half seven. I just decided to get
here early and get to first period before everyone spills in

and starts asking me about Saturday. I don't want to think about it. And I've seen the news; seen the headlines displayed massively across the front of this week's edition of the *Eastwood Observer*. It's horrible. Big, bold, black words telling the whole town that Jackson is dead, that "local teenage girl Evelyn Reed" found the body.

I barely slept all weekend, tossing and turning and thinking about Jackson, dreaming about the blood under my fingernails and waking up screaming and sweating, Mom rushing in and smoothing the hair off my sticky forehead.

Eyes heavy with sleep I didn't get, I heave textbooks out of my locker and into my bag and pull homework out, filing it away in the tiny metal box for later.

"Lynny!" A voice cries behind me, horrible enthusiastic for this early on a Monday morning, but I know who it is instantly.

Swinging myself around, I manage to miraculously not fall over when Benji Hassan launches himself at me, tackling me in a hug. Benji has spent all the last week in Georgia visiting his Nonna. He's my other best friend. My loud, outspoken best friend.

"Benji!" I say, getting a noseful of the smell he always comes back with of cookies and Nonna's floral perfume and the stale old smell of old people's houses. It usually sticks on his clothes for a few days after he comes home, and I make the most of it. I've met Nonna a few times, mostly at Benji's birthday parties and the occasional family dinners. She's an icon of a woman: openly gay, always wearing floral dresses that reach her ankles and fluttering around with her dyed pink hair pinned up in a curly topknot. It's magnificent.

"God lahd did ah miss you," Benji says, letting me come up for a few lungfuls of air. His southern accent is always strong when he gets back from Nonna's, but it goes back to just a bit twangier than the rest of us after a few weeks.

"I missed you too,"

"Mae not here yet?"

"Nope," Mae usually doesn't show up to school until the last possible minute.

"'Course. Barely realised the time, just thought, oh *gahd*, I gotta get here and greet my favourite gahls!"

I laugh. Benji is just like his Nonna in every way except the gay part: he's been going out with Ivy Laurier since the fifth grade. I'm pretty sure they'll get married as soon as they graduate and stay together until they die of old age. I like to pretend I'm not jealous, but I think most people are.

"How's Nonna?"

"Wouldn't shut up about Ellie-May from the yacht club, again,"

Ellie-May. Nonna's been convinced they'll be the next great pensioner love story for the past four years. Fun fact: women in their sixties can still have crushes on people. I think it's utterly adorable.

"And Frieda?" Frieda is Nonna's chunky Maine-Coon. He spends most of his time eating prawns and farting.

"Freida is still fucking iconic," Benji grins. "Ivy here yet?"

"Not sure." I scrunch up my nose. "I thought you came to see me,"

He bumps my shoulder, teasing. "I came, and I saw. Now I need to kiss my girlfriend, or ah *will* go mad as a hatter,"

Nodding, I shut my locker and check the time. Twenty minutes until first period. "Of course, of course. Tell you what, I'll help you find her, and catch you up on the weekend's events,"

He's read the news, right? He must have heard it from someone. I don't want to tell him; I really just want to pretend it didn't happen. Benji and I make our way down the West corridor and into the halls that surround the courtyard. Ivy, who is absolutely certain she is going to go to Harvard, usually spends her mornings in the study group which is in one of the small study rooms. That's in the Science Wing, which is on the other side of the school. We have at least five minutes to talk until then.

"Before you try and tell me, Lynny, yes I heard about what happened on Saturday. I know you don't wanna talk about it, but you know I'm here for you, right? It's really crappy what happened,"

I nod. Don't tear up don't tear up.

"Thanks, Benji."

He winks. "No problem. Anything interesting go down?"

"Ooh, there's a new boy starting today,"

"Oh?"

"Yeah."

"Care to elaborate? Have you seen him? Possible romantic interest?"

I blush and hate myself for it. River? Not the guy who picked me up off the road when I was covered in blood and literally talking absolute nonsense. Nope.

"His name is River. I will absolutely not be going out with him. Nuh uh."

"Oh, *Lynny*, how you break my heart you horrible, delightful creature."

"I can be single and happy, Benji, not everyone has to find their one true love at the age of literally eleven,"

"I was two weeks away from turning twelve, imbecile,"

"Oh, shut up." I joke, knocking into him.

"So, you've met this River, have you?"

I blush again. What is *wrong* with me?

"Maybe."

"Pray tell,"

"Uh, well, on Saturday night he found me and took me to the Sheriff's station. So I went to his house yesterday to say thank you,"

Benji stops. Right there, in the middle of the hallway, so the increasing number of people arriving have to walk around us. "Good God. *Lynny*. You've done it. You've found your one true love,"

"You idiot, Benji. It's too embarrassing to think about. Besides, I don't know the guy— he could be some kind of axe murderer for all I know."

He goes quiet as we approach the classroom. "Well, thank you for being so chivalrous as to walk me to class, oh sexy one." He jokes.

I snort a laugh and poke him through the door, already seeing Ivy's pale, elfin face light up through the frosted glass. He pats my head, as he always does to remind me of how he's almost a foot taller than me, and then disappears. And I lean against the wall outside, reeling.

River and me?

Why am I even thinking about this? Who talks to a guy literally twice and starts thinking *that?*

Absolutely and completely disgusted, I set off down the corridor towards physics.

****

You have to be kidding me.

You have to be effing kidding me.

Izzy Beaumont is staring at me. She's standing by my desk, staring at me like I'm some kind of art piece that she doesn't quite understand.

"Are you okay?" She asks. There's a condescending, nasally tone to her voice, as there always is. Of course she, of all people, would pretend to care.

I nod tightly. "Yes, thanks."

"Are you sure? I wouldn't be."

"I'm not you."

Izzy Beaumont is our school's version of the Queen Biatch. Her older sister, Lauren, who was the same age as my sister, used to hold that title, but as soon as she left for college she passed it down to Izzy. And now Izzy is standing over me, looking both confused and absurdly delighted.

"Right. You can talk to me, you know?"

I smile in what I hope is a polite way, but I also want her to know how much I want to stick my foot so far up her ass it—

"Earth to Evie? You look like you're about to pull out a machete and go to town on her." It's Mae, nudging me with her elbow. I blink and stop staring at Izzy, who is giving me a weird look.

"I don't really need your help, thanks, Izzy." I say. She huffs.

"Didn't want to help you anyway. Everyone knows you're a psycho."

And then she walks away.

Mae scoffs. "I'll kill her. I'll take out her intestines and shove them down her throat,"

"Please do." I'm suddenly very tired, even more so than before. I just want to put my head down on my book and fall asleep.

"Does everyone really still think me, and my Mom are psycho?" I ask.

Mae shakes her head, but she's really the wrong person to ask because she wouldn't say anything to hurt me if I put a gun to her temple. "No. Izzy is just, well, Izzy. She does what she wants, says what she wants, and what she needs to say to feel cool."

"Right." I'm not convinced.

I fell apart in the middle of our town's only grocery store a couple of weeks after Bethany died, and about twenty people saw it happen, filmed it, and posted it everywhere. Then my Mom went bat-shit crazy on some tweens who threw litter in our font yard, and no one has ever forgiven us. That's the thing with small towns: you are defined by the worst thing that has ever happened to you, and no one ever moves on.

*****

Psychology is fourth period. And River is in my class.

He sits in the empty seat next to me and pulls out a notebook missing half its pages and a pen that looks like it died a long time ago. It's the first time I've seen him today.

"Hi." He says.

"Hello." I say.

And he flips open his notebook to a clean page.

"How are you?" He asks me.

I nod. "Better, thanks. Thank you again for Saturday, I—"

He waves his pen around dismissively. "Seriously, don't mention it. It literally is what anyone else would have done."

I almost say "not in this town" like I did before. But instead I smile at him and look down, back to where I'm finishing off the homework I forgot to do over the weekend.

"You really were right about no one liking you." He says. The bluntness of it makes me blink twice before I can answer.

"Uh, yeah, I guess."

"Right. Sorry. Didn't mean for it to come out so, um—"

"Blunt?"

"Yeah. Sorry." He flicks his pen up and it lands on his book. "I've been asking about you."

Okay, kind of creepy. I arch a brow. "You have?"

"I mean I was too nervous to talk to you in person, so I brought you up in conversation earlier."

"Who with?"

"Um, Izzy, I think?"

I snort a laugh. "You're kidding."

"No?" Poor guy, he looks so confused.

"Izzy Beaumont? Yeah, she hates me. I won't be surprised if she said I killed Jackson myself,"

"Er, she kind of did."

My eyes widen. "Oh, shit. She did?"

"Yeah." There's a pause. "I didn't believe her, or anything,"

"Good. Izzy is probably the least reliable person in this school for facts about me. She's hated me since literally freshman year."

"Why?"

"Dunno." This is true. I don't know, but I'm holding out hope that it's some kind of deep philosophical reason that explains why she has treated me like the spawn of literal Satan for the last four years.

River is quiet for a minute, and our psychology teacher Mr Black walks in. He's in his forties but bald, and a short and plump man who sets his bag on the desk and takes his jacket off.

"Morning, class." He says.

There's a grumbled reply. Mr Black rolls his eyes, good-natured as ever, and pulls a whiteboard pen out of his pocket. He turns to the board as he speaks.

"I promised y'all last week that I'd tell you what this semester's project is, and this semester it *is* a project and not just me rambling on at y'all for hours on end." He starts writing, "The topic for this semester, is surprisingly very on par with recent news."

And he steps away from the board.

And announces,

"Your project this term is profiling murderers."

The board behind him reads, *WHAT MAKES PEOPLE KILL?*

8] AS IT STANDS

What makes people kill?

Anger?

Hatred?

Passion?

I write all of these ideas down in my notebook, and then chew on the end of my pen as if it will give me any more inspiration.

The library is empty apart from a few freshmen who have managed to still not find another place to awkwardly eat their lunch. Evie and I are basically the only ones here apart from the librarian, who's eating her lunch in the corner, heavily invested in what looks to be a *Fifty Shades of Grey* book.

"Hey, you're getting distracted," Evie throws a pen at me, and it hits me squarely on the nose.

"Sorry."

"As you should be."

I look down at the page I'm working on.

Anger? Hatred? Passion?

I'm sure Mr Black will give me an A plus for this absolute masterpiece. He's asked us to spend until the end of the year researching and presenting a detailed investigation into the psychology of murderers, using any example we choose.

We're to work in partners, and Evie assigned herself to me the minute he said that. Not that I'm complaining, since she *is* the only person I know in that class, but the unfortunate thing is that she's even more lacking in inspiration than me.

"The Zodiac Killer?" She asks, going down the list of well-known serial killers she's reading from a criminal justice textbook.

I shake my head. "Everyone'll be doing that. We won't get the creativity marks."

She nods, "Very true, very true."

"So we need something more obscure."

Evie slams shut the textbook she's reading, tossing it back to the pile of books in the middle of the table that she's already been through and running a hand through her hair.

"I don't think this shit library has the deep stuff— the small-town serial killers who aren't famous at all, but are very intriguing."

"No. This isn't a murder mystery book, Evie." I say, smiling.

49

She smiles back and stands up, closing her notebook. "I need coffee. Don't you?"

"But lessons start again in ten minutes?" I say. Unless Cathy's Diner is now officially a fast-food place, I'm not sure how we're going to manage that.

"What do you have after lunch?" She asks me, leaning over the table, hands pressed against it, knuckles white with the pressure.

I dig through my bag for my timetable and hold it out in front of me.

"Independent study and then business,"

She smirks. "Well, I've got independent study and then AP Math, so what do you say we get out of here until last period?"

The New Brunswick version me would have said absolutely not. *No way in hell.*

But Eastwood is testing me, pushing me.

So I nod. "Sounds good."

Evie grins and swings the strap of her backpack over one shoulder, leading the way out of the library and into the hall, which is busy. We weave a path to one of the back entrances, one that stems from the rear-end of the North corridor.

"I've never skipped school before." I say, truthfully, as she pushes open the door. The world outside is frigid and still.

It's just me and Evie and these empty streets.

At my words, she turns to me and smiles. "Neither have I."

I'm shocked into silence for a few seconds. She seems like the kind of person who's daring and free enough to skip school whenever she pleases.

"Really?" We stride around the side of the school building, out of the tree cover and into the parking lot. Evie heads towards her car, a purple, beat up Volvo Estate, and I follow.

"Where are we going?" I ask.

She doesn't turn around, keeps on ploughing forward. "It's a surprise,"

Frowning, I jog a little to catch up with her bouncy pace. "Why are we walking so quickly?"

"Parking lot warden's shift starts in five minutes, and I'll bet he's sometimes early."

"Oh," I keep jogging towards her car, overtaking her, and she starts running to catch up with me and then there's the two of us, running like idiots to get to her car, grinning like idiots because *look at us we're skipping school this is amazing.*

When we finally reach the elongated purple metal monstrosity, she unlocks it and I have to wrench the passenger side door open to get it to pull free, and then we're on the cream leather seats and still grinning.

Evie, slightly out of breath, shoves the key into the ignition and a second later the engine turns over. I plug in my seatbelt and lean my head back against the headrest, running a hand through my now windswept hair.

"Ready?" She asks me, and she puts the car in reverse and just like that we've skipped school.

*****

She drives into Redwood. Redwood is a slightly smaller town, around five minutes down the highway (but highways in rural Maine are wider than usual roads, and there's hardly anyone on them except the occasional tractor and runaway). I'm still very surprised at the amount of trees in this part of the world. They're everywhere, like the metal bars on a prison cell. From far away, Redwood looks like a giant grove of deep red pines. Beautiful, but I'm starting to wonder if there is anywhere near here that isn't ninety percent foliage.

"It's pretty, right?"

I blink at the expanse of pines, the overwhelming presence of nature, and am forced to nod. "Yeah, it is."

Even though it's January, and the trees are all missing their leaves, there is still an overwhelming sense of beauty in the town.

She continues on Redwood's main road, following down to where the buildings thin out and the forest threatens to take over again, not allowing the town to take any more space. She's forced to turn onto Halliebottom Road. Halliebottom is lined with small, far apart houses, and I wonder what could possibly be down this deserted road until she turns into the parking lot of a cabin off the road.

Halliebottom Emporium reads the sign outside.

"Is this it?" I ask, pointing at the squat wooden structure.

"Don't judge a book by its cover, River."

And I learn the truth behind that statement as soon as we step out of the car and wander down the path to Halliebottom Emporium. Evie reaches for the door handle and swings it open, a bell shrilly announcing our presence. Inside, the place is huge. Like, way bigger than the outside suggests. It's a shop with an attached cafe, by the looks of it. Antiques and quirky little objects are stacked to the ceiling, and the cafe is a corner of the chaos, with chalkboards announcing prices and one single worker, stationed behind a shop desk.

The girl behind the desk looks vaguely familiar, but I can't place her.

Evie lunges forwards and hugs the girl, and I stand by the door, taken aback.

"Evester! Oh, my little Evester." They let each other go, and I get an eyeful of the girl. She's taller than Evie (though that's not very difficult to accomplish) and has dark blonde hair French plaited to her elbows and a green and brown striped summer dress on, even though it's in the twenties outside.

"Hey, Nevae."

And then it clicks.

Nevae Bradbury. She was Bethany Reed's best friend. I remember seeing her in the articles I saw, the ones from when I chucked Eastwood, Maine into Google just out of interest. Where I saw a younger Evelyn standing, solemn, beside her mother and then, another picture, of Bethany with her best friends: Nevae Bradbury and Jackson Miller, the kid that died over the weekend.

Nevae looks strikingly different from the girl in the photograph: that girl had platinum blonde hair that was trimmed to sit on her shoulders, and she wore heavy makeup in blacks and reds.

She spots me finally, looking curiously over Evie's shoulder.

"Who's this you've brought, Evester?" Her tone is mildly teasing, but Evie blushes.

I blush too, for absolutely no reason whatsoever.

"Nevae, this is River. River, this is Nevae."

I step forward, sticking my hand out. Nevae shakes it, smiling. "Nice to meet you, River. Welcome to Halliebottom Emporium,"

I look around me, again absorbing the madness. "It's lovely. You own the place?"

"No. My fiancé does," She says.

Evie grins at me. "Oh, you should meet Henry. I bet you two'll love each other,"

I nod and smile politely and follow Evie to the back room.

That room is slightly tidier than the shop, and a very tall guy with slicked black hair and golden skin sits behind a desk in there. He grins when Evie waltzes in and gets up to hug her. "It's been too long since you came down, little duck." His accent sounds vaguely Italian.

He sees me over her shoulder and smiles. "And you've brought a friend?"

"Yep." Evie scurries over to stand next to me. "Henry, this is River. River, this is Henry."

Henry steps out from behind the desk, shaking my hand very firmly. It's mildly intimidating. "Henry Di Santis. Nice to meet you, mate."

I nod. "And you."

Evie claps her hands together. "Right, well, lovely to see you Henry, but we came for coffee, so coffee we shall go and get."

Henry nods and smiles and sets a hand on my shoulder when Evie leaves, to stop me from following her. "You look after our girl, yeah?"

I nod. "Yeah, 'course."

He lets me go, nodding, and I leave. Evie's standing at the counter, pondering the menu whilst Nevae busies herself. Evie hands me a menu and points at one of the things on it.

"I think you'll like that one," she's pointing to the *Winter Pumpkin Delight* and I can't think of anything more disgusting, but I order it and Evie orders a *Frosty Latte* with extra coffee and I chuck in two pain au chocolates and pay for us.

We take a table by one of the two massive windows and Nevae sets the drinks down in front of us. She then drags a chair over from another table and starts picking bits off of Evie's pain au chocolate and eating them. I try my drink and, surprisingly, it's not disgusting.

"So, are you two dating or something?"

Evie chokes on her drink and I set my coffee down, going red.

"Uh, we, like, just met."

"Like just met as in met five minutes ago or just met as in met over the weekend and became immediately infatuated?"

Evie baulks. "No need to make it awkward, Nevae. We met on Saturday, okay? Just friends."

Nevae winks. "Oh, that's what I said about Henry when we first met."

"Just shut up, okay?" Evie says, but she's smiling. And I realise I'm smiling too.

Nevae turns to me. "So, did you just move here or something?"

I nod. "From New Brunswick."

"Very cool. I went there once."

"Oh? Where?"

"Saint John, I think. It was beautiful, oh my god."

"I grew up in Saint John, it's stunning, I'll give you that." I say, excited. I haven't spoken about my hometown to anyone since moving here.

Evie has a bit of whipped cream on her nose. "I need pictures, like, yesterday."

I grin, pulling my phone from my pocket. But there's a text from my Dad on the screen.

Where are you? Police want to talk to you.

My stomach drops.

The police?

9] FOUL PLAY

evelyn

JANUARY 11th, 2021, 2:12pm

River is in the Sheriff's station. I think he's being interviewed, but I don't know why. I know that he got a text from his Dad and then we had to rush back to town, and I barely got a chance to say goodbye to Nevae and Henry but now I'm outside the station, in the Volvo, wondering where he fits into this.

Because the police can only be wanting to talk to him about Jackson, right?

Maybe they figured out that it was him and his Dad that picked me up from the road on Saturday and now they want to make sure my timeline is right. If they're questioning my timeline, though, that means they're looking at me. And if they're looking at me, then they suspect me.

They suspect me.

Why?

I have no motive. I'm definitely not a killer. *(They don't know that, dumbass).*

The afternoon is slow and cold and torturous, and I keep remembering it's only Monday, that I have a whole week to go, and this whole ordeal seems one hundred times more tiring.

River is in there, and if our stories don't match up then I might go to prison.

(Don't be ridiculous, they can't put you in prison with that little evidence)

I'm trying to reason with myself, and so I decide to worry about him instead of myself.

What if they think he did it?

What if he did do it?

That thought is terrifying, so I banish it from my mind and focus on other things.

Like, why did I bring River to meet Nevae and Henry? That's like bringing him home to meet my parents, except my Dad's gone and my Mom doesn't really count. So Nevae and Henry are basically the next best thing.

I know they met at the end of senior year, after Beth died. Henry was the deputy that was assigned to the suicide initially and they met through there. Henry is three years older than Beth, and moved from Cosenza, Italy to live with his birth Mom five years ago.

Henry quit his job at the Sheriff's station a year ago and bought a shack in Redwood. Halliebottom Emporium, it became. Antiques shop, cafe, bookshop. It's my own little heaven. I work there when Nevae visits her grandparents every Thursday to Monday. I know they live in Bangor, and her Nan is sick.

I think about how AP Maths starts in twenty minutes, and if I don't move this darn car to school then I'll be late. There's no reason for me to sit here, anyway. They'll likely have River back in time for the end of school anyway, and I'm sure his Dad will drive him.

There is no reason for me to sit here.

I start the Volvo's engine and pull away from the curb and onto the main roads.

*****

I don't hear from or see River again until Tuesday. We have psychology third as always, and I'm waiting in my seat when he slopes in, bags under his eyes and wringing his hands out. I'm silent when he sits next to me and I'm silent until Mr Black walks in. If he doesn't want to talk, then I don't want to talk either.

*****

We spend the whole of psychology silently flipping through textbooks, making notes, not really exchanging more than pleasantries. I can tell by River's posture, by the stiff set to him that wasn't there before that something happened yesterday, something that made him put his guard up.

I mean, fair enough. I don't expect that small town murder investigations are very light at all, but every bone in my body yearns to know what the hell happened, and why he hasn't told me about it. As soon as the bell rings and signals the end of that period, I gather up my stuff and get up to leave. When I step out the door, River wraps a hand around my wrist and tugs me next door, into the library. Startled, I stumble after him.

"Sorry I've been rude, Evie. I didn't want to say anything and risk it being overheard,".

My heart lifts a little with relief. "It's okay, I understand. What happened yesterday?"

"Um, they called me in for questioning about, um, about Jackson."

"Why?"

"Someone said they saw me, on Saturday, in the forest around the time he was murdered."

"*What?*"

This is completely ridiculous. My heart is racing.

River blinks, as if the reminder is too much. "Yeah."

"Who?"

"They don't know, it was an anonymous tip. But it was the only lead they had, so they called me in,"

"And what did you say?"

"I said that I didn't know what the hell they were talking about. That I arrived with my Dad in the town in the afternoon and spent the whole evening with my Nana. She's my alibi."

"And then they let you go?" I'm so distracted by the idiocy of this that I ignore the fact he said *Nana* which means he's got relatives in this town. I'm not surprised—no one just moves to Eastwood, Maine by chance.

"Yeah, they did. Said they'd ring up my Nana and ask her if it's true."

I nod, biting my bottom lip. "Well, then. Crisis averted?"

"Crisis averted. But I'm still very interested to know who called in that tip."

I realise something then, and it sends shivers down my spine. "What if the person who called in that tip was the actual killer? You know— to take the heat off themselves, and put it all on you?"

He nods. "It would make sense. But that's terrifying because it means that—"

"That the real killer knows who you are." I finish.

The temperature in the library drops several million degrees.

*****

When I get home, the first thing I do is make my way upstairs, to my room. Mom's working late tonight (like every night), so it's up to me to find myself dinner and do the dishwasher and make sure my clothes are clean for tomorrow. I turn on my laptop, intent on checking my emails— maybe Mrs Johnson has emailed me back my physics essay score.

I have one email.

It's definitely not from Mrs Johnson.

1 NEW MESSAGE
To: evelynareed2002@gmail.com
From: nodancer2119@gmail.com
    R.E: Revenge.
    Jackson knows what he did.
    I think if you looked a little
harder you would be able to figure it
out too, Evelyn.
    Much love,

    -   L

10] BREAKING POINT

JANUARY 13th, 2021, 5:47pm

"Evie, I really think this isn't the best idea," I say, "maybe you could sleep on it? Think again in the morning."

"River," She groans in frustration, still pacing around her room. "Think about it— it's original, no one else will be doing it, and we might even bring some justice to this godforsaken town in the process,"

She's right, but she's also being mildly idiotic. "Maybe if we don't get killed ourselves in the process!"

"I don't care!" She cries.

And then there's silence.

"Shit. I didn't mean it like that, I swear—" she rushes.

"I get it. You're all emotional. I would be too."

I got a call from Evie ten minutes ago. She'd decided that we should do Jackson's murder for our psychology project. She said this email she had received was a clue, and a big enough clue that we would be able to take off with the investigation.

I'm still trying to convince her that it might have been a prank, and it's not a very good idea to interfere with a murder investigation. But if I've learnt anything about Evelyn Reed, it's that she is a horribly stubborn person, and she definitely won't back down very easily.

"Think about it— if we find the murderer, then me and my Mom won't be the town's crazy family anymore, and no one will believe that you, like, actually killed Jackson or whatever."

"Yeah, but, what if we don't find the killer? Then what will our project be about— it'll be boring and uninteresting, and we definitely won't get a good mark."

"So we make a backup project. One we can submit if this one doesn't work out right."

She's indignant.

"And what if that email you got was a prank?" I ask, something akin to desperation clawing at my voice and straining it. "What if it's a false lead and we spend three months going down a very dangerous rabbit hole?"

"Then we spend three months going down a very dangerous rabbit hole." She says. Evie looks me dead in the eye and I can see the raw emotion in them. She wants to do this. She wants to do this more than anything else in the world, I can tell. I don't believe that I'll be able to convince her not to.

So I nod, sighing a deep and steady sigh. "Alright. But think about it again in the morning, okay? This could just be the adrenaline talking."

This is definitely the adrenaline talking. Evie nods. "Thanks, River."

"No problem." I say.

11] OLD WOUNDS

evelyn

JANUARY 14th, 2021, 8:09am

I'm just shoving my haphazardly done physics homework into my bag when James Cabot knocks on the door. I can see him through my bedroom window, standing on the porch, looking warily around the house.

My heart picks up a bit. Maybe he's just following up from Saturday.

Yeah.

That's it.

Calm. *Calm.* I hear the front door opening and Mom's light, welcoming voice. I stand by the door to my bedroom intent on overhearing their conversation, but it turns muffled the moment they enter the living room.

And then,

"Evie!" Mom's voice easily dances up the stairs. Heart dropping, I make my way down the carpeted stairs and into the living room. On the three-seater, Deputy Cabot is sitting with one leg crossed over the other, poised and perfect. The tension on his shoulders is so potent that I can see it from across the room.

Something is wrong.

I take a seat on the two-seater across the room from him and Mom flutters back into the room with a tray of coffee.

"I'll keep this short, since I don't want to make you late for school, Evelyn. And you, Nicole."

Mom smiles, sipping the boiling hot liquid and trying to hide her wince from the promised burning pain.

I don't reach for my mug, too sick with nervous energy.

"We got the autopsy back on Jackson Miller last night." He says.

I blink. Okay. What does this have to do with us?

"Oh, the poor boy. Didn't deserve that at all," Mom says with a lilting voice, tinged with sadness. Jackson spent a lot of time at this house with Nevae and Bethany. Bethany, who died just like Jackson. Tragically, in Eastwood Forest.

"No, Nicole. No, he didn't." Cabot shifts, his every move drenched with the hesitation of discomfort. "Do you remember when we got Bethany's autopsy back?"

"Yes." I say. "She had Polonium-210 in her system, but nothing else. It was taken that she tried to poison herself, and because she excelled in chemistry it wasn't a stretch to believe she knew that it was lethal."

"And then, when she realised it would be too slow, she jumped in the river to finish the job." Mom says. I don't miss the bitterness in her voice. She never speaks about Bethany, but I know that she disguises her sadness with anger. Anger at her daughter, for doing what she did. Anger at me, for being a constant reminder of Bethany. Anger at Dad, for running when life reached its hardest in the months following her death.

And, largest and most potent of all: anger at this town, for ripping us to shreds for falling apart.

"Yes. Well. Something came up in Jackson's autopsy that seemed... familiar."

The silence that statement leaves in its wake is so painful I almost cry out.

"Jackson, too, had Polonium-210 in his system."

Mom bristles. "So, it was suicide too?"

"No one but you two knew that Bethany had Polonium-210 in her system. I need to know the truth here, did either of you tell anyone? You won't be in trouble if you did, you didn't promise secrecy or anything like that,"

We both shake our heads. No. It never left my lips, not even to Mae. I assumed her Dad told her and never brought it up. And even if I had told Mae, she wouldn't tell anyone except maybe Benji, and Benji wouldn't tell a soul. Not something like this.

Cabot appears to age several hundred years in that minute.

"Well, then Jackson could not have known about the Polonium-210. And he was failing chemistry— didn't have a scientific bone in his body."

"What are you suggesting, Deputy Cabot?" Mom sounds annoyed. I wonder if it's a facade to show the anxiety I know is brewing and sizzling under her skin.

"The police have yet to find the gun that Jackson was shot with. I'm sure you can understand that Jackson was shot in the forehead, and so could not possibly have hidden a gun somewhere that fifty professionals couldn't find it with a bullet in his skull. And the sheer volume of Polonium in his system would have made it impossible to hold a gun, let alone aim it and throw it with such strength."

My mom looks like she's going to throw up.

I'm not really feeling much of anything. I had already assumed that Jackson was murdered— I know most of the town feels the same way. But having it confirmed, having the dynamics of the crime drawn out so blatantly is something I couldn't have prepared myself for.

"We overlooked the Polonium-210 detail to an extent in Bethany's case. She could have just taken it, and fallen in. Or maybe she took it, realised how long it would have taken, and then jumped in, as you say Nicole, to make it, um, happen, uh, faster."

Cabot, too, looks like he's seconds away from hurling. My hands are bleeding from little crescents from my fingernails. The blood is slick in my grip.

"The Polonium-210 in both of their systems was the same, or close to the same, quantity. Same strength, stolen from the same laboratory in Bangor. All details only privy to us, you, presumably Bethany and Jackson's killer."

"I'm confused. Why does any of this matter to us? Bethany couldn't have killed Jackson."

"No, but Jackson's killer could have killed Bethany."

Mom drops her mug. I become unable to move, think, breathe.

"We've reopened Bethany's suicide case, on presumption that it may have been murder. And whoever murdered Jackson, is responsible for her death as well."

And I know in that instant that River and I are going to solve this case, or I will die trying.

And I know in that instant that this bastard is going to *pay*.

1 NEW MESSAGE
To: evelynareed2002@gmail.com
From: nodancer2119@gmail.com
R.E: Revelations

I know you know. I know what you're going to do now that you know, and I need you to know that you can't. You shouldn't. Because then I'll look at you, and I'll have to level the same weapons at you that I did at them.

Much love, stay safe,

L

12] WHERE DO WE GO FROM HERE?

JANUARY 14th, 2021, 8:18am

In the morning, Evie has not, in fact, changed her mind. She finds me in the corridors at school with flushed cheeks, wild hair, and a strange look on her face. "River, I need to talk to you."

Of course, my first expectation is that she's going to admit she was being crazy and change her mind about the whole pursuing the case thing, but instead she drags me into an empty classroom, shuts the door and turns to me.

"Cabot came to my house this morning," she says.

I frown. "Who?"

"He's one of the deputies at the Sheriff's station,"

Oh.

"What did he say? Have they cleared me?"

She shakes her head. "I— no, not yet. But they will— once your Nana gives her statement or whatever. He— oh god. He came to tell us that they got the autopsy back on Jackson, and there was something consistent between his and Bethany's autopsies that told them that it's very likely that Bethany was murdered, too. That she didn't kill herself."

The silence is deafening. All I can hear is my blood rushing in my ears. Bethany was murdered? Two victims instead of one.

Evie's sister was murdered.

"They've reopened her investigation, River. As a homicide." She says. Her voice wobbles a bit at the end. She looks away and a piece of hair falls free from behind her ear, hanging in front of her face. A curtain. It's made painfully obvious to me then that we're doing this investigation, whether I like it or not. If I say no, then she'll do it herself. And I don't want her to get killed.

"I'll do it." I say. "I'll do the investigation with you, Evie. I swear to God I will."

Evie looks back up at me and she's not smiling, but her face is lighter— her eyes rounder, brighter.

"Thank you," she says. Quietly, as if she's afraid I'll change my mind. As if my acceptance is delicate— our friendship fragile. As if she doesn't know how to navigate it without it breaking down in front of her like everything else in her life.

And she blinks, and that Evie I've come to recognise in her is back— defiance, readiness to do anything it takes for justice. "We need to go into the woods."

"We do?"

"Yes. If we're going to find out who killed Bethany and Jackson, we need to find the weapon."

"Haven't the police already found it?"

Evie gives me a conspiratorial look. "The Sheriff's station got Jackson's autopsy back this morning, and Mae's Dad told her that he was shot. Like, with a gun."

"Right."

"He also told her that they've crawled the whole forest, but they haven't found the gun."

"So you think we'll be able to find it? And what if the killer just took off with it?"

Evie smirks. "Everyone knows that when you kill someone, you dump the weapon at the scene so no one can find it in your possession and realise the truth. If the police haven't found it, then they aren't looking hard enough."

I laugh, despite the fact that this definitely isn't the time. "God, Evie, you do terrify me sometimes."

She smiles back. "Well, pull up your big girl panties, because we're going out to the woods tonight, Mr River."

"I think I have plans." I say, joking.

"Oh, you dick. Cancel them, there are more important things than your plans." She's joking, too. I hope she is, anyway.

I chuckle. "I have to babysit until seven, but you can come over earlier if you'd like? I could make dinner, and we can talk about how the hell we're going to solve this case? And then, if we haven't found a better—safer—plan, then we can go into the woods and look for the weapon."

She nods, looking pleased. "Yeah. Sounds great. See you then, Mr River."

I quirk a smile. "Lopez, Evie. My name is River Lopez."

*****

Hadley has formed a friendship with Evie. Well, as close to a real friendship as you can get with a two-year-old. They're on the couch, Hadley sat on Evie's stomach whilst she plaits the dark, knotted hair falling in waves down Hads' back. I can see them across the hallway, and it makes me feel all warm and fluttery inside. Hadley doesn't take to strangers easily, but she adores Evie.

She's not the only one.

Stop. Stop it.

Evie laughs at something Hads says, lips turned up and hazel eyes bright. Her own hair is tied neatly at the base of her neck with a frayed green ribbon, with stray pieces of hair resting on her freckled cheeks. High, arching cheekbones that are sharp as a razor turn her face into a weapon that's kind and gentle— her beauty isn't overly feminine, but it's lovely. Her feet are kicked into the air on the other end of the couch, dusty pink socks peeking out of the end of large, ripped jeans.

Evie.

"What are you staring at?" She asks. She's looking at me. Hadley turns and pins me with a cheeky look.

"Yeah, creep," Hadley says, youth rounding the words. I don't know where she learnt "creep" but it's funny. Evie laughs.

"Your sister's a real girl boss, Lopez."

I smile at the two of them. "Yes, she is. She takes after her brother."

"So you're a girl boss now?" Evie teases.

"Of course."

***

After dinner, it's pitch dark outside already, but in a way it's definitely smart to go in the dark since then no one will be able to see us, or if they do and call the police or whatever then they'll probably never be able to say confidently that it was Evelyn Reed and River Lopez, of all the possible duos in this town and surrounding areas.

We're being smart.

If we're doing this, at least we're doing it with a shred of common sense.

I park the truck down Devil's Pathway. The dark is an effective cloak, maybe too effective since I can't see two feet in front of me. Reaching a hand into the back seats of the truck, I fish around for a torch and pull one out, switching it on. The light flickers. The battery is running out.

I ignore the sinking feeling this puts in my gut and press it into my hands, gripping tightly. Evie looks nervous. "God, why is this so terrifying? We're literally just looking for something."

"We're breaking into a crime scene. Which is definitely illegal." I say.

She sighs. Closes her eyes. "You're right. Duh. You're always right. Shit, let's do this."

And she pushes open her door, letting the cold air spill in. It fractures the warmth; shatters the dreamlike state I was in before. This is reality.

I've never done anything illegal before, except for when I went over the speed limit once.

"You know, my sister knew the boy that died here," Evie says, picking a path with me down the pitch-black track. The torch projects a faded yellow light across the loose gravel and dying plants littered across the road. It is achingly obvious that no one comes down here anymore.

"Really?" but I'm not all that surprised. This town is so small that I've gotten the distinct impression that basically everyone knows everyone.

"They were friends. Dunno how close— I only met him once."

There's a silence. A long, stretchy, spooky silence. We're both listening for any sign of another person being out here, but most of the forest has been sectioned off in the search for the gun. Sure enough, there's only a few minutes until we break off from Devil's Pathway, which must be metres from the river (I can hear it churning incessantly) onto a smaller path and into the deep recesses of Eastwood Forest.

And then there's police tape: yellow and lurid. Watching, teasing, leering at us.

"You ready?" Evie says. And it's like we're readying ourselves for a literal war, not for just one measly illegal act.

Teenagers break the law all the time, right? And not many of them end up in prison for it, right?

Shut up, River. Stop overthinking this.

We'll walk out of this forest tonight with some answers, hopefully. And then this investigation will be easy and safe, and Evie will be right.

Yes.

"Oi! Who's there? I've got a gun!"

Everything comes to a standstill. And then Evie stumbles on a root, crashing down next to me.

"Oh shit." The voice murmurs.

Crack.

Like a sonic boom. And then

screaming

PART 2

THE

ANSWER

IS

THE

HARDEST

PART

12.5]
DISAPPOINTMENT

bethany

SEPTEMBER 22nd, 2017, 5:33pm

News on the block is that Lauren Beaumont is throwing a party in a few hours. This is a horrible thing for two reasons: one, because it means that Nevae and Jackson will definitely drag me along with them and two, because Evie wants me to stay home tonight with her and watch *Dirty Dancing* for the seventh time, which I am absolutely not opposed at all to doing.

But Lauren throwing a party means I'm going to have to cancel on my sister, and that just makes me even more of a disappointment and an altogether horrible human being. I get home late from school, since I spent an hour in the library trying to finish off a physics assignment due after the weekend. When I open the door and slip in, away from the storm that's brewing in the dark clouds overhead, Evie is on the couch in the living room, reading.

She looks up when I walk in, hair down (it rarely is), eyes sleepy. With any luck she'll succumb to the Friday night exhaustion and fall asleep before I have to leave.

"We still on for tonight?" She asks, looking excited.

"If you can stay up long enough," I try to sound light-hearted and jokey. It seems to work because she smiles through a yawn.

"Yeah,"

I set my school bag by the door and ruffle her hair on my way to the kitchen. In the kitchen, Dad's leaning against the counter, drinking coffee and reading the news.

"Hi, Dad,"

He looks up. Smiles. "Hello, daughter. I assume your study session was productive, then?"

I nod, pouring myself a mug of bitter coffee. "Yep, I wrote two thousand words about physics."

He arches a brow. "Sounds very intellectual,"

I try not to think about my failing physics grade and how when my reports arrive this semester Mom and Dad will realize that I've been lying about my grades this whole time and they'll either get me tutors and force me to work my butt off or hug me and tell me they don't want me to be perfect.

I don't really want to know.

A few minutes later Nevae texts me, making sure I will be present at the party tonight. She's going to pick me up at eight, and I don't have a choice in the matter.

I almost text her back, telling her not to bother, that I'm done doing things I don't really want to do, but I don't.

Instead, I kiss my Dad on the cheek and go upstairs to pick an outfit.

*****

The party is in full swing when Nevae parks her Fiat outside. I left Evie on the couch, where she had passed out, with a full pot of cookie dough ice cream in the freezer and a note apologizing in case she wakes up before I get back.

I'm a horrible sister.

So I fully plan on getting piss drunk tonight so I don't have to think about how much of a failure I am. I've got on my usual party attire: tight denim skirt with flowers embroidered on the back pocket, and a lacy white crop top that shows off the smooth skin of my stomach and the dip of my belly button.

Lauren Beaumont's sprawling house overlooks Eastwood Forest, but it's dark, so you can't see any of it other than a vague and dark ominous shape. There's a chill in the air, the kind of bitterness that promises autumn, promises snowstorms and a whole grumpy town wishing for summer's almost-heatwaves.

I shiver.

I wonder if Nicolas will be here.

If he cares for his social standing at Gingham Memorial, he'll be here. But he doesn't strike me as the kind of person who would care whether he's considered the "in" crowd or not.

The huge house by the forest is pounding. The bassline of the music coming through the open front door gives the house a heartbeat, and I am glad that the Beaumonts are rich enough to not have neighbours within almost a quarter of a mile. The sound doesn't travel far, dampened by the swamps of trees that run down the sides of the house.

Nevae, clad in a pair of flared jeans and a t-shirt, grabs me by the wrist and drags me up the steps and into the swarm.

Jackson is the first person we find, pressed against the wall outside Mr Beaumont's study (locked on party nights like these), with a half-empty urine-coloured bottle of beer in one hand and the other on the hip of a junior who's whispering something in his ear.

Nevae drags me up to him and smacks him on the shoulder, so he pulls away from the junior in surprise, blinking at us like he's just woken up from a really long nap.

"Hey, Ella, mind if we get back to this later?" He asks the junior, who flicks her ponytail over one shoulder and nods glumly, wandering off towards the kitchen. I watch her go, wondering what it's like to make out with a stranger in a stranger's house.

"What plans did you cancel this time?" Jackson asks me, grinning. I resist the urge to flick him in the ear, instead smiling like a polite person.

"Movie with Evie,"

He scrunches up his nose, downing the rest of the beer. "Sucks."

I send Nevae a pointed look, "Yeah, it does."

Nevae sighs, hugging me to her tightly. "I'm sorry. This is the last time I drag you out of family plans, I promise. I'm going to pine after Elodie for a bit, okay?"

I smile and watch her go. "Healthy pining from a distance only! She's a bitch, and you know it,"

Nevae winks and struts back out into the throng. Jackson whistles lowly. "That girl is going to get her heart broken again."

"Yeah." I say. "She is."

At that moment, Aiden Islington, someone I don't know all that well, strides into our space. "Miller. Reed." He addresses us.

Jackson and him do that bro-hug thing that I will never understand, and then Aiden turns to me.

"Care to dance?"

I'm blushing, but before I can protest we're forced out of the way, further into the house, because the door is thrown open and Nicolas Lopez walks in.

He looks dapper in a pair of blue skinny jeans and a graphic t-shirt. His hair is loose and free like always, curling over his forehead. His eyes, wide and blue, scan the crowd and then they land on me, and I turn away from his gaze. I can still feel Aiden's presence beside me, waiting for me to go through with this dance.

So I turn to Aiden and take his hand, letting him lead me into the packed living room. Nicolas calls out to me, but I ignore him. By being blatantly rude, I'm trying to prove to myself and maybe even to him and Jackson and even Nevae that I am capable of making new friends and even boyfriends.

I let Aiden pull me to his chest and wrap a snaking, sneaky hand around my waist. Not low enough to be sexual, not high enough to be purely platonic.

"I haven't spoken to you recently." He says in my ear, having to speak loudly over the pound of the music.

"I haven't spoken to you ever." I say.

He laughs. I feel his breath against my skin, hot and tinged with the sharp smell of alcohol.

"Touché. Feel like changing that?"

He's flirting with me. I'm proud of myself for making such an accurate observation when I know I am lacking horrifically in the romance department. We sway for a moment in silence, and I allow myself to be happy. To be proud. Proud that I'm putting myself out there with a boy I don't know, dancing with a boy I don't know, with the distinct possibility of sex in my future. In this moment, with nothing but Aiden's breath, my buzzing thoughts, and the too-loud music, I find myself forgetting about the Evie I left behind and my parents, who will wait up until past midnight for me to come home, and then shout at me, but be secretly as proud as I am that I'm out here, socializing, making new friends outside of the ones I am friends with simply because we have known each other for so long that our friendship is obligatory.

"You know my name, at least?" Aiden says.

"Aiden." I don't reveal his last name for fear of sounding *too* eager. Flirting is a dangerous game; one I know nothing about.

"And you are Bethany."

Normally, I would chastise him for using my full name. But on his lips, the syllables that make up *Bethany* that before sounded clunky and too fancy for me sound sexy. New. Romantic. *Bethany* from his mouth sounds like someone that isn't me. Someone who *is* sexy and romantic and new and everything that I am decidedly not.

We dance for several more songs, quietly sharing information about ourselves. I learn that he has a younger brother, Noah, in my sister's grade. I vaguely think I already know this information, but I am too intoxicated by our proximity to really remember. I learn that he lives on New Road, not more than four minutes' walk from my house. This is good information to have, because it means that if I ever need to fulfil all the teen romance films I've ever watched then I can sneak away to his house in the dead of night for dead of night sex if we ever make it that far.

My heart is beating too-fast, too-excited by the time we step away from each other.

My body feels cold without his pressed against it, and I almost grab him back, pull him flush against me, grin against his chest, whisper more empty words across the space between us.

But instead, I let him go. He winks. "If you feel like getting out of here any time soon I'll be at Amber Park for the next few hours." And he saunters off out of the front door, leaving me dumbfounded at what on earth just happened.

I think I've evaded Nicolas entirely until I'm in the kitchen and he's tapping on my shoulder, and I turn around, heart still racing from the encounter with Aiden.

"Hi." He says. Like he knows something I don't. Like he saw all of what just happened and is about to ridicule me on how badly I handled the situation.

"Hi." I say.

"So…"

"So."

"Aiden Islington, huh?" He says it like it's a joke and I'm supposed to laugh along good-naturedly.

I smile politely and nod. "Yes."

He smiles politely back at me and reaches around me for a bottle of beer, one of the lukewarm ones by the fridge.

"You having fun?" He asks, popping the bottle open with one of the bottle openers scattered on the kitchen island. He has to shout in my ear over the pounding music and roar of people's voices.

"Yeah,"

"You don't sound very convinced."

"I am, I'm just not intent on sharing my sexual encounters with *you*." I say, and he laughs like he's supposed to. And then he reaches out a hand and tugs on my sleeve.

"Want to go outside?"

I suddenly want nothing more than to escape this sweaty house and give my heart and my mind some time to slow down and process exactly what just happened, so we walk together through the living room, and then the small sitting room and then through patio doors into the Dupont garden. There's a pool, covered over for autumn and winter, and then a huge expanse of grass that disappears into the darkness. Nicolas leads me to the edge of the pool, where some other guys are gathered.

"These are my friends," he introduces.

I don't really question it, I'm too busy revelling in the breeze and the cold and the feeling of Aiden on my skin.

We sit by them, and I notice it's a group of guys from our grade with two girls on two of their laps.

"Guys, this is Bethany." Nicolas introduces. "Bethany, this is the gang."

Nicolas Lopez is a druggie.

I always knew the druggie kids existed in Eastwood. Hell, I've probably sat next to a fair few high kids. But this is different. I don't trust Nicolas; I wouldn't even go so far as to say that we're friends. But I thought he was better than this, better than wasting away his youth on drugs and alcohol. Maybe that's a really pretentious thing to think. Crap, it's a horribly pretentious thing to say. But still— I never pegged him to be involved in this kind of thing.

And yet here we are, huddled illegally by the pool in Lauren Dupont's backyard after the first romantic experience of my high school career. And I'm being offered amphetamines by Marie Blaine, Poppie Masters, and Nicolas Lopez.

What a mad, mad world.

"Um, no thanks." I say.

Nicolas frowns. "Don't you want to have fun?"

"Not really."

Poppie Masters, who goes to Loye Valley CC, barks a laugh. "She's not going to take one, Nic. I've heard about girls like Bethany. Too tight-skirted and good for us."

"Where'd you find her?" The other girl, Marie, asks, smirking.

And something hot boils up in my stomach. I want to prove them wrong; I do. I want them to see that I'm not the goody two-shoes. Evie is. I am not my sister.

I can be my own person with these people, right? They won't expect me to surpass Evelyn in grades or find a hobby that will get me a free ride to Yale.

Nicolas bumps my shoulder with his. "Yeah, come on, Beth. You only live once, amirite?"

"Yeah, I guess." My resolve is cracking. Fracturing.

I crave something to take the tension away.

So I hold my hand out for the pills and knock them back with beer.

That is the moment I fall.

13] YOU'RE STILL AROUND

evelyn

JANUARY 14th, 2021, 8:42pm

Pain.

It's blinding.

Burning.

But if I was dead, I wouldn't feel the pain, right?

"Evie? Fuck, goddammit. Evie!"

All I see is Bethany. Pale face, small eyes forced into wide almonds. *"Evester!"*

"Evie, stay with me, alright?"

"Evester! Bet you can't catch me,"

"Evelyn goddamn Reed keep your eyes open, you idiot."

"Evie, shut up. I wish I was as smart as you."

"I think it just grazed your side, okay?"

I'm going to end up just like Bethany.

"I'm not going to let anything happen to you, Reed. You hear me?"

"I think I need to go away for a while, yeah?"

Bethany. River. *Bethany.* River.

Reed Lopez. There's familiarity in *Lopez*, like I know something that I'm forgetting.

"River." I'm gasping and my throat is burning but it's okay because I'm alive and I can feel all my extremities. My limbs are flexing, nose scrunching, lungs gasping. I passed out. I'm not dead. Or dying. I'm being dramatic— he's being dramatic.

It's still dark, but the limp glow of River's torch illuminates my legs and the blood seeping from my side, through his jacket. He must be cold.

"What the actual hell? Did you shoot me?" I ask him.

He actually *laughs* at that. "God, no, you idiot. Some guy in the forest did. One of those guys with the big guns who take it upon themselves to protect the town. When, really, all they're doing is causing more trouble,"

"Oh," For some reason I thought this shooting thing would mean something more. That there's a trigger-happy lunatic killer out there, or something. But this is a bit, well, boring.

And then I move a bit and pain shoots up my side. I gasp. "Shit, was I, like, shot?"

"The bullet grazed your side. You'll probably need stitches."

"Did you call an ambulance?"

River shakes his head. "I didn't really get a chance, what with dragging your ass through the woods, and then waiting to make sure you're still alive. You were out for a few minutes at most."

I nod. "Don't call one. I'm fine. Our health insurance ran out last year."

"You need stitches, though."

"I'll do it myself, or something. I think we have some of those butterfly strip thingies."

He nods, but he's frowning.

"Oh, stop being such a worrywart. I'm fine. Or I will be after I down a shot of vodka and get cleaned up. I suppose we'll have to postpone the find-the-gun operation, then."

"Postpone?" Incredulation is dripping from River's voice.

"You don't think we should go back there?"

"You just got *shot*, Reed. *You* think we should?"

"Well, yeah." I manage to prop myself up on my elbows. The ground is freezing against my butt. "How else are we supposed to get shit done?"

He shakes his head, his face screaming in resignation and exhaustion. "We'll talk about this tomorrow."

I bark out a breathy, sharp laugh. "That's your response to everything I say, isn't it? We'll talk tomorrow. God, Lopez, stop being such a Mom for once."

He flinches. "Just shut up and let me look at your side."

Suddenly feeling very tired, I flop back on the ground and wave a hand. "Do whatever, Doctor Lopez."

He chuckles at that, peeling away his sweater and then mine. Great, my third favourite-sweater, ripped and ruined. Ruined like so many other things.

"The good thing is this world's thickest sweater stopped most of the damage," he says.

I feel cold fingers against my burning skin, prodding at the swollen area. I'm afraid to look.

"The bleeding has mostly stopped. Maybe you were right— I don't think it's quite deep and wide enough to warrant stitches, but still." He's lying. I can tell. He's trying to make me feel better, but it's not working at all.

"It's bleeding a shit ton."

His face scrunches in defeat. "Yeah, it is."

He wraps his sweater around my midsection, tying it in a neat knot. "Is your Mom home?"

"God, Lopez, first you're taking all my clothes off and then you want to get in with my Mom? Calm down,"

He laughs. It's a scraping sound, like he doesn't do it a lot, or hasn't in a while. "Shut up, Reed. Shut up because if I have to sit on this frozen-ass floor for much longer *I'll* shoot you and make sure it actually hits you this time."

He swoops an arm around my shoulders and, with me mostly leaning on him and biting my lip against the sharp flames of pain, we become erect.

"Shit." I say, gasping.

"You okay?" River starts to hobble towards the truck. It's closer than I thought it would be. He must have managed to drag me the incredible twenty metres we made it into the forest. That plan really did fail miserably. Of *course* some Eastwood hero dude would be waiting for us. Hell, it was probably old man Arnold Windsor and his ridiculously long shotgun.

"Of course I'm okay. I'm perfectly fine." I gasp as he hoists me up into the seat, grappling for a foothold. "Everything's fucking okay."

"Don't make me wash your mouth out with soap."

I laugh as I finally sit, upright, in the seat. "I'm sorry if I get blood all over your seats,"

"This really is becoming a trend with you, Reed."

Yeah, it really is.

What a horrible, horrible pattern to repeat itself. My eyes are burning before I can stop them.

I almost got *shot*. I could have *died*.

River starts the truck's engine. "You okay?"

But I *didn't die*.

Maybe I should have died. Maybe I deserve it. Maybe— I clear my throat. Shake the horrible thoughts out of my head. Send River a tight-lipped smile that physically hurts me to produce.

"Yeah, sure."

I'm not. Oh, shit, I'm not okay.

14] FATHER FIGURELESS

JANUARY 14th, 2021, 9:01pm

"Stop screaming!" I say, exasperated. Evie is perched on the bathroom countertop, wincing and gasping.

Dad's in the living room with a sleeping Hadley. All he said when Evie and I hobbled in was if we needed a lift to the hospital, and when we said no, he promised us mugs of coffee and dug the first aid kit out of one of the boxes in his closet.

So now I'm trying to clean and bandage Evie's side, and she's being very dramatic about it.

"It *hurts*."

"I hadn't noticed."

And it looks like it does hurt— the skin is jagged and ripped in a line about two inches long. The cut isn't life-threateningly deep, but I can still see the shiny pale fat under her skin. My hands are shaking a little bit. The

THE ENIGMATIC END TO BETHANY REED

tanned skin around it is swollen and red, puckering up with the threat of impending infection.

"You don't want sepsis, do you?" I say, gently holding the antiseptic to the bleeding gash again. I feel her stomach tense under my hands, and swallow.

"You kids alright?" Dad calls through the door. "Bit of an unsuccessful first date, huh?"

He laughs to himself.

I wonder why he's not freaking out more.

"We're good, thanks!" I say.

Evie smiles. "Your Dad seems wonderful."

"Yeah?"

"Yeah."

"Is your dad around, or?" I say. It could be digging too deep, too personal, but she just sighs.

"No. He left not long after Bethany died,"

I frown, digging around in the first aid kit for what I'm looking for. "Oh, I'm sorry. That's a dick move."

She lets out a breathy laugh, wincing at the strain. "Yeah. He lives in Bangor now— but I haven't seen him since I was fifteen,"

"That sucks."

"What about your mom? Did she come with you from Canada, or?" She asks.

I don't know what to say. Do I tell her the truth, or is that severely oversharing? So I just smile. "She's not in Canada, she— um,"

"You don't have to say." Evie butts in quickly, cutting me off.

I come up with the butterfly strips and open the packet. "Ready?"

"As I'll ever be,"

I press the first strip to the cut and try to hold it closed, but it slips and strains under the pressure.

I hate it, but she needs stitches.

"You need stitches, Evie." I say.

"No hospitals." She says. Sharp, hard. "*Please.* I can't afford it at all."

"Well, then, I'm going to have to stitch it up,"

"I trust you." Without hesitation. The words are quiet, calm. They hang stagnant in the air, waiting. I suck in a breath. Can I really do stitches on someone? I've sown up holes in jeans and socks before. I can do a simple stitch, but—

"Please, River. Just do it." She says. Her teeth are gritted, and the gash has started bleeding again. She really needs a hospital. But she just might be alright if I can stop the bleeding and stitch it up. I have fairly steady hands. When I'm not nervous, or under pressure.

I let out a hysterical laugh, lifting a sweaty hand to wipe my sweaty forehead. "Oh, god, am I really going to do this?"

She smiles, her skin shining as well. "Yeah, Lopez. You're going to stitch me up."

"If you die, I don't take responsibility."

"You're being dramatic. It's just a needle,"

But she doesn't sound too convinced that it's all going to be fine, either.

"Right." I say, setting everything down. "Hold that against it, okay? I'm just going to get the sewing kit and a lighter."

I leave the room, legs trembling. Dad looks up at me from the couch when I jog into the living room.

"She still alive?" He jokes.

I wipe a hand across my forehead. "Yep. Where's the sewing kit?"

He looks alarmed by that. "Do you need, um, help in there?"

Dad can sew about as well as he can cook. I shake my head. "No, thanks. We'll be alright."

He points to the drawers in the corner, under the window that looks out to Evie's house across the street. "Sewing kit's in there, son. Don't seriously maim anyone if you can help it."

I nod, biting my lip. "Yep, thanks Dad."

Kit in hand, I hurry back to the bathroom. Evie's looking pale, and I can see her hand shaking as it holds the gauze against the blood. The counter is smeared with red. It looks like the scene of a murder, which is horribly ironic.

"Right then, let's do this. You good?" I say.

She nods, her bottom lip tightly gripped between her teeth. "Just do it, please."

I open the kit and pull out a needle and thread. I don't have a way of sanitising the thread, but I hold up the lighter and stick the needle in the tiny flame until it goes red.

Then we wait, for a few minutes, until it's cool. I hate that my hands are shaking, but I wash them well and it takes me a few more minutes to poke the black thread through the eye of the needle.

"Hurry up, for God's sake." Evie says.

I hold up the needle and pray to anything that will listen that the thread doesn't slip from the needle and make this ten times more difficult than it already is.

I place a hand on hers and move aside the gauze. The wound is bloody again, so I wipe away the excess and use two fingers to try and keep the cut closed. She winces but doesn't say anything.

"Breathe, okay? Don't hold your breath, or you might pass out, and then I'll just end up stabbing you."

She nods. "Yep. 'Course. Anything for you, Doctor Lopez."

I grip the needle and position it next to the wound, angled to go down into the skin. The tip goes in, disappearing beneath the flesh. It feels oddly smooth as I angle it across the wound and up through the other side.

Evie is whimpering, knuckles white against the counter. I hate this. I hate this.

It takes me twenty minutes to do the whole cut and it's messy and horrible and will leave a nasty scar, but it's done. The bleeding stops.

"We're done." I say, dropping the bloody needle in the sink. She lets out a huge breath, and I can see the muscles in her stomach relaxing. I wash my hands again and reach for a large adhesive bandage from the first aid kit. The cut gets one last wipe and then is finally covered.

I don't have to look at it anymore.

But I do have to look at the haunting collection of bloodied gauze in the sink and the mess of two destroyed sweaters on the floor and the coil of stained thread.

"Thank you, River." Evie says. Her voice sounds hoarse. Pained.

"It's no problem, really."

"You're a good friend. And I bet you'd make a good doctor," she throws in a sad, small smile at the end there and I let out a shaky laugh.

"Yeah, right." I say. "Never doing that again, if I can help it."

We take a second then to breathe, not saying anything, just admiring the fact that she's still alive and I just stitched someone up. Successfully. Kind of.

Then I blink, sigh, and nod to the bandage.

"You have to change it twice a day, okay? And check for infection every day. That's excessive redness, pus, red streaks, or fever. Okay?"

She nods, gritting her teeth as I help her down from the countertop. "Thanks, Lopez."

I smile. "All in a day's work,"

She helps me pack everything away and pile all the bloody bandages and her ruined sweater into a trash bag and then follows me out into the hall. She has a limp, and probably will for a few days.

"You have a nice house." She says, admiring the pale grey painted hallway. "It's weird, I've lived opposite this house my whole life and it's been empty for four years. I guess I wondered what it looked like inside."

"Yeah, well, they renovated it last year, I think, to try and get it to sell."

She hums as I lead her into my bedroom, and I curse myself for not tidying up my room this morning. It's a mess, but she doesn't seem to mind at all. I dig out a spare t-shirt from one of the boxes by my bed, handing it to her.

"Thanks," she says, pulling it over her head. I only then realise that she's been just in a bra this whole time. My cheeks flush with the realisation.

Dad's in the kitchen now, and he has made toast with surprising success. There are three steaming mugs of coffee on the side. Evie takes one, holding it in her hands.

Some of the colour starts to return to her cheeks. God, Evie and coffee. It must be the only thing keeping her alive. Except maybe my masterful attempt at stitches.

"Hi, Mr Lopez," Evie says brightly.

"Evening, Evie." Dad says, smiling. "What did you two kids get up to, then?"

We've spoken about this lie. It slips off my tongue with scary believability. "Evie is such a horrible klutz, oh my *god*."

She laughs along, eyes crinkled. "Don't be a meanie, River. We went into Loye Valley for coffee and then I slipped on the riverbank and ripped myself open on a fallen branch. And I think it's incredibly important to note that the branch was very much obscured in darkness, so anyone could have made the same mistake,"

Dad laughs as well, and I throw in a chuckle for good measure. "Oh, you silly thing. You're alright, though?"

"Yep. All that blood was just my body being very dramatic. I'm fine, just a small gash."

He smiles and nods. "Well, I'm sorry your little outing went so awry. Did you two get to eat, at least?"

Evie's stomach chooses that moment to rumble noisily. Her smile takes on a sheepish quality. "Um,"

Dad's bellowing laugh echoes out. My own mouth twists into a grin. *This*. These are the kind of moments that we moved for. We never would have achieved something this close to normality in the depressing confines of our five bedroom in suburban Saint John.

He reaches behind him and plucks two slices of not burnt toast from the toaster, setting it on a plate and gesturing to the measly collection of spreads.

"Ooh, butter please," Evie says.

And we sit down at the table with a sleeping Hadley and have hushed conversations about school and life in general and despite the horrible events of the night, it's the best few hours I've had since we moved.

15] BITTERNESS

JANUARY 15th, 2021, 8:18am

On my eighth day in Eastwood, it feels like my eight-hundredth. In a week, I've made friends. I've become overly involved with a strange girl from across the street. I've begun investigating a murder that's turned into two murders. I've barely slept.

And yet I've developed a kind of liking for this town. Not your usual warm liking, filled with fondness and attraction, but the kind of liking that hasn't really figured itself out yet.

Tentative. More knowing than loving.

More understanding than enjoying.

Eastwood is my home now, and this is a fact I have become very certain of. New Brunswick is also my home.

You can have two homes; it's like having two best friends, in that they both occupy separate sections of your heart. New Brunswick will always be my favourite place, my childhood, a symbol of some of the best, most monumental moments of my life. But Eastwood will probably always be the place that I really, truly felt at home, however much I hated it.

One week and I already feel like this.

But it certainly feels like much more than a week has passed. It feels like I've been sleeping in this uncomfortable double bed for decades, eating breakfast on the way to school in the truck for centuries, picking up two lattes from Cathy's on the way to school for millennia.

There's ten minutes left of this life skills lesson, first period and already I'm exhausted enough to go right back to bed. Running on a few hours a night is wearing me down like a pencil. Worrying, worrying, worrying. It was worse last night, when I had to stitch Evie up and even though she has assured me plenty of times that the pain's not too bad, and there's no sign of infection— I'm worried. *Worrying worrying worrying.*

Part of me now understands why the town sees her as the crazy one, crazy, broken, mentally damaged. It's painfully obvious that the death of her sister and the constant reminders of it and its damage have worn her mind down to just the saddest remains of what it was.

Another part of me aches to know the real Evelyn Reed: the girl that was there before grief shaped her into a shell. I hate to think that the Evie from before is gone. I hate to think that she will feel like this forever— let the weight of grief move in permanently.

I myself have seen more grief than one can imagine, but the suburbs of Saint John were kind to my family. We grieved in a community that understood the pain and its repercussions. Evie and her mom were ripped to shreds for feeling what is completely normal.

That judgemental side of Eastwood is the side that I despise. The judgemental side of Eastwood is the reason why she only goes to Cathy's when Hailey is working. Why she avoids the grocery store in the town, and ventures into Loye Valley.

The bell rings to end the lesson and I join the cacophony of students packing up their stuff. The human nature corridor is cold and bustling, coating my arms in goosebumps.

Evie is beside me a moment later. "Morning, Lopez."

"Hi," I say. We sidestep a group of fluttering sophomore girls. "How are you doing?"

She blinks, as if confused, as if she doesn't know what I'm talking about. But the moment of weakness is fleeting and within half a second she's back to keen, concentrated Evie. "I'm alright. Mom's a mess, but she always is."

"Oh,"

"Yeah."

"What about with the email? Are you going to take it to the Sheriff?" I ask, already half-knowing the answer.

"I think that last email confirmed one of two things. Either the emailer really *is* the killer, or I'm being stalked,"

Both of those leave sick, horrible feelings in my gut. I don't say anything, swallowing hard.

"Because whoever wrote it knows that Bethany was also murdered— or at least that that's what the police think. To know that, you'd either have to be the one behind it all or have overheard the conversation in my living room this morning."

"Or be a policeman or be stalking any of the deputies." I say.

She looks at me, frowning. "Are you doubting me?"

Yes. "You're tired. Can we talk about it later?" I say, desperate to stop the pinched, pained look on her face when she thinks about all of it.

There's a moment of silence. A nod from her.

"So, do you want to meet up this weekend, or?" I pose. If we're going to do this then we might as well rip off the Band-Aid and start working on the case as soon as possible, hopefully with less disaster than the last time we tried.

"Sure. My place or yours?"

"Actually, my dad has been bugging me to invite you over for dinner one night. We could do Saturday afternoon and evening?" I ask. We're approaching the maths corridor now. I've got algebra next. I think Evie has statistics. We'll be going to different classrooms.

She nods earnestly to my question. "Yeah, yeah that sounds great. Tell your Dad I'm looking forward to it!"

And then she's pulled into Mr Sanderson's class, and I push open the door to Miss Adams'.

*****

9am rolls around and Evie and I settle down in the courtyard for psychology. We're allowed to go basically anywhere in the school to work on our projects, and we chose the courtyard because it's January. No one else is going to be out here, so we get maximum privacy.

The only downside to that is there's frost on the ground, and our breaths steam the air. It's fucking cold. No, *freezing*.

"Where do we even start?" I ask Evie as she unwraps a brand-new notebook from its plastic cover.

"At the beginning." She says, without hesitation, as if she's spent the last few days thinking very very hard about that exact question. I wouldn't be surprised if she had.

"What do you mean?" I ask.

"Well, we know the first murder was in 2018. Senior class of 2018. So, we need to find out exactly what happened to my sister in that year, and who knew Jackson and Bethany well enough to want to kill them specifically."

And then she goes horribly pale.

"What?" I ask.

"Nevae. Oh, fuck." Evie looks like she's going to be sick. "Nevae Bradbury. There was always the three of them, all the time: Jackson, Bethany, and Nevae. How on earth did I miss this? I know that she couldn't have done it, because—well, you met her— but she could be the next victim. Oh, *shit*."

She spends much of the rest of the lesson writing a couple of pages worth of notes— background information, mostly, whilst explaining to me most of what I need to know. About Nevae and Bethany and Jackson and their friendship.

When the bell rings, Evie's skin is still pale, and her eyes are still wider than usual. She pulls a permanent marker from her bag and scribbles something on the white cover of the notebook. When she tilts it towards me, she says, "I think this is what our project should be called,"

And I smile because the name she has chosen is so very Evelyn Reed.

*****

Having spent an hour after class with Evie in the library going over some of the logistics of how we're going to do our project with Mr Black (submitting weekly updates, but more independence than the other groups with more relaxed deadlines due to the personal element to our project), I'm home later than usual.

"I'm home!" I call, swinging the front door shut and kicking off my shoes.

Dad's voice comes from the kitchen. "In here, son!"

So I walk into the kitchen, and my heart drops through the floor and into the ground, out the other side, and into space.

Nicolas Lopez is in our house.

TEXAS STATE UNIVERSITY

Where dreams come true.

01.05.2021
Nicolas Lopez
Apartment 19B, Cromwell Heights
Norman Road
Houston, TEXAS

To Mr Lopez,

It is with regret that I have to inform you that, following a rather unfortunate string of incidents, the administration office at TSU have been forced to revoke your scholarship and place at this institution.

We hope that you will thrive elsewhere, as it has become apparent that this college isn't a good fit for you. We need you to collect any belongings from campus, clear out your library cubby, and hand in any assignments (finished or unfinished) to your professors by the end of this week. You will not be attending classes after Friday.

Best wishes,

Samuel Arrington

Samuel Arrington, Student Director T

16] BROTHERS LOPEZ

river

JANUARY 15th, 2021, 5:38pm

I have not seen my brother since he was fifteen, and I was freshly twelve. I know that I've hated him since basically the day I was born. I know that he has done terrible, terrible things and it is unlikely that we will ever be close with one another.

We may be brothers, but the *man* standing in front of me now is as much a stranger as the man I passed on the street outside who gave me a tight smile, filled with pity because he could see me getting out of Evelyn Reed's car.

Nicolas Lopez is the same height as me, but he is broader in the shoulders than me, filled out by manhood. We could not look more dissimilar. Where I have Dad's Hispanic face with the round chin and skin the tone of molten honey, Nicolas is sharp and angular like he's cut from stone. His skin is pale and freckled, eyes blue and bright.

My own are dark brown, more likened to the warm tones of autumn than his stark wintry colouring.

"River." Nicolas says. It sounds like he hasn't said my name in centuries. His voice is deeper than it was last time I heard it, rawer and rougher.

I don't reply.

Dad looks horribly uncomfortable.

"It's, um, it's nice to see you." Nicolas tries again. "Uh— you're all grown up! I almost didn't recognise you."

He sounds sad.

I don't give a single shit.

"Why are you here?" Is the only thing I can bring myself to say.

"I, uh, I was in town. Decided to come and visit."

"How did you know this is where we live?"

Dad clears his throat. "I sent him our address, River. Decided that it was time to rip off the Band-Aid and get to know my own son again."

"How could you forgive him?" I'm shocked at the harshness in my own voice.

"People change, River. People get better, you know."

It's such a Dad thing to say that I almost laugh.

Maybe I'm going a bit hysterical.

I can't stop staring at Nicolas Lopez. Startled at how different we look, how so much time in such different places has shaped us into opposites. Where he is pale and angular, I am soft and coloured. Where his hair is dark and wild, mine is brown and neat. I cannot stop running over our dissimilarities in my head, how stark and bold they are now that we are grown.

"You've grown." Nicolas says, again.

I nod. "It's been five years, Nicolas."

"My friends call me Nic, now, by the way."

"We're not friends,"

"I never said we are."

"Why now, Nicolas?" I ask, because it's a question that makes sense and there isn't a lot that makes sense to me at the moment.

"I felt like seeing family. Familiar faces. Thought I'd welcome you to the states."

"Well, you're not exactly a welcoming sight," I say.

Nicolas flinches, as if that particular sentence is more impactful and hurtful than anything else I've thrown his way. And I almost feel bad. And then I remember my mother's face, all beaten and bruised to the point where I cried when I saw her, because that wasn't my mother.

And I hate him.

I hate him.

17] PERSONS OF INTEREST

evelyn

JANUARY 15th, 2021, 8:09pm

The most recent email has been playing on repeat in my head for hours. I think it's branded itself on the underside of my eyelids, on the forefront of my brain, on every surface I look at, dancing in the sky and the frigid, empty air outside my window.

I need a distraction.

Usually, this would include stealing a bottle of white wine with Mae from her parents' wine collection, sitting on my front porch, drinking from clouded glasses so it looks like lemonade to anyone walking past. Getting tipsy, having long conversations into the night, until Mom comes home from her shift at the bar and shoos us off to bed.

I don't know if she's the person I need to talk to right now. Lately, every time I've seen Mae I've seen her father and only been able to think about what I'm keeping from her— the emails, the suspicions, the depth of my friendship with River. So instead I pull on my Converse and lock the door behind me, slipping our only front door key under the mat.

It's cold outside. Cold enough to make me believe that it's going to snow tomorrow. Or maybe even tonight. Maybe I'll get caught up in it and it will soak through the thin canvas of my shoes and turn my feet pink and numb.

Maybe I'll just walk until I'm south of here, in a state where it doesn't snow. Where everything is clean and visible and clear, and you don't have to read between the lines.

My fingers are turning stiff already, but I mosey down Hastings Road anyway. All the lights are on in River's house, and in Mae's. I cut off onto New Road, in the direction of Morning Road and the Sheriff's station. I'll probably walk past it, stare at it, thinking about what would happen if I handed in everything I had about Bethany and Jackson.

They'd thank me, but I wouldn't miss the suspicion in their eyes— why did I find these things now? Why was I looking? Why was I interfering?

I keep walking.

I walk past Ella Lopez's house on the corner of Beaumaris and Morning, past Cathy's Diner where I used to work evening shifts. Just as the peaks of Elizabeth Gingham come into view, unused chimneys illuminated and reaching into the sky, and I've been walking for almost an hour, I see Benji.

He's hunched over on a bench, but I wouldn't miss those dark jeans with Ivy's messy, loving embroidery work weaving down the leg. I wouldn't miss the buzzcut, the horrible posture.

But something's wrong with this image. Where he should be perky, upright, smiling, this Benji is staring at the asphalt as if it's going to swallow him whole. As if he wants it to.

"Benji?" I ask.

My voice fractures the silence he was likely seeking solace in, and momentarily I regret saying anything. I should have kept walking, left him to his thoughts, not disturbed what was obviously an important, emotional moment for him.

But then he looks up and, in the dull light of the streetlamps, I see he's crying. Glistening cheeks I've seen thousands of times in the mirror, and the dark green of a bruise blooming on one cheek.

My heart just about falls to pieces.

I hurry over, taking a seat next to him on the bench, not even waiting for words before I'm pulling him against me, hugging him tightly.

"Oh my god, Benji." I say into him.

"Lynny— I—"

"Shh," I say, "you don't have to say anything."

Except he kind of does, because by the looks of it someone hurt him, and I want to hurt them.

"Who did this to you?" I ask a few minutes later, loosening my hold. He leans his head against my shoulder, his large frame almost comically warping itself to fit against my shortness.

"No one, Lynny. No one but me."

That's how it begins. Stories like Benji's begin with scenes like these.

—

When I get back to the house a little under an hour later, having walked Benji home and hugged him until he stopped crying, Mom's car is in the driveway. It's an old Ford Fiesta, a rusted black. It blends into the darkness of the night sky effortlessly. I grit my teeth and my hands curl themselves into tight fists as I make my way up the porch steps. They creak under my weight.

I love my mom, I do. But ever since Bethany she's become so withdrawn and thrown herself so fully into her work that we're nothing more than roommates that occasionally see each other in the house. When I wake up, she's leaving for work cleaning houses in Loye Valley, and when I get home she's already left for her evening shift at the bar. Since our conversation just after Jackson died, I haven't shared more than a few polite words with her.

The front door squeals as the hinge shifts open, the sound too loud in the echoey foyer. Why is she home early?

I undo the laces on my Converse slowly, trying to think of what to say to her. *What have you been up to, Evie?* Oh, nothing, just investigating a murder— my own sister's murder.

I am a horrible liar when it comes to my mom.

She's in the kitchen. As I slide the final shoe off my foot and place it carefully by the door, I hear the sound of a mug settling heavily onto the granite countertops.

"Evie?" She calls a second later. Her voice is strained and tired, but soft.

I bite my tongue and walk into the kitchen. Mom is leaning against the counter. Her hair, as wavy and messy as mine, is in a tight ponytail that tugs on her worn features. She looks like a taller, more tired version of me.

"Hi, Mom." I say. It feels like I'm in trouble, even though she doesn't have any idea what I've been up to the past week.

"It's nice to see you properly." She says. She's smiling.

An invisible weight lifts from my chest. We're just mother and daughter, having a conversation.

"You too. You look tired. What are you doing home from work early?"

"The bar closed early today. I'm only an hour early,"

"Oh,"

"Where were you? I thought we could have a girls night, or something."

Girls night? My mom hasn't suggested a girl's night since Bethany was alive. I'm so taken aback that it takes me a few moments to string together a suitable response. I'm only half lying.

"Oh, I was out— a friend needed me."

"Which friend?"

"Uh— Benji."

"Oh. is he okay?"

The memory of him, folded, looking so horribly broken flits back into my mind. But I bite back the truth and nod. "Yeah, just needed some homework help."

Mom clucks her tongue, and her smile is teasing. "I thought I got you a mobile phone for this kind of thing."

My phone is eight years old and cracked in multiple places across the screen. It only turns on when it wants to, and it's currently in my back pocket, dead.

"It died." I say.

She nods. There's an awkwardness in the air as both of us try to think of something to say.

Finally, Mom clears her throat. "I—uh— I'll just have a shower, and then how do you feel about watching Dirty Dancing? We have popcorn, I think."

My heart shudders. *Dirty Dancing* was Beth's favourite film. She used to watch it all the time. Why would Mom suggest watching it again?

But I don't want to risk fracturing this perfect little bubble of peace that we've acquired, so I nod and watch as she climbs the stairs, half a mug of coffee abandoned on the counter.

18] HITTING HOME

river

JANUARY 16th, 2021, 8:33am

Our new house is much smaller than our massive stone suburban in New Brunswick, so Nicolas spends the night on the couch in the living room. He hasn't met Hadley before. She doesn't know about her half-brother, and I don't want her to. He doesn't deserve to meet her. I don't want her perfect innocence to be tainted by the shadow that Nicolas seems to lug everywhere with him.

I haven't spoken to him since I was twelve, and he beat my mother, Hannah, absolutely senseless. Nicolas was sent to live with family, and I never heard anything about him ever again. The Lopez's aren't exactly close, from what I've heard there hasn't been a family gathering on Dad's side of the family since whatever sent Dad away from Eastwood and forced him to cut off all contact with his own mother.

It must have been bad: I'm pretty sure that our family just sort of carries bad luck around in their pockets.

My second Saturday in Eastwood begins with the sun streaming in through my bedroom window. After a week, I'm pretty much moved in: my double bed has new, clean brown sheets on it, and I've decided to go to the hardware store this weekend and pick out paint colours for mine and Hadley's rooms. All my school stuff is strewn across my desk, and it looks lived in. Homely.

I'm so surprised at this thought that I shoot upright. And then my phone vibrates, and I look down at it, and it's Evie's daily photo of the wound on her side.

> still alive ;)

I smile. It looks better, actually— the swelling has gone down, and she's taken off the butterfly strips, so it's just a long, jagged, painful-looking cut more than the sickly, gnarly gash it was before.

> good to know. we still on for tonight?

ofc! will be there seven on the dot. u need me to bring anything? wear anything nice ? is this a casual dinner? bro no i'm so lost.

I remember, briefly, that Nicolas will probably be at this dinner, and I suddenly don't want her to come. Which is stupid.

Evie can hold her ground against my brother.

> you're good. don't bring anything except yourself! just wear normal clothes, we're not a fancy dinner family.

> oh, and my brother will be there, fyi. and he's kinda a dick so yea

She quickly texts back an affirmative along with several emojis expressing her confusion at me never mentioning I have a brother. I don't answer, instead tossing my phone onto the bed and getting up. I stretch nice and big and yawn, looking outside. And then doing a double take.

It's snowing.

Like, the foot deep doesn't stop for days kind of snowing.

Shit.

I mean, we got the yearly snowfall in New Brunswick, but most of the time it happened over winter break, and I didn't have to worry about driving to school in it, and it wasn't this heavy.

God, it's practically a blizzard outside. No wonder it's so bright in my room; the snow reflects bright white light into the space. There's definitely a chill in the air: more than normal. My arms are covered in goosebumps as I gape outside.

It's beautiful. I thought that Eastwood was the kind of town that was doomed to be ugly forever: that not even the bright sunny kiss of summer could turn it into a place worthy of photographs, but this—

"River! Are you up?" Dad's voice calls through the wall.

Shaken out of my stupor, I call back, "Yeah!"

"Good. I'm just going to the grocery store. I've got Hadley with me!"

I shout back an affirmative and then my heart drops as I realise that leaves Nicolas and me in the house alone together. Not so fun.

But I stumble into the bathroom and turn on the shower, letting the mirror steam up and the heat wrap me up all cosy. I've got a free day today— not doing anything except for dinner later, so I decide that I'm going to devote the whole of the day to exploring my new home.

The shower is blisteringly hot, which I think is the best way to have it. I stand under it until my skin is pink and sore and then wash and step out. I catch a look at my face in the mirror and stare.

There are bags under my eyes, and my cheeks are looking slightly sallow. Perfect excuse to stop by Cathy's for lunch.

After getting dressed in a pair of jeans and my favourite sweater (blue, with a funny graphic involving a

cabbage), I sit on my bed and look up Eastwood on
Google Maps.

It's literally just a spot of grey in a sea of green with a
slightly larger spot of grey (Loye Valley) next to it.
Redwood, which sits on the other side of Eastwood, isn't
even visible through the green, it's so small. I could drive
the hour to Bangor and actually get some of the city air
that was everywhere in Saint John. But that's not exactly
local, and what if Dad needs me? What if Evie needs me?
Not an option. I could go into Loye Valley and try to find
coffee and maybe a good bookstore. I had to leave a lot of
my books in New Brunswick because there wasn't enough
room for them in the truck, but my bookshelf looks
garishly empty without all four hundred and eight of its
occupants.

Yeah, I'll do that.

*****

I must be an Eastwood native now, because as soon
as I drive into Loye Valley and see how much bigger it is
than Eastwood I think it's like a city. Which is ridiculous,
because Saint John was about 120 square miles and Loye
Valley can't be more than 2 miles wide.

Still, the roads are wider and straighter and there's
more than two main roads. Eastwood has Gretchen Road
and New Road, and the rest are short, squiggly lines
bordered by houses on all sides. I'm very grateful that the
truck still has its snow tires on, and there's no problem in
trundling down already-ploughed roads. Luckily, it seems
that Ashwell County is accustomed to snow, so everything
is still open despite the disruption. And there is a lot of
snow— the blizzard conditions have waned, but it's still
flurrying quite heavily.

There's barely any cars on the road, but I'm not sure that Loye Valley gets particularly busy even when it's not snowing.

I follow one of the town's main roads, Springwood Leys, all the way to its end. At the bottom of the road is a collection of eclectic looking tiny cafes and shops, not all that different from Halliebottom Emporium in Redwood. This seems as good a place as any to hunker down for a few hours. I park the truck across the road and cross.

There's a row of five or six square, squat buildings all decorated busily with ivy, fairy lights and wonky wooden signs. Charming. They're all lit up, with *We're Open!* plastered across the doors. I reach the third one in, which is apparently a cafe, and inside the place is warm and empty except for a girl working the counter.

She looks a bit older than me, maybe Nicolas's age. She's got blonde hair pinned up on her head with streaks of blue weaved in. Her name tag reads *Marie*.

She smiles as she sees me. "Finally. We could use some customers today. Welcome to the Coffee Cubby, what can I get you?"

I wander up to the counter, "I'll have the largest latte you do with an extra shot of coffee, please."

She nods, getting to work behind the counter. "You from around here, then?"

"Yeah, I live in Eastwood."

A funny expression crosses her face. "Cool."

"Are you?" I'm trying to use my Canadian charm to make conversation, so it isn't so silent and awkward.

"No. I live in Abbey Saltville, just up the road. I used to live in Eastwood, though. Near the Sheriff's station? I went to high school there, actually."

"When did you graduate?"

"2018. Couldn't wait to get out," she laughs.

"No, me neither." I say, but there's an absence to my voice now. *2018*. That was the year Bethany was supposed to graduate. I take a deep breath, and swallow. "Did you know Bethany Reed?"

Marie freezes. "Uh. I'm not really comfortable answering that."

So that's a yes then. "Oh, don't worry. Sorry, just me being nosy."

She places the latte in front of me with shaking hands. "Here's your coffee."

I hand over a ten-dollar bill. "Keep the change." I pick a seat in the back of the cafe and put my earphones in to show that Marie doesn't need to keep talking to me and think about how weird that was.

I shoot Evie a text.

> hey. did your sister ever mention a girl called Marie from her grade?

maybe. Marie Blaine?

> possibly

> i mean, how many Maries could have been in their grade lol

very true. why do you ask?

> just met a girl in loye valley called Marie, said she gradyated in 2018 and when I asked her if she knew bethany, she got all weird.

i mean, most people probably aren't that willing to talk about a classmate that comitted suicide/was murdered.

> true.

still a bit weird though, you're right. i know of Marie Blaine, she lived on manor drive, not too far from Benji. i thought she moved further away than that,

19] SMALL WORLD

evelyn

JANUARY 16th, 2021, 9:44am

"We should search Bethany's bedroom." I say, around lunchtime. The snow is still coming down, thick on the ground. River and I are in my kitchen, drinking hot, dark coffee and pouring over the case. The notebook I named the other day is open in front of us, pens scattered haphazardly across the counter.

River looks vaguely concerned, which is a look he frequently sends my way. "Are you sure that's a good idea? I mean— have you even been in there since, you know…"

"No, I haven't." This is true. Bethany's room is exactly the same as it was that day when she got out of bed and went to school and never came back. I am too terrified to go back in there, and before now I haven't had a reason.

He sighs. "You shouldn't push yourself or move too quickly just for a school project."

"It's been three years, Lopez. I'm not moving too quickly. If anything I'm moving too slowly,"

He arches a brow. "You really want to go in there?"

"I do." I don't, not really. Well, I want to try and get a lead on the case, but my heart aches and pulls painfully at the idea of actually going into Bethany's bedroom and seeing it the way she would leave it in the morning: a mess, with the window shut tight and bedsheets everywhere. There would probably be makeup on her desk, homework on the floor, phone charger strewn across the bed. Curtains open.

Another, smaller, part of me wants to step into a world where she's still alive. Where she's about to come home and go in her room and finish an assignment, or something.

"There could be something in there— a tie to another person we're not thinking of looking at."

River nods. "Someone like Marie Blaine."

"Yes! There could be something in her room that makes Marie a suspect, something we can use or something I can use to contact her." I know that Marie was in my sister's grade, and I want to talk to her. I want to be insensitive and dig too deep and be a horrible person. The thought makes me feel sick, but the desperation is still there. Clawing. Climbing up my throat.

There are some things that Nevae doesn't know about, and I always feel shitty about asking her about my sister when it's clearly painful for her. But Marie Blaine is a faceless nobody I have only ever heard whispers of. It's easy to break the hearts of people you don't know.

River still doesn't look sure, so I stand up to emphasise the fact that I am really actually very ready to do this. And he stands up as well, which feels like a good sign.

"Come on," I say, and I start walking. Through the living room, into the tiny hallway. Up the stairs, which creak too much, too familiarly. Ignore two of the three doors crowded around the top of the stairs. The one on the right, that leads to my bedroom. The one straight ahead, that leads to the bathroom. The one to the left, we stop in front of.

"This is it?" River says.

"This is it." I confirm. My throat is closing up, like I'm deathly allergic to the white wooden panelling of this door, to the thought of what lies beyond, to the idea of any trace of my sister being left on the planet. When she died, Mom ripped out everything that reminded her of Beth and threw it up into the attic. I haven't seen anything belonging to her since 2018. This feels like too much too fast too suddenly, but I won't cry so I push open the door.

It smells musty. The window is tightly shut.

But other than that it is exactly the same as the last time I saw it. Unmade bed, pale yellow sheets strewn haphazardly. The bed is pushed against the wall, under one of the eaves. The small gap between the bed and the wall is filled in with a precarious, thin bookshelf. Her desk is pushed under the window, a mess. I choke up.

My cheeks are suddenly wet. There's pictures, like there always was, covering the wall above her bed. Pictures of her favourite movie characters, smiling faces of Nevae and Jackson. And the biggest picture— a portrait of me and her, taken on the only family holiday we've ever been able to afford: a four-day trip to New York four summers ago. Me and her are wearing shorts and caps and smiling widely at the camera from in front of the statue of liberty.

It's too much.

It's not enough.

"Are you okay?" River asks, and then he curses. "Of course you're not okay, shit. This was a bad idea, oh my god."

"No, it's fine." I say. Wave him off like he's an annoying fly. "I'm fine. We need to start looking before my Mom comes home and finds out I've done this."

"Are you not allowed?"

"Mom doesn't want anyone in here. She got mad every time I suggested it before."

He frowns but doesn't say anything else.

We're both still standing in the doorway, staring at the room. It feels weird. Like we've just walked into a time capsule. Like this in this room Bethany is alive. Nothing has changed here. She isn't dead as long as we're in this room.

I feel sick, suddenly, like someone has punched me in the gut.

"Are you good?" River asks me again, poking me in the back with a single long finger.

I nod, pulling my hair back into a low bun and exposing the sweating skin of my neck. "Let's do this."

*****

I make River start on the underneath of her bed whilst I dig through her desk. Everything is coated in a thick layer of dust. I've hauled open one of the large windows built into the eaves and now the room is fresh and slightly too cold. Not so warm and musty and difficult to breathe in.

As the minutes turn into half an hour, all we've found from the months surrounding late 2017 and early 2018 are an invoice for some repairs to the Volvo, and a couple of receipts for things like journals and pens.

It's gotten easier. My eyes dried up a while ago, and since then the thickness in my throat has faded as well. I'm just laser-focused on the task at hand, not allowing myself to think about the last time Bethany was in this room. The last time she sat down at this desk to do homework and messaged Nevae and rang Jackson and came down for dinner in the sweats folded in her closet and

"Evie." River says.

I swing around, looking at him. He's crouched by the bed like he has been for a while, but he's holding something in his hand.

Something small and black.

A phone.

Except, no, the police took away Bethany's phone and it was a slim phone, one of the early 2010 models. This— this is something else.

He hands it to me, and I look at it. It's lightweight and small. The screen lights up when I hold down the power button.

I turn it over, looking for any sign of a manufacturer or an owner or anything.

"Evie— I'm pretty sure it's a burner phone," River says. Quietly. As if this information is going to bruise me, and by saying it softly he's helping soften the impact.

"No. Why would she need a burner phone? Those are for drug addicts and criminals. Not high school girls."

At that moment, the phone flickers onto its lock screen. It doesn't ask for a password.

There are two apps: phone and message.

My hands are shaking furiously as I press on the grey icon of the messages app.

●●●○○ PREPAID 4G **1:01AM**   3% ▭

‹ Messages   **JM**   Details

This is getting ridiculous

Hello??

Beth?

God, has he got to you, too?

> jackson? i thought we agreed not to text on here anymore

Oh, thank god. i thought i'd lost you.

> definitely not dead

Yet.

> Stop being dramatic

I'm being realistic.

> what do you want, miller?

I just needed to know you're okay.

> i'm fine. now leave me tf alone

◻ Text Message   Send

Evie drops the phone.

"Shit." She says. "Oh, *shit.*"

"What?" I say. "Who's Aiden?"

"Aiden Islington. Shit, it must be him." Evie says. Her voice is weak, frail, fragile with the weight of all of this.

"Who's Aiden Islington? Can we talk to him? He sounds like he knows something. *Oh.* Wait. No. He's the guy Jackson was warning Bethany about? Then he must be our guy, right?"

"No." Evie is shaking her head. "It can't have been Aiden."

I frown. "Why?"

"Because he died three months before Bethany's murder."

****

Eastwood is a death town. People keep dying. People have died. People go down like dominoes.

From what Evie has told me, I know this:

Aiden Islington was killed in a hit-and-run in Eastwood Forest. This is why Devil's Pathway is called Devil's Pathway. Some clairvoyant spiritual witch lady decided that the track was infiltrated by demons, because how else could someone have fit down that road and killed Aiden, and then gotten away quickly enough that no one saw them?

From Nevae's messages, it's clear that Bethany was going out with him before he died. Evie didn't know this. She's a bit upset.

Disappointed.

Disappointed in herself, that her sister didn't trust her enough to talk about boys— something sisters should talk about.

Disappointed in her sister, for not feeling like she *could* tell Evie these things.

Disappointed in me, because I was there with her, and she was sort of just projecting emotions on everyone.

I leave her house in the early afternoon, but instead of going straight home I decide to walk down to Cathy's. I don't want to see Nicolas. I don't want to see my Dad, or even Hadley. I want to be by myself and think.

I can't keep going on like this, right? Surrounding myself with death and grief and sadness? There is nothing about my new life in Eastwood that is the least bit happy, or not somehow associated with murder.

"Hi, how can I help you?" The server says. I notice it's Hailey, Mae's girlfriend. She smiles when she sees me. Today her red hair is in French plaits and the flyways are sticking to her glossy lips. As always, her smile is big and bright.

"River, right? How are you?"

"I'm alright, thank you. I'll just have a large latte with an extra shot and a brownie, thanks,"

She nods, getting to work. "You settling in okay?"

I nod. "Yep."

"Mae tells me you've been hanging around with Evie," She's smirking.

I try to catch on to the humour and grin back. "Yeah, I guess."

Hailey arches a brow. "Should I be worried?"

"No. Don't worry."

"Well, if you say so." She holds out the card reader for me to tap my card on. "You know she used to work here?"

This surprises me. "Really?"

"Yeah, back before her sister died. The manager's a dick, though, so he kicked her out after the whole grocery store fiasco," Hailey's eyebrows are furrowed, and her lips are down in a small frown. Her smile is gone, and it takes some of the light out of the room.

"Oh. That's horrible." I say.

She nods, "Yeah, it is. From what Mae tells me, she's struggled to find a job since."

There's a sort of vaguely awkward silence then whilst she fiddles with the coffee machine.

She turns back to me a moment later. "And listen, River, our Evie's been through a lot. If you two are, you know, then you take care of her, yeah?"

"'Course." I say. She hands me my order. "But you really don't have to worry— there's nothing going on there. With us."

Hailey winks. "Yeah, that's what they all say."

*****

I google Aiden when I get home and start writing up a factsheet on him, since he's now officially associated with this case. I wonder if the police have looked at him, or if he's still completely unrelated to them.

And then I'm thinking about the police.

Sheriff Mohamed Whittle and his army of deputies. Will we really be able to solve this case quicker than them? Is what me and Evie are doing even legal?

I mean, we're not technically interfering.

We're just giving it our own shot, away from their investigation.

Still, this whole thing leaves a sour, heavy feeling in my gut.

*****

One minute past seven pm, there's a knock on the door. Evie is here.

This day feels like it has lasted a century, but here we are. Dinner with Evelyn and the Lopezes. This is a match made somewhere near to hell, and the chances of it being at all successful are frighteningly low, but I decide that having Evie around will make me less inclined to kill Nicolas during dinner.

Sound logic, River. Truly.

I open the door and there's Evie.

I'm hit suddenly by the realisation that she's pretty. Very pretty. Beautiful, maybe.

It's not the fact she's wearing more makeup than usual, or her hair is pulled up neatly or the fact she isn't wearing baggy jeans and muddy Converse that makes me realise this, but the nervousness in her eyes and the bouquet of wilting roses in her hands and the fact that she's here, about to witness me try not to kill my brother, who she didn't know existed until literally this morning.

"Hi," She says.

She's wearing a dress. Black, knee-length, patterned with little white flowers. And she's wearing sheer black tights, feet tucked into a very battered pair of black boots. I'm surprised at that, because I didn't think she owned any shoes other than her pair of Converse.

"You look nice." I say. "Hi. Thanks for the flowers,"

She smiles. She's wearing lip-gloss— her lips are shiny. And even though she's wearing a noticeable layer of makeup, the smattering of freckles still shows. Her hair, usually a frizzy, wavy brown wilderness around her face, is pulled tightly and neatly into a ponytail with a few wisps hanging around her face.

She steps past me into the hallway, and even though she's been here before it suddenly feels as if this is her first time— that she is a stranger to this family. Which is so dumb, and is just a testament to the nervous, anxious feeling in my gut.

"You've settled in nicely, then,"

"Yeah." I say. And then, calling into the kitchen. "Dad! Evie's here!"

There's a curse and then Dad's rushing out into the hallway, almost knocking a dead plant from its place on a shelf by the front door.

He smiles when he sees Evie, looking flustered at the flowers in her hand. "Oh, hello Evelyn. Lovely to see you again."

"Hi, Mr Lopez. I brought you some flowers. How're you settling in?"

She starts off the conversation with impressive smoothness and then they're conversing as if they've known each other for years instead of days.

I stand by the kitchen door as Dad pours her a glass of white wine that's mostly diluted with lemonade, and she leans against the counter, cooing over Hadley and complimenting the smell of the chicken he's cooking on the stove.

"River, why don't you introduce her to Nicolas?" Dad says after a few minutes.

Evie, who has a half-empty glass of wine in one hand, looks up at me. She looks terrified and intrigued at the same time. Eyes wide, but face set in her usual determination.

"Oh, um. Okay. Sure." I say. My hands are almost shaking. I don't want these two parts of my life to collide.

I don't want Evie's kindness to be tainted by Nicolas' darkness.

Evie steps towards me until she's standing next to me. Her tights make her feet soundless against the floor (she insisted upon taking off the boots inside the door, so she didn't make a mark on our carpets). I'm close enough now to get an inhale of her perfume when I breathe in. It's sharp and I can tell it's cheap, but it's also flowery and lovely at the same time.

Once we're out in the hallway, alone, she smiles. "I like your Dad a lot."

"Me too." I say, smiling back. I'm subconsciously playing with my phone, in my hand. Eyes darting everywhere except her face. Over the cracks in the walls, the areas where the damp is starting to seep through the fresh paint. Evie clears her throat.

"How come you never told me you have a brother?"

"Before the other day I hadn't seen him in five years, Reed."

She arches a slender, dark brow. "Oh. Sorry."

I know she can tell by the tension in my voice that the reason behind his five-year absence from my life is not a pretty one, but she doesn't push it, and for that I am thankful. I'll tell her about my many stepmothers one day, but tonight isn't for emotional conversations like that one.

I lead her into the living room, where Nicolas is sitting on one of the couches with a beer in one hand.

"Um." I clear my throat. "Nicolas."

He turns to me, the couch squeaking under his weight, and then seems to do a double take.

"Who's the lady friend, River?" He asks, clearly amused. But there's something there, behind his eyes, that seems akin to fear.

"This is Evelyn. Evelyn, this is my brother— Nicolas."

Evie looks suddenly pale. "Nicolas Lopez?"

"Evelyn *Reed*?" Nicolas says.

She turns to me. "Why didn't you tell me that your brother was my sister's best friend literally right before she died?"

Something tells me this evening isn't going to go as smoothly as I'd hoped.

"I— *shit*, I didn't know." I say. The room is spinning a bit. I turn to Nicolas. Face him head on. "You've been to Eastwood before?"

Nicolas stands up. He looks confused. Upset. I don't care. "If you'd paid any attention at all to me in the past five years you'd know that I lived here for a year. 2017 to 2018."

"The year Bethany died." I say. And it hits me then that Nicolas and Bethany would have been in the same grade and if he was going to school here then it's entirely possible that they crossed paths. But it sounds like they did a lot more than just see each other in the halls sometimes.

"You look just like her." Nicolas says.

I move to stand in front of Evie, as if I can protect her from the living reminder of her sister.

But she moves to the side, rushing forward until she's a hairs length from his face. He looks down at her. She sneers up. "*You.*"

"Me." Nicolas says, looking vaguely terrified. It would be amusing if I wasn't so damn afraid.

"I heard her talk about you." Evie says. "She hated you. I don't know what you did but I know it was enough to make my sister upset enough that it was believable that she *killed herself*."

"Is everything alright in there?" Dad calls from the kitchen. The room falls into a tense silence.

"Yeah, Dad. All good." I say.

Evie is still standing there, hands in fists by her side. I move forward, next to her, reach out an instinctive hand to uncurl the tense muscles. Nicolas moves past us, into the kitchen, continuing a false facade of okayness and normalcy. Evie relaxes, hands moving free of their sticky, sweaty fists under my touch. She hugs me then. Arms around my neck, head buried in my chest and before I really know what's going on I'm hugging her back. Tightly. Glad that there's someone she can find comfort in. Even more glad that it's me.

She's just added another reason to the extraordinarily long list of reasons that I hate Nicolas.

"Are you okay?" I ask.

"Yeah," is all the answer she gives.

Document 3: Aiden Islington Fact Sheet

River Lopez, 01/16/2021

Name: Aiden Islington

Born: Unknown (sometime in 2000-2001)

Date of death: 18th November 2017

No one has yet been convicted for the crime. Killed in a hit and run on Devil's Pathway, Eastwood Forest, in November. Body was found by a dog walker whose identity was kept anonymous.

Publicly named suspects included Richard Wells, who has been convicted of drunk driving numerous times and tracks left on Devil's Pathway matched those of his 2006 Volvo Estate; as well as Izzy Bark, who was home from Uni at the time and was reported to be seen driving past the forest late on the 18th of November. But there was never enough evidence to actually convict someone.

Aiden's younger brother Noah still lives in Eastwood and is currently a senior at Elizabeth Gingham Memorial High. His older sister, Joy, (according to her public Facebook page) lives in Portland with her husband and three daughters.

ISABELLA MAI BARK
Born: 09/09/1995

(most information drawn from her Facebook accounts, as well as the Facebook accounts of her friends/family)

Currently lives somewhere near Boston, Massachusetts.

Used to live in Redwood, Ashwell County. Posts from 2013-15 show that she was friends with Aiden Islington's older sister, Joy Islington and was also frequently pictured with Henry Di Santis. This group of friends did everything and went everywhere together. Parties (see images 1 to 3), study groups (see image 12), and frequent visits to the Islington household (see images 4-11). I managed to find the Facebook account belonging to Joy Islington and asked her a couple of questions about Izzy under the pretence that I was writing an article for the school newspaper about Aiden. I managed to bring up Izzy a few times during conversation.

Quotes from Joy Islington about Izzy Bark:

"We were friends mostly because we'd been friends for so long. You know? Like— it was an obligation more than a friendship"

"She was a bit headstrong; I think. She was definitely very secretive towards the end of everything. It's weird, I never thought too much about it, and then Aiden died, and I started to think about all of my friends really hard. Izzy stuck out to me. I realised then that she'd been sneaking around at the house, and it occurred to me that she brought up Aiden a lot more. Maybe they were sleeping together. Maybe. Hey, could you not include that maybe? It's just— it's not very positive. I guess I've just always kind of wanted to get it off my chest, you know?"

RICHARD WELLS

Born: not known

I was unable to locate Richard on Facebook, but I did come across his Instagram account. One of his posts dated November 25th, 2017, detailed how he had totalled his 2006 Volvo Estate by hitting a deer head on in the woods whilst drunk. I sent him a message asking him if I could talk to him about Aiden Islington, and, surprisingly, he replied.

"That part of my life was really horrible. Genuinely. I'm ready now to talk about it, but only if your aim is to prove me innocent, and not guilty. People need to know the truth."

I asked him then if he wanted to talk over messages, in real life, or over the phone.

And he sent me his address:

14 Echo Hill Avenue

Deepwater, Ashwell County

 Maine (ME)

21] WELLS, RICHARD

evelyn

JANUARY 20th, 2021, 4:19pm

Seventeen miles up the Clerwood lies the small, sleepy town of Deepwater. I'd never heard of it, but it's where Richard Wells lives. If he does turn out to be the killer, then River and I are walking straight into a trap. But at least we're doing it with our heads held high (and I'm pretty proud of my outfit today, so there's that).

Deepwater turns out to be the small cluster of houses on the side of Echo Hill. The sign at the entrance to the town tells us it has a population of two hundred and thirty, which surprises me. The view is gorgeous, and it's a hundred times more inviting than any of the other towns nearby.

I drive up the main road (Deepwater Road). There are only two other roads in the whole town: Echo Hill

Avenue, and Spruce Street. Both aptly named for the proximity to Echo Hill and a very large spruce forest not more than a mile from here.

I check the address on the dashboard again, even though I've looked at it a hundred times since River sent it to me a few days ago.

Number 14 Echo Hill Avenue.

The tall street sign signals for Echo Hill Ave and I turn down the street. It's not very long, and fourteen must be near the end. The houses are not dissimilar from the ones in Eastwood and Loye Valley: short, panelled, *beige*. Just beiger. The difference here is that the people walking down the road look *happy*. Kids grinning, dogs trotting along with tongues lolling from mouths.

"Evie, it's there." River says from beside me, and I slam on the breaks right in front of a two-story house with a wooden front door and plant pots on the porch and a big sign on the mailbox reading *14 Echo Hill Ave. Wells*. *Wells* is written in bright red paint on the metal, and I know we're in the right place to find Richard Wells.

There's also a 2006 Volvo Estate almost identical to the one we're sat in in the driveway. It's just dark blue and not purple. There's a dent on the front.

He's expecting us, but it still feels like we're intruding. What if he has a family? And we're marching in there, half-suspecting him of murder?

I turn the Volvo's engine off. The finality of the gesture grounds me, reminding me that we're here and we're doing this, no matter what.

River places his hand on top of mine and squeezes, once, before lingering a second and then pulling away. My hand, resting on the gearstick, feels cold without him.

"You ready?" He asks me.

I nod, not trusting myself to speak. If I open my mouth, then I'll probably express my nerves, and then I'll drive home, and I won't have learnt anything.

We're here to ask Richard Wells about his involvement in the Aiden Islington case. He thinks we're here to prove him innocent to an audience on our "blog" or something. This is only half-true.

We're here to find the truth. Unbiased. To no one but ourselves.

I tuck my phone into my pocket and crumple up the address on the dashboard. We're here. No point in keeping it if we're not coming back.

Stepping out of the car, I take in the house again. It's so... normal.

I don't know what I was expecting, to be honest.

River's by my side a second later, like he always is.

Wordlessly, I step up to the porch steps and then up to the front door and raise my hand and knock once, twice, three times in quick succession. *Like gunshots.* Like a bullet, grazing my side. Like—

"Hello?" A woman has opened the door. She has dark hair and dark skin and when she smiles it's with warmth that I've never seen in strangers before. Other than the Lopezes, that is.

"Hi. We're here to see Richard Wells?" I say, trying to keep the quiver out of my voice. Keep a brave face, Reed.

The woman smiles. "Yes, yeah, of course. He told me about you— River and Evelyn, is it?"

She opens the door wider when we nod, and gestures. "Here, come in."

So, we do. Me first, and then River. The house smells like red wine and chemicals and laundry detergent. It's off putting.

The entryway has hardwood floor, covered with a threadbare rat. When the woman shuts the door, it rattles in its frame. She smiles at us again.

"I'm Dayna, Richard is my husband. He's probably in his workshop. Hold on, stay here— I'll be back in a second." And she flits into what must be the kitchen. We hear a door slam— a back door, probably.

We're left alone, in silence. Well, not quite silence. There's a grandfather clock by a set of steep, carpeted stairs that ticks loudly, echoing off the hard floors and empty walls.

"You okay?" River asks me.

I nod. I am. I'm a bit terrified, but I'm okay. "Yeah. You?"

He nods, but I can tell he's as nervous as me. What if Richard Wells did kill Aiden? What if this lovely Dayna is married to a killer?

What if—

"Hello! Hello! Sorry for my, well, disorganisation— time ran away with me." A man comes bustling into the entryway. He's short and broad, skin rough and stubble decorating his chin. The first thing that really strikes me about him is that his eyes are huge. Wide, buggy blue things that are set far into his face, surrounded by smudges of black. Insomnia? Stress? He's smiling, exposing a set of yellowing teeth, and the shirt he's wearing is wrinkled. He stretches out a hand.

"Richard Wells, nice to meet you both."

I shake it first, and then River. River smiles kindly. "I'm River, this is Evelyn."

Wells nods. "Yes, yes, I've been thinking about you two a lot since Saturday. Strange, how you two are so interested after all this time,"

River's smile remains, unflinching. "Yes, well, we live in Eastwood, you see, and we were doing a bit of research into the town's criminal history for a podcast we're doing. And we came across Aiden Islington's case. And your name was all over it, sir."

Wells looks stricken. "Why don't I make you two a cup of coffee? And we can sit down in the living room and talk about this properly,"

"Yes, yes, of course, sir." River says, nodding earnestly. I don't really know what to say, so I follow them both into the kitchen. It's full of yellow tiles, aged, and cupboards that have fallen victim to some pretty severe water damage.

"Coffee for you both?" Wells asks, pulling three mugs from the cupboard above the coffeemaker. We both nod.

"Yes, please, sir, that would be great. Two sugars for me, black." River says.

"No sugar, black, please." I say. It's the first words I've spoken to him and he turns and looks at me when I speak.

"You sound familiar. Beg my pardon, but what's your surname? Evelyn…"

I don't want him to know the truth, so I lie.

"Rayna, sir. Evelyn Rayna." The lie slips off my tongue as easy as the truth would have done. Wells pauses, thinking, and then nods.

"Yeah, I haven't heard of you. Sorry about that—suspicion runs high when you've been through what I have, you know?"

River nods stiffly. I don't do anything. This is all so strange. And probably dangerous, if he does turn out to have killed Aiden.

But at the moment he's just a chaotic man making us coffee. In a house that smells of chemicals.

As if he can hear my thoughts, Wells turns and speaks again whilst the coffee brews. "Excuse the smell. Dayna and I have gotten used to it over the years, but it's formaldehyde."

"For taxidermy?" I ask. This is weird. Beside me, River tenses. Dead animals? Okay, this guy just got a whole lot weirder.

Wells smiles, "Yes, for taxidermy. It's not as weird or horrifying as you'd think, actually. I have a license and everything, and I don't kill anything myself. It's all roadkill, or people's pets or things. It's good pay around here, surprisingly enough."

"When did you get into that kind of thing?" I ask.

"Well, it must have been around the time that, you know, Aiden died."

Don't tell me he has a stuffed Aiden in his garage. Oh my god.

Okay, maybe that's just a little extreme. And gross. Ew.

"Oh?" River says. Wells hands us a mug of coffee each and I hold mine, letting the warmth seep into my chilled bones. He gestures for us to follow him, and we enter the living room. The smell of laundry detergent is stronger here, and the chemicals are all but gone.

We take seats on squeaky couches and a spring settles itself painfully in my tailbone.

"Funnily enough, the night Aiden died I did hit something with my car, accidentally. That is, of course, why the police thought I was a suspect, and why you're even here now."

In the silence he leaves there, I think back to the Volvo on the driveway and the dent in the front. What did he hit if not Aiden Islington?

"What did you actually hit, then?" River asks.

Wells turns around, towards the wall behind him. There's a deer's head, fixed to the peeling wallpaper. I hadn't noticed it before— but now I can't look away from its staring, terrifying eyes.

"That." He says. "I hit that deer,"

"And that's what started the whole taxidermy thing?" I ask.

He nods. "Yeah. There was a, uh, a documentary about taxidermy on the TV the night before so when I hit the poor deer, I thought *hey, why not*. And I dragged it into the back of the car, stupidly enough. It took months for the smell to go away completely."

"Why were you in the forest anyway, then?" I ask. I've unconsciously leaned forward on the couch, closing the space between me and Wells. Closing the gap where the truth sits.

My question unsettles him. He fidgets in his seat, taking a long sip of coffee. He's stalling. Why?

"I, uh, was hunting." He says.

"Hunting's illegal on this side of the river. Why are you lying, Wells?" I say, without missing a beat.

"I ain't lying." His voice is gruff in a way that it wasn't before. "Hey, I thought you were here to prove me innocent, not poke holes in my story." There's an accusatory tone to his voice. I don't like it. I want to leave. If he really did just hit a deer, then the reason he was in the forest shouldn't matter, right? Besides, he has no motive. No means. I don't even see how he could have known Aiden even existed.

"Maybe we should be going," I say, admitting defeat. What did we really think this trip would achieve?

River holds out a hand as I move to stand up. "Wait," he says, "Richard, why were you in Eastwood at all?"

"Visiting an old friend." He says. "Arnold Windsor."

22] REACHING

river

JANUARY 20th, 2021, 4:42pm

Arnold Windsor.

Here's what we know about Arnold Windsor:

He's Hailey's father.

He found Bethany's body.

He might have shot Evie.

He's close with Richard Wells, who was suspected of Aiden Islington's murder.

He fits into this investigation a little too closely.

"He's just another old white man around here who's a little too trigger happy and a little too rich." Evie says. We're back in the Volvo, having said hasty goodbyes to Wells and deeming him innocent. No motive, no means, and a corpse to prove his alibi.

But Arnold Windsor? He doesn't look particularly innocent. But again, he has no motive.

I have a headache.

"What now?" I ask, eyes focused out of the window. It's sunny for once, and the view is incredible from halfway up Echo Hill.

"We have hours until either of us need to be back in Eastwood," Evie says. She turns to me, and smiles. "Why don't I show you Echo Hill? We could get coffee on the way out of Deepwater and spend the afternoon at the top of the hill."

That sounds amazing. Coffee, Evie, and a beautiful view? Count me in.

"Yeah, sure. Is there even a coffee shop here, though? It's pretty empty." I say.

Evie winks. "If you know me, then you know that I could sniff out coffee in the freaking Sahara Desert."

She turns the Volvo off Echo Hill Ave and follows the main road for a few minutes. There are probably about fifty houses on this road, all spaced apart to make the road as long as possible. Just before the exit onto the highway, she turns onto Spruce Street. And I'm not at all surprised to see a small coffee trailer parked halfway down the short, narrow road. There's a queue of about three people, so she parks a little way away and turns to me.

"What do you want?" She asks, reaching into the glovebox for change.

I shake my head, reaching for my wallet. "No, I'll pay."

"River," she says, deadpan, "you've been buying me a latte every day you've lived here. Let me get you a coffee— to say thanks for following me all the way out here."

She's not going to back down— if I have learnt anything about her in the fleeting time we've known each other, it's that she is incredibly stubborn and even more determined.

"Fine, alright." I relent. "I'll have an iced latte, please."

Evie winks. "Coming right up, Lopez. You stay here, make sure no one steals my lovely Volvo."

If there was a word I would use to describe the old, ratty thing, it wouldn't be "lovely" but I just smile and wave her off.

I watch her jog down the street and join the line. Her hair is down today, since there's no wind to push it in her face. She's wearing a short, tight green and blue striped shirt and a pair of baggy, ripped jeans. Effortlessly beautiful.

Staring at her is creepy, I know, but I just— I can't look away.

The person in front of her steps forward, an elderly man with white hair and dark skin, and she steps up as well. A second later, a familiar figure saunters into view.

Izzy Beaumont.

There's suddenly a sour taste in my mouth. I watch dumbly as Izzy catches Evie's attention and I can't hear what they're saying, but I can identify the afflicted look on Evie's face and the smug look on Izzy's. Abruptly, Izzy turns to the people around them and starts gesturing with her hands.

I push the door open and step out onto the street. Her words hit me immediately, stark, loud, and bold.

"Don't you people know who this is? It's Evelyn Reed. She caused massive public distress three years ago! She's a maniac."

And my blood is boiling over, simmering, and simmering and bubbling.

Evie looks like she's about to cry and the people around her are starting to back away. I hurry forward, jogging over to where they are. The elderly man in front of Evie turns to look at her, and he's the only one that doesn't back off. There's a spot of affection in me for him.

"Izzy." I say. Just as loud and firm as her. She looks at me. Snarls.

IS she even human?

"Izzy, stop it. Please." I say.

Evie tugs on my sleeve. She's next to me, close to me, looking up at me. "River please let me handle this."

I nod, silent. Izzy is sneering at us now.

"Oh, of course, Evelyn Reed is still too much of a *fucking coward* to fight her own fucking battles. Is that what's going on?"

This isn't right. There is something seriously wrong with this girl.

"Izzy, why are you doing this?" Evie says. "Why are you so obsessed with me and making my life hell?"

"Because you deserve it. Because you're a snivelling wreck who falls apart in public and can't keep herself under control. Because I *hate you*."

"But why? Why do you hate me?" Evie's voice is so impossibly gentle. Her usual defiant anger so wonderfully in check. The elderly man steps up to order, but the server is looking at us like she can't decide whether to tell us to get the drama away from her trailer or if she should let us stay so she can see how this plays out.

Izzy looks between us. "It's none of your business. I just want everyone to know that you're a time bomb— it's only a matter of time before you blow up again, in public, and scare all the little kids. You know, I still think that you killed Jackson, Evelyn. I think you're too emotionally unstable to be allowed in public. Why doesn't your cow of a mother keep you on a leash? Huh?"

She's spitting her words out and Evie is quiet by my side.

Anger is a living thing inside of me. I go to step forward, to give this horrible girl the time of fucking day, but a hand reaches out across my stomach and holds me, firmly, in place.

Evie looks at Izzy. I can see the sadness in her eyes— and something tells me it's not just for herself, but for Izzy, too. "Izzy, if you're not going to say anything nice, then I'd really appreciate if you could leave. My business has nothing to do with you. My grief is not yours to deal with. When I "blow up" I promise you'll be the first one I'll call. You know, so you can warn everyone in a twenty-mile radius. But for now? I really just want some damn coffee and I don't have time for you, okay?"

Evie smiles sweetly and Izzy, struck speechless, expels a sigh. And she throws us one more bitter look before turning on her heel and walking away. The elderly man accepts his drink from the server and smiles at Evie.

"I'm sorry for your loss. I don't know what you lost, but whatever your grieving— may God help you, dear."

And he wanders away.

Evie lets out a shaky laugh. "Coffee?" She asks.

I nod, smiling. "Yeah, coffee."

*

She wasn't wrong about Echo Hill being beautiful. The top of the hill is so high that you can see Eastwood, Redwood and Loye Valley amongst the thousands of trees that stretch for miles. EGMHS is a big square in the midst of it all, its unused chimneys reaching up like trees. I can just about locate what could be Hastings Road, one of four prongs that stick out from Morning Road. And the Clerwood, winding through it all.

Eastwood Forest is even more breathtaking from up here. Pines, oaks, birches. All of them reaching, reaching and reaching. Endlessly. Whatever they're trying to achieve, they're not quite getting it. Maybe they never will. Maybe they'll keep climbing, keep searching forever. Until they fall.

"It's pretty, right?" Evie says, in my ear. We're sitting close to each other, because it's exposed up here and the wind's picked up and we have coffees clutched in our hands and she's warm against my side.

"It's beautiful." I say. And I'm half talking about the trees and half talking about her smiling face looking out over her home proudly.

From all the way up here, our problems down there look tiny.

For a few hours, it's easy to pretend that they're not there at all.

So, for a few hours, until the sun starts to disappear in the horizon, we forget about the grief and the horror. I tell her about New Brunswick and my old school and my Nana. And she tells me the happy parts of her childhood— how Bethany would read to her by the river and hide with her under the covers.

About a childhood of fond memories with Mae.

A bittersweet collection of snapshots of a life before it was ruined.

And it's a blissful few hours.

Document 5:

Arnold Windsor (fact file) - Evie.

Arnold Windsor and Richard Wells are close friends. When we went to talk to Wells, he mentioned that he was in Eastwood at the time of Arden's murder to visit Windsor, and that's why he was in the woods, and that's why he was suspected of Arden's murder.

Windsor is also the man that found Bethany's body, less than six months later, about half a mile from his house.

We need to talk to Arnold Windsor.

But first my plan for what to do next is to talk to Nevae Bradbury, because she is the only person left of the trio: Bethany, Jackson, and Nevae. She has to know something about Arden, and maybe shed some light on the whole thing and the players involved. I have never spoken to her about directly her time at EGMHS and with Beth and Jackson. Maybe I'll even ask her about Nicolas and what he did.

23] FORGIVENESS

evelyn

JANUARY 27th, 2021, 5:21pm

It's one week later, and Nevae is twenty minutes late.

I'm more worried than annoyed. Since last Wednesday's visit to Richard Wells and the odd encounter with Izzy Beaumont, River and I have done copious amounts of research, and I have wildly procrastinated putting actual real effort into finding contact details for Marie Blaine. I've resorted to calling Nevae. We're meeting up for after-school coffee, and I'm going to ask her about my sister and high school and about Marie. After I've spoken to Nevae, I'm going to hold myself in check long enough to talk to Nicolas Lopez, the bastard.

I'm going to be selfish and put Nevae through memories that she doesn't want to think about for my own personal gain.

My hands are shaking.

We're eating at Cathy's, because I know they used to meet up here a lot and I thought (again selfishly) that it might trigger Nevae's memory a bit.

But she's 20 minutes late.

And I'm worried. Because River and I have also realised that Jackson and Bethany were two pieces of three. If Nevae isn't the killer, then she's the most obvious third victim. Which is sickening. Henry would be left behind, and I can't imagine a Henry without Nevae. And since Bethany's death we've become close. She's a close friend.

The thought of Nevae dying makes my heart feel like it's being split down the middle with a serrated blade.

Just as I'm contemplating calling Henry and making sure she is, in fact, still alive, the door opens and with the chilly air comes Nevae Bradbury. Cheeks flushed from the cold, she waves to me and goes up to the counter to order a coffee. When she's got it, she takes the seat across from me in the booth.

"Hi!" She says. "How are you?"

"I'm good." I say, wringing my hands under the table. "How are you?"

"Good. You said you wanted to talk to me about Bethany, right?" She says. Straight to the point then, okay. Good.

"I do, yeah. I'm sorry to put you through this, but I've just always wanted to know more about who she was like in high school."

Nevae smiles sympathetically, reaching out a warm hand to place on my shoulder. "Awe, Evie. Of course I'll tell you about what she was like. I know in those last few months you didn't see her a lot, and I'm glad that you're ready to talk about her."

"I didn't see her a lot anyway." I can't help but say, and Nevae's sympathy only intensifies.

"That's mostly my fault, to be honest. I kept dragging her off to parties. I thought I was doing her a favour, you know? Giving her a chance to live. It was stupid. You were more important than having a decent social life, but I was naive at the time. I just wanted to impress everyone."

"I get it," I don't, but I'm trying to get her to open up.

Nevae softens. "Oh, Evie. I really am so sorry. I shouldn't have taken her away from you, and oh god,"

I rush to object. "Don't be sorry. Really. When someone dies, people twist their actions into selfishness when really that's far from what really happened. Seriously— you did basically nothing wrong, but Bethany's death made you think you had, anything to make the impact, well, impact less?"

Nevae lets out a strangled, struggling breath. "You're so smart, oh gosh. Bethany always said you were smart, you know."

"She did?" This time I'm genuinely curious. I always worshipped Bethany— I saw her as the better part of our duo. Perfect. Poised. Elegant. Everything I couldn't be.

I was clumsy and unfinished compared to her. But maybe that was just the impact of having an idol: I was willing to break myself down into my most inadequate parts just to have someone to look up to.

"She was in awe of you, Evie. Have I really never told you this?" Nevae rests her chin on her hands, looking into the distance with an eye of wistful memory. "Bethany was so jealous of you— she spent so long trying to be more like you, to get your parents to like her as much as they loved you."

"That's bullshit. Why would she want to be like me? I was childish, and idiotic, and *fifteen*, for gods' sakes!"

This is so much new information and I have half a mind that Nevae's just telling this to me to make me feel better because Bethany isn't here to discount this herself.

But there's something so close to genuine memory on her face that lets me believe her, just for a second.

"None of that mattered to her. She just wanted to be smart and put-together like you. She really thought that if she did better in school, she wouldn't be such a disappointment to everyone."

"But no one was disappointed in her."

"She didn't know that, Evie. It's really hard to believe something when your whole life you've told yourself the exact opposite."

I'm going to cry. My voice shakes when I speak, "She really thought we were disappointed in her?"

Nevae looks as heartbroken as I must do. "I don't want you to think of her as unhappy, because I don't think she was. But she was forever striving to be like you— she thought you were perfect."

"But I wasn't. She was."

"Maybe you two just see perfection in each other. That's beautiful, really,"

When she puts it like that, it is. I see perfection in Bethany because she was beautiful and older, and she saw perfection in me because I impressed our parents.

I wanted beauty.

She wanted praise.

The knowledge that I could have made her happier by showing her more love breaks my heart and is so horrible that I wish Nevae never told me. But there's also a part of me made giddy from the knowledge that Bethany, who I always idolised, wanted to be more like *me*. There's a part of me that is actually desirable.

"Are you okay?" Nevae asks me. I must have been quiet for a while.

"Yeah, yeah, I'm fine. Thank you so much for telling me all of this."

"You're welcome," she smiles. She's fiddling with her coffee mug, light fingers dancing across the patterned ceramic. I watch, transfixed in the silence before her next words, "I'm just sorry I kept it all to myself,"

And back comes that point: death makes people feel selfish.

A moment more of silence ensues, and then she clears her throat. At once, the mood lightens as she speaks. "So, how are you?"

I smile. "I'm alright, thanks. Been busy with school and stuff. You?"

"I'm good. It's been a bit hard, you know. What with all the stuff about Bethany coming out again— I'm just tired, is all,"

I completely understand. "I get it. How's Henry?"

The mention of her fiancé makes her perk up more. "Oh, he's doing great. We both are. I've picked out a wedding dress— I'll show you a picture."

She digs around in her purse for her phone and switches it on, a moment later bringing up a photo of her in a wedding dress. I almost cry. It's beautiful— a modest dress with long sleeves and a fitted top that flows outwards in a narrow gown decorated with floral-patterned lace and pools at her feet. In the picture she's grinning—cheeks rosy and face glowing. She looks stunning.

"Oh my god," I say, "Henry is going to *freak* when he sees you in that dress, oh my god."

She grins, putting her phone away. "I know, right? I paid a fortune for it, but it's totally worth it,"

Nevae wraps her hands around her mug and takes a sip. "I really hope they catch this bastard before the wedding, because I want to have a wedding that's not full of fear. You know?"

I nod, thinking back to my revelation— that she's the next victim. "Yeah, I know."

I think about warning her that she could be next, but the words just won't come out. She looks so happy. Nevae rarely looks as joyous as she does right now, talking about wedding dresses over coffee. Thinking about her fiancé back home, with the kind eyes and broad shoulders.

So I don't say anything to burst her bubble.

God, I should have said something.

24] LIARS MAKE EXCELLENT THIEVES

river

Nicolas is still here. Living in our house. Eating our food. Pretending like he did nothing wrong— like he's still the same brother that I knew ten years ago, fifteen years ago. It's sickening.

Hadley calls him by name now— craves his presence like any other sister to her older brother. It's sickening.

Dad did the weekly groceries the other day and asked if Nicolas wanted anything, like he asks me. It's sickening.

I've spent most of the morning anxiously checking my phone, anxiously checking to see if Evie has any news from when she spoke to Nevae earlier today. Anxiously checking to see if she's gotten another email, has died, been attacked, or just about anything that seems to happen in excess in this town. It's kept me busy, kept me distracted, kept my mind focused and concentrated on one thing, which is good. It's been a long week of stilted conversation with Evie, waiting for the other shoe to drop.

She swears to me it's fine that my brother is someone who made her sister's life hell, and I didn't tell her. She swears to me that she doesn't doubt that I didn't know all this time that Nicolas lived in Eastwood, made friends and enemies out of Bethany's friends and enemies. But I know her well enough now to recognise the tiny seeds of doubt in the sea of brown and green in her eyes.

It's enough to make my stomach feel sour, bitter, and wrong.

I hate this. I hate this situation. I hate this town. And I hate myself.

Pretty much exactly two hours after Evie texted me to say she'd gotten back from her meeting with Nevae, my phone vibrates on the kitchen table with an incoming call from her.

I almost trip over in my haste to pick up the call. I press my phone to my ear. "Hello?"

"Hi," she says, in that quiet but strong way of Evelyn Reed.

"Are you okay? How did it go with Nevae?"

"I'm alright." There's a pause. An intake of breath. Shaky. Something's wrong. "I, um, I got another email, though."

My heart drops through my stomach, slides down my legs, and disappears into the ground. "Oh shit. Where are you? Can I come over?"

"I'm fine, Lopez. Stop being a worry wart. I'll come over to yours in a bit. I just need to, um, yeah,"

"Right. Yeah. Okay." I swallow thickly. "What did the email say?"

The stretch of silence then is almost enough to send me over the edge. "I— I need to tell you in person,"

Oh.

"But you're okay, right? You're not in any danger or anything."

"Not right now, I don't think. Listen, I've got to go. I'll be at yours in about ten minutes, okay?"

"Yeah. Sure. See you then, Reed."

She hangs up. I let the phone fall back onto the table and run an anxious hand through my hair. Ten minutes. Where is she? I stand by the window, watching the rain, watching the street outside.

When she shows up, it's not in the Volvo or her mom's car. It's by foot, wearing nothing but a t-shirt and a pair of baggy jeans. The dirty mustard of her Converse shine through the rain. I run to the door, swing it open, and pull her in. Mommy River mode kicks in, and I barely say hello before I'm tugging her into the bathroom adjoining my bedroom and planting her on the bathroom counter, throwing towels at her that are warm, fresh out of the dryer.

I don't miss the lingering look she gives the counter and the way she winces, looking down at her stomach.

"Calm down, I'm not going to die of hypothermia, you weirdo." She says, smiling. The amusement in her face is so genuine that for a moment I relax. And then I notice that her shirt is clinging to her skin, making her shiver, and I'm in my room digging through drawers until I find a sweater and joggers that she can wear. I hand them to her and give her a stern look.

"Reed, why did you go out in the rain in a t-shirt?"

"Okay, *mom*, I forgot a sweater."

"You have a car."

"I don't have gas money."

"I could have given you a lift."

"I didn't want to bother you."

You never bother me is on my tongue as quick as a reflex, but I bite it back. It's too personal, too intimate. So instead, I sigh and let her get changed, making my way to the kitchen and putting the coffee on. When she emerges a few minutes later, her soaked hair is up in a bun that looks haphazard and messy. All the makeup has come off her face and left behind a raw version of her.

I hand her a steaming mug and she takes it, smiling softly.

"Are you going to tell me what's going on?" I ask, leaning my hip into the countertop. There's a silence so long that I momentarily believe that she's not going to answer me.

And then she does, "Can we sit down somewhere? My legs are tired."

We go into the living room, and she curls up on the couch in the corner, legs tucked up against her chest. I forgot to give her dry socks, so she's pulled the way-too-big sweatpants over her feet. I sit next to her, back against the arm of the couch, facing her, hands wrapped around my mug, but every muscle in me is far too tense to drink it.

So I sit and watch her as she takes a few tentative sips and looks down at her nails, down at her phone, at the time, at anything other than me.

And then she says, "I spoke to Nevae."

The silence stretches like a rubber band pulled and pulled and-

"She told me about Bethany in high school, and about how Beth, erm, she admired me. Wanted to be like me." She wipes a tear from her eye angrily. "It's stupid, but like— I hate myself for not realising she loved me that much? I always admired *her*, thought *she* was the better of us. And now I just regret that I didn't know that about her, and I never told her how much I admired her. It doesn't make sense, really, I know, but yeah."

I want to reach out and hold her hand, offer her some kind of comfort, but I don't.

I wait for her to continue.

"So yeah. Erm, I was a bit of a mess when I left Nevae and, yeah, I was going to text you and tell you everything I swear, but then I opened my phone and there was the email."

She opens her phone and swipes a few times and then holds it out to me, so I can read.

1 READ MESSAGE

To: evelynareed2002@gmail.com

From: nodancer2119@gmail.com

R.E: Think Better

Bethany deserved it. The moment you see that is the moment you get to know a bit more.

Maybe next time, spend a bit more time looking. And, whilst you're at it, give me back what she stole.

Much love,

L

25] CLOSET FULL OF GHOSTS

evelyn

JANUARY 27th, 2021, 7:00pm

I think it's entirely possible that I may be the killer's next victim. If these emails are true and real and coming from the killer, then why me? Why target me for any other reason than I'm next? Did Bethany get emails like this? Did Jackson?

I hate the thought that I'm going to be snatched from my mother and father like Bethany was, but I can't help the logical side of me from thinking it. Believing it. Letting the possibility manifest itself beneath my skin, living there like a parasite, taking and taking and taking.

River moves closer to me, places an arm around my shoulders, pulls me so my head falls onto his shoulder and he's squeezing me, hugging me, holding me together.

"Thanks," I say. It comes out as a whisper, my throat harsh with the promise of sobs.

"Are you okay?"

"Yeah." I say.

"Maybe you should go to the police with these emails, Evie."

Give me back what she stole.

River's right. God, he's right. I should take these to Mohamed and let him do the dirty work. Let myself relax and let someone else deal with it.

"I don't want to." I say.

River looks at me. My eyes are shut tight against the wave of tears, but I can feel the twist of his neck and the weight of his gaze heavy on my skin.

"It's stupid. I shouldn't be upset over a stupid prank." I say. More to myself than to him.

"What if it's not a prank, though?" River says. I can feel each of his breaths, and it's nice but also kind of weird. "Wouldn't it be better to be safe and tell the police?"

"What does it mean though? If it *is* the killer, then why me? Why talk to me?"

He doesn't say anything. We both know what's gone unspoken. *I'm next.*

*****

It's nearly midnight. I'm knee deep in Bethany's bedroom.

I stared at the email for about two and a half hours at River's house, and then took myself home around eight. I think I might have figured it out:

Maybe next time, spend a bit more time looking. We've only physically searched two places in the investigation, the woods (which was less of a search, more of a mission cut off before it even started), and Bethany's bedroom. And I'm not too keen on going back to the woods, so Bethany's bedroom feels like the best place to start.

But this does mean that if I end up finding something, and it's something that's to do with the killer, then the killer knew it was in here. Which means that the killer has been in Bethany's room.

Which means it was someone close to her.

Which is sickening.

So I search. And I search.

And I don't find anything.

Until about two am.

There's a box, right at the back of her closet. I missed it before because her closet is one of those ones that's built into the wall, where the closet space extends off to the side where you can't see. My hand brushes over it when I reach in to fish out one of her t-shirts. I feel the plastic, and the corrugation on the box's lid. My fingers hook around the box and pull it out into my eyeline.

Visible through the translucent pink plastic, are notebooks.

About five, stacked on top of each other. They look well used, but old enough that they ended up at the back of her closet, forgotten. Either that or they contain something secretive, something Bethany went out of her way to hide at the back of her closet to be forgotten.

It's heavy as I pull it onto the floor, and sit down next to it. My fingertips sting as they push against the sharp edges of the lid in an attempt to pry it off. Years of disuse give way as there's a satisfying *pop* and the lid comes off in my hands.

They're journals.

I know this because they're dated in Beth's neat cursive handwriting.

2015 Freshman Year/Sophomore Year

2016 Sophomore Year/Junior Year

2017 Junior Year/Senior Year

2018 Senior Year

I feel a pang of grief, looking at the familiar loops and swirls of her handwriting. These must be journals or diaries of some kind. And they go right up to 2018. Considering she died less than a month into that year, the dates on them confirm that she hid them purposefully— it wasn't time that pushed them into the back of her closet, it was a will for secrecy and the protection of something she wanted to keep hidden.

I reach in and lift all of the books out, placing them on the floor in chronological order. They're all thick and weathered apart from 2018. I reach in and lift out that one, keen on knowing what her thoughts and actions were in the week leading up to her death.

Will this tell me who killed her?

I open it to the first page.

01/01/2018

I don't feel like celebrating. Like, at all. Nevae and Jackson spent last night at Lauren's party, but I stayed home. They called me boring. I agreed.

02/01/2018

There probably isn't a lot of point in me starting a diary again this year. I haven't got nearly as much to say as I did before.

01/03/2018

Today was the same as yesterday, and the day before. Mundane. Boring. Just like me.

01/04/2018

If you ever find these, Evie, because you're looking through all of my things, know that I'm sorry for being a terrible sister all those years. Ignoring you. Letting you down. I'm not surprised if you hate me, if you've hated me for your whole life. I don't think I'll make it to next year. There's no point.

Just promise me that you won't go down easy. That you won't let me go down that easy.

I can't tell you who to look for, but I can tell you that you should ask Jackson where to start.

I love you more than words can say, Evester.

I love you more than words can say.

"I love you too," I whisper, barely audible even to me. *I love you too.*

26] FOR HER

river

JANUARY 28th, 2021, 9:12pm

"This is the last entry she wrote before she died." Evie says. We're in her living room. On the couch, with coffee, the rain coming down in rivets through the inky dark outside.

I have read the entry about ten times, poring over it, not really absorbing the meaning behind the words. I don't ask Evie if she's okay. I've asked her that too many times in the last week or so. When I read it for the first time, I just hugged her. That's how close we've gotten— I know when she needs a hug, and I know when she needs me to physically hold her together more than she needs verbal consolation.

"What do we do?" Evie says. More to herself than me, I'm fairly certain. The words hang in the air, suspended from strings made of doubt stretched thin. *What do we do?*

Who are we kidding? We're *teenagers*, trying to solve a murder that feels so complicated and difficult that I'm not even sure we'll make it halfway without help. But it seems to be keeping Evie busy, keeping *me* busy, so it can't be hurting too much, right?

Evie shifts, setting her mug on the coffee table. Her house is smaller than mine, and more suffocating. It's well maintained, but all the walls are painted the same shade of lilac, scuffed with twenty odd years worth of life. I wonder, briefly, how long she's lived in this house, in this town. If it's as much a prison to her as it is to me.

"I don't know." I say in response to her earlier question after a few minutes, because the silence is too much. For the past few days, I've quite frequently thought to myself *why why why why why why*. Why am I doing this? Why am I putting myself in danger like this?

For Evie. My brain tells me. My stupid, hormonal, teenager brain. *For Evelyn Reed, who I met less than a month ago, who is ninety percent emotional baggage and ten percent a funny, nice person to be around.*

But it's true. I'm doing it for Evie, and to make myself feel like I'm doing something good, something for someone other than myself.

"We could go to the police," I suggest, again, because I'm a broken record and I'm tired.

She just shakes her head. "You know we can't, River. You know they won't be able to help, not really."

And she seems so convinced of this fact that I just nod, accepting what she believes to be the truth like it's something out of the Bible.

"Who do you think it is?" She asks after a few more moments of silence.

Her question surprises me. It's such an obvious question to ask when you're quite literally investigating a murderer, but when I actually think about it, I don't have a clue.

"I don't know, to be honest." I say.

Could it be Richard Wells, who hit a deer with the same model car that killed Aiden? Could it be Arnold Windsor, who found Bethany's body and *may* have shot me in the stomach? Or is it Nevae, who was close to Jackson and, possibly, to Aiden?

Marie Blaine?

Izzy Beaumont?

"I still think Richard Wells is hiding something." She says. "And Arnold Windsor. I don't know why, it's just— I have a weird feeling about them."

27] THE BEAUTIFUL PEOPLE

evelyn

JANUARY 28th, 2021, 00:56am

About three hours after River leaves, there's a knock on the door.

Mom's at work, covering a late shift at the bar.

I'm home alone, and I'm scared. I jump up from my position on the couch and silently make my way to the kitchen window, moving aside the blinds to peek out onto the porch. The dim, yellow security highlights a familiar face— wide face, big eyes.

It's Benji.

Hurriedly, I rush to the door and unlock it, pulling him inside before he even has a chance to talk. His tall, broad frame is trembling and he's crying again. I think back to that time I found him on a bench, bruised and crying, not willing to talk.

Anger burns in my veins. Who is doing this to him? Has grief really made me so horribly selfish that I haven't thought about him? About who did this to him? Why didn't I do more to help?

"Oh my god." I say.

Benji blinks, silent. "Evie— I, um, I'm sorry— I just didn't know where else to go."

I nod, nod, can't stop nodding. "It's okay, I'm glad you came." I lead him to the living room and usher him onto the couch, then I make hot chocolate (his favourite kind) with shaking hands. When I'm done, I burn myself on a bit because my hands are so unsteady. In the living room, I hand him one mug and sit on the couch opposite him, the threadbare material rough under my feet.

Benji sets his mug on the coffee table.

"What happened, Benji?" I say, gently. Trying to ease the truth from his tight, unrelenting grasp.

He takes a shuddering, gasping breath that seems to wrack his lungs and fracture his ribs. "I— *oh, god.*"

"It's okay." I say. I rub his back gently. "Do you want me to call Ivy?"

"No, thank you. I don't— I don't want to worry her,"

"Is this about her?"

"No." He lets out a dry, hoarse laugh that looks almost painful. Like Ivy doing this to him is so absurd it makes him hysterical. I've never heard such a harsh, disjointed and *wrong* sound coming from Benji before, and it positively terrifies me.

"What, then? Benji— let me help you."

"I can't tell you, Evie."

"You can. Do you want me to call your step-dad? Your Mom?"

He goes quiet. "No, thank you."

There's a tension in his shoulders at the mention of his father. I know Benji doesn't get along with his step-father that well, but—

"Oh my god. Benji, did he do this to you?"

No reply. My heart drops. My stomach roils. *His step-father did this to him.*

His step-father is a big, strong ex-wrestler with spotty, rough pale skin always a horrible shade of pink. A dickhead, but I didn't think he was capable of— of doing something like this to his own son. Especially a son as wonderful as Benji.

I feel so stupid. And useless. And horrible. How long has this been going on for?

Benji shifts in his seat, and winces. I immediately go to his shirt, lifting it up. An ugly bruise sits on the skin, so fresh and awful that it is bright and saturated on the dark skin.

"Oh my god. Benji— we have to go to the police."

He shakes his head desperately. "No, *please no.* They'll never believe me. A black teenager like me, getting beat by his white father? They'll never believe me."

"Mohamed will."

"He's not powerful enough to put my father in jail by himself, Evie. Be realistic, please. You don't understand. If I thought people would believe me and I would get justice, then I would have told you and then the police a long time ago."

A long time ago. Just how long has this been going on?

"Why now, then? Why not three months ago, why now? Why are you telling me this now?"

He sucks in another sharp, painful breath. "Because, Lynny, he kicked me out of the house." Silence. Grim, ugly silence. "I just need a couch to crash on for a few weeks until I turn eighteen and can get myself an apartment, or something."

I'm nodding before he's finished. "Yes, yes of course you can stay here, Benji. Of course."

"Don't you need to ask your mom first?"

"I don't think she'll mind." My mom loves Benji like a son, and she's hardly here anyway— she'll agree. She has to.

Benji hugs me tightly. "Thank you, Evie. Thank you so much."

"It's okay, Benji. You[re safe here. Your father can get you here."

"Please don't tell anyone else, Lynny. I'm not ready for everyone to know,"

"Not even Ivy?"

"I'll tell her. Just, please, not Mae and River."

I nod. "Yes, yes of course."

He falls asleep about an hour later, with his head on my lap. I watch him, watch his eyes moving beneath his eyelids, his chest rising and falling, and I think about how ignorant I am.

How did I miss this?

Am I really that terrible of a friend?

28] ELECTRONIC MAIL

evelyn

JANUARY 29th, 2021, 5:18pm

Her *emails*.

What was I thinking about yesterday? I was wondering if Bethany and Jackson had gotten the emails too. And if they had, then it was confirmed: I was next.

The thought has been nagging at me all day, picking at my mind, pulling at it in every class. So as soon as I pull the Volvo up to the front door, I climb out and leg it through the front door.

I'm the only one here— Benji is at football training, and Mom's working again. He spent the night on the couch, and I spoke to Mom when she got home late last night. I was as vague as possible, and she insisted that he stay for as long as he needs. And then I went upstairs and cried.

Today, I stayed at school later to help River finish off the factsheet for Richard Wells and our weekly update sheet, as well as his factsheet on Aiden himself. Helping him create a clearer picture of what's going on, what's happened, and what we're missing.

So It's nearly five thirty when I pull my hair up onto my head into a frightfully messy bun and enter Bethany's room again. It hurts less now to see it all, now I've rooted through it all and left a mess on the floor. My own mess. Proof I've reclaimed this room and taken its power to hurt me.

So I dig through her desk until I find the MacBook I've left in lieu of more useful things, and sit cross legged on the dusty sheets on her bed.

I open it up, and am extremely grateful to discover that there isn't a password required.

A notification pops up as soon as I've logged in.

It's from her emails, and I double click to open it before it disappears, my heart picking up speed in my chest.

1 NEW MESSAGE
To: bethanynicole@gmail.com
From: nodancer2119@gmail.com
R.E: Hello Evelyn
I told you not to pry, because now I'm looking at you, and you're not going to like me looking at you any more than I like it.
Tell River I say hi.
Tell Nevae I say *watch out*.
L

I'm terrified.

My hands are shaking. My heart is racing. My legs are shaking. My entire body, trembling under the weight of the threats of this *L* who I'm not even sure is real. I click off that email, and am met face to face with seven emails, all from L.

And all I can think is *oh my shit I'm going to die.*

I read each email, starting from the first one, and working my way down.

> From: nodancer2119@gmail.com
> 10.11.2017 R.E: Hi!
> Could you send me the notes from the video in class today? I forgot to take some— not enough coffee!
> See you tomorrow
> *L*
> From: nodancer2119@gmail.com
> 10.18.2017 R.E: Hi again.
> I know you told me not to talk to you, but I realised I still had your email address: Aiden told me what you said. I hope you know you've made a mistake.
> *L*
> From: nodancer2119@gmail.com
> 10.25.2017 R.E: Not really good enough, tbh
> You just keep making it worse for yourself, don't you?
> *L*
> From: nodancer2119@gmail.com
> 11.18.2017 R.E: Good day to die
> Today seems as good as any.

L

From: nodancer2119@gmail.com
11.19.2017 R.E: Mysterious man
Stop.

Bethany, just *stop* before anyone else gets hurt. You're being ridiculous. Someone is going to get hurt.

L

From: nodancer2119@gmail.com
1.1.2018 R.E: Here's to us
Not bad. Well played, and all that.

I will get you back, though. I hope you know.

L

From: nodancer2119@gmail.com
1.7.2018 R.E: Hitting home
In 72 hours you're going to see your lover again, Bethany. I hope you're excited. I hope your fever goes down— I wouldn't want to be looking like a sick wreck when you reunite.

L

It feels kind of stupid now, that I didn't figure it out before: L killed Aiden first. And then my sister. And then Jackson. And now L is going to kill Nevae.

Bethany wasn't this person's first victim— Aiden was.

18th November, 2017, the day Aiden died: *Good day to die: today seems as good as any.*

Today seems as good as any to kill Aiden.

It's not uncommon for a killer's M.O to change after their first kill— they're still young in their killing days, still experimenting, figuring out what they like and don't like.

Maybe not so drastic as changing from hit and runs to drowning to a bullet in the head, but still. That email is practically a confession.

I quickly forward all eight emails to myself, and then screenshot them and send the screenshots to River. Then I read all of the emails three more times, until I'm satisfied that there's nothing I'm missing— no hidden piece of information I've skipped.

Could Richard Wells have killed all of them? Aiden, Bethany *and* Jackson? Why?

If he hit a deer in the woods the first time, then what are his excuses for all the other times? Was he even in Eastwood when Bethany died? Is this, potentially, where Arnold Windsor comes into things? Could he have killed Bethany, working in a team with Richard Wells, to eradicate the town's drug-addicted teenagers? My head hurts just thinking about all of it—all of the possibilities. All of the terrifying, possible conclusions to draw from this whole mess.

29] THE EMPTY MINDED

FEBRUARY 1st, 2021, 11:12am

Mr Black wants an update. Most of what we have that's actually useful to the case, we can't show him because he would force us to turn it all in to the police and pursue something else. Most of what we *can* show him right now is history work— details from the original investigations, and a tentative finger pointing to the fact that we've worked out that Aiden was the first victim, not Bethany.

He's pleased when he reads it. His bushy eyebrows arch, and a small smile tugs at the corner of his mouth.

He's surprised at how much we've managed to squeeze out of two "closed" cases, and he doesn't even know that we're sitting on bigger things: the emails.

I get a horrible, sick feeling every time I think about the fact that Evie's probably on the killer's list of victims. But she's only had four emails so far. That's three less than Bethany had when she died.

Three emails, though, isn't many.

The thought of Evie ending up in that forest, dead, is too horrible for me.

And yet I can't quite stop thinking about the fact that the killer might have already tried once. That first time we were investigating, when we went to try and find the gun in the woods and she got shot. Was that supposed to be an attempt on her life?

The logical part of my brain says no. A killer that's evaded capture for so long knows better than to fire blindly into a dark forest with a witness, and that was only after one email. Now there's four emails, and no sign that the killer was at all satisfied with the almost-tragedy in the woods.

The class is once again dismissed to spend the lesson working either in the classroom or the library. Evie and I choose the library like always, piling books and sheets into our arms and tucking pens into our pockets.

On the way to the library, she slows down a bit so we have more time just the two of us.

"I'm not sure I've actually said thank you," she says.

I arch a brow. "What? For what?"

"For doing the case with me. You didn't want to, and it means nothing to you, so— you know— thanks and all that."

I smile. "You're welcome, and all that."

"Seriously, though." She says. "You don't need to help me with all of it. I know we're doing it for this project and everything, but I'm happy to go at it alone. I don't want to put you in danger or anything."

"We're friends, Evie. That's what friends do for each other."

She doesn't say anything after that, staring at the ground with a smile tugging at the corner of her mouth. Something tells me that people don't say that to her very often.

*****

Jackson's funeral is taking place this weekend. It was just announced on all the Islington siblings' social medias as well as the Sheriff's department. There's going to be a public memorial service in the churchyard on Saturday afternoon. The town is welcome to attend.

Evie's going to go. I'm not. I didn't know Jackson— it wouldn't feel right.

Nicolas is going. He knew Jackson, if only briefly, and they weren't friends.

When he told me this at dinner last night, it stirred something within me. Right. Yes. Nicolas did something to Bethany to make her hate him, so Jackson probably wouldn't have been willing to befriend Nicolas because of that.

Very slowly, the pieces that make up the senior class of 2018 are coming together.

Evie made a document showing who was in that group of people, and how they relate and connect to each other. There are a few names we still need and many gaps we need to fill in, but this thing in my chest that fills up every time we find something new or write something down, feels a lot like progress. And it's a sweet feeling.

Document 6: the Eastwood Three and their connections

Bethany Reed:

- Romantic relationship with Aiden that ended either when or slightly before he died
- Negative relationship with Nicolas Lopez/ he did something to her

Jackson Miller

- Wanted Bethany to stay away from Aiden, and probably Nicolas as well. (protective of them)

Nevae Bradbury

- ? no information yet

Aiden Islington

- Why did Bethany go for him?

30] RESPECTS

evelyn

FEBRUARY 6th, 2021, 1:43pm

Grovespring Church of Peace sits just a little bit outside Eastwood, in the midst of a village that burnt down somewhere in the twentieth century. The church survived, being the only structure made out of stone, and now it's a stout little church surrounded by acres of cemetery and forest.

It seems like the whole town has shown up. My mother is by my side, gripping my hand so hard it hurts. She rarely goes out in public in the town now, and if she does it's always with me next to her, giving her strength, and never to social gatherings that everyone else attends. We get too many stares. Too many whispers. But Jackson Miller was a good person, and he deserves Bethany's family showing up to his memorial to pay our respects. He deserves at least this from us when we didn't reach out to him in the years following Bethany's death. After they graduated, Nevae and Jackson lost contact when he went to college in Michigan and Nevae stayed behind when she met Henry.

Still, we could have at least spoken to him when we heard he was in town.

Of course I only regret that when he's dead.

Of course.

That's how grief works— it forces you to think about every little thing you could have done to prevent it from happening, or kicking yourself for not knowing the last conversation you had was the last time you'd speak despite the fact that there was no way you could have known.

Grief is a cruel, cruel thing.

Even though basically no one knows that it was me that found his body, I can't help but feel like most of the whispers following us around are about me. Snarky jabs in my direction, tugging at me.

Mrs Miller is standing closest to the casket, staring at the large photo of Jackson standing on a gold painted easel off to the left. It's his senior graduation photo— him with one arm around an off-frame Nevae. His dark curly hair is messy and he's smiling and the roundness to his cheeks and their pink glow stabs me right in the heart.

I don't deserve to be here.

I'm just contemplating leaving when Mrs Miller turns and spots us, immediately rushing over to where we've stopped walking.

She hugs my mother, and then hugs me. I never really knew her very well, but both of us knew Jackson.

"Evelyn, dear, thank you so much for coming." She says sweetly. "And you, Mrs Reed, thank you. Jackson loved your girl so much,"

Mom tenses beside me, and I can see her eyes glistening with unshed tears. "I'm so sorry for your loss, Mrs Miller, I know how hard it is to lose one of your own."

As they embrace again, I take the chance to step away and scan the churchyard until I find Nevae and Henry. They're sat in seats near the front, alongside some of Jackson's other school friends— and Nicolas.

Nicolas Lopez.

Why is he here?

He doesn't have the right to be here.

Nevae reaches up a hand and waves me over to her, and I break my death glare at Nicolas to make my way over to her and Henry.

She reaches up and hugs me, smelling of roses and vanilla. I almost cry.

"Are you okay?" I ask her.

She nods, but doesn't say anything. Maybe because if she tries, she'll cry. Which I understand. They might not have spoken in a few years, but they were best friends before. Nevae lost her best friends one after the other, and there's no way that she's okay with any of it.

Henry catches my eye over her shoulder, and I smile sadly at him. I'm glad that she has someone, even if he doesn't fully understand what she's going through.

About ten minutes later, one of Jackson's older cousins calls the audience to attention, and the service begins. There's a lot of poetry read through cracking voices, and words said by family members that unearth parts of Jackson that I never knew.

It hits me just how little I knew about him. Yeah, he was my sister's best friend and spent a lot of time at our house, but I don't really deserve to mourn him because he was never my best friend.

*****

After the service finishes, I go to Halliebottom with Nevae and Henry and we sit around a small table in the corner whilst Nevae flutters around, cleaning and getting ready for the day's late opening— postponed in solidarity for Jackson and the memorial.

Henry and I sit opposite each other, watching Nevae over the tops of our coffee mugs. He looks concerned, brows furrowed. Frowning.

"What's wrong?" I say. Even though there's a million reasons why nothing is right at the moment.

"I'm scared she's gonna be next, Evie, and there's nothing I can do about it

31] OCEAN, DROWN ME

evelyn

FEBRUARY 13th, 2021, 10:10pm

A week later, Nevae is dead.

The news reached me via a phone call from Henry. I don't know why he chose to call me first, but he did.

They found her by the river, strangled.

Choked.

I'm standing in the kitchen, my phone in my hand, shaking. *Nevae is dead.*

"*She's gone, Evie. Nevae— they— I was right, Evie, I was fucking right.*"

Henry's words to me are burnt into my mind, and I'm sure they'll be there for years to come. *Nevae is dead.*

He *was* right. And I hate myself for not doing more to protect her. I mean, River and I saw it coming weeks ago— but we assumed we had time. Three years happened between Bethany and Jackson, so what would stop another three years from going by before Nevae?

Stupid. *So, so stupid.*

I feel like there's a million things I should be doing right now instead of standing in the kitchen like a fucking lemon. I should call River.

Yes.

I hold the phone up to my ear. It rings four times before the call goes through.

"Evie?" River's voice cuts through the static of the line and the sound of his voice makes me feel both suddenly comforted and emotional. "What's wrong?"

It takes me a moment to get the words out, my voice stiff and scratchy like I haven't used it in centuries.

"Nevae— I— Nevae, she's dead. River, they killed Nevae." A sob chokes its way from my throat. *"Nevae was murdered."*

There's a long, agonizing silence. And then, "I'll be there in a second. Hold tight, 'kay? Is your Mom home?"

I shake my head even though he can't see me, pressing a hand to my mouth to stifle my sobs. "No. She's at work." Benji is out with Ivy. I'm alone. So, *so alone.*

"Okay. Stay there, I'll be there in a second."

A minute later there's a knock on the door. I will my legs to hurry to the door and force my shaking hands to pull the deadbolt across and turn the key, releasing the door from its constraints. Pulling it open, I'm left face to face with River.

He steps forward, not even speaking before he's gathered me up in his arms, hugging me tightly against his chest. "It's okay. It's okay." He keeps saying, even though I know *I'm* okay. It's Nevae that's not okay.

I cry for centuries.

By the time he lets me go, I've left a damp patch on his shirt. I reach up a hand and rub at it instinctively, until he takes my hand and holds it in his, pulling it away from his chest and letting it rest between us. I lean forward, forehead against his sternum, breathing deeply.

"Are you okay?" He asks me.

"Better."

"Look at me."

I do. Eyes the color of strong coffee swimming with something akin to concern and the bitter presence of fear.

"I'm next, aren't I?" I say.

PART 3

HELP

ME,

MA.

I'M

DROWNING

31.5] LOVE

bethany

OCTOBER 15th, 2017, 12:38pm

Nevae finds me in my spot by the Clerwood, watching the water ripple and waiting for Aiden to arrive.

She appears behind me and I think that she's Aiden until she places a hand on my shoulder and says,

"Bethany, you've got to stop talking to Aiden."

And my body is yearning for drugs and I'm frustrated and hot and sweating despite the chill and Nevae is the last person I want to see right now, so I just squeeze my eyes closed and beg her to disappear.

"Beth." She says.

My chest heaves. My stomach roils. Anyone but her, please. "Go away. I'm waiting for someone."

"Beth, I'm worried. So is Jackson."

"I'm fine."

"You're not. Look at you! You're sweaty and shaky and practically foaming at the mouth. You're ruining yourself for someone who probably doesn't even like you back!"

I'm suddenly enraged and I want to hit her but I can't because she's Nevae. She's my best friend. But Aiden loves me.

"Aiden loves me. He loves me more than anyone else ever has,"

There's a stretch of silence so long that I let myself think that she's left me alone, finally.

And then, so soft and quiet I almost don't hear her, "I love you, Beth. Jackson loves you. Evie loves you. Your parents love you. I just wish you'd see it and stop destroying yourself."

32] I BEG OF YOU

river

FEBRUARY 14th,   2021,   11:12am

It's on the morning news.

Riverside Killer Strikes Again

Riverside Killer. They've given the guy a nickname and everything.

It's sick. All of it— it's *sick*. Nevae isn't even so much as referenced in the headlines— they care more about the person that killed her than the fact that it was an innocent young woman that was killed.

I feel sick.

I didn't even know Nevae that well— I only met her once, but she was nice. Kind. Absolutely did not deserve to be choked to death on the side of the river and then not even spoken about on the news. So no one else knows she existed.

I stayed at Evie's last night, even Benji showed up at about ten to comfort Evie, until nearly midnight, when her Mom came home and heard the news. Then I went home, gave Dad a brief rundown on what had happened and then climbed in bed, but I didn't get much sleep.

We're going to Nana's for lunch today, so I'm forced to swallow down bitter bile and wash Hadley's hair, then let it dry, and then twist it up into a loose low bun. I'm just tying a red ribbon around it to secure it in place when Nicolas appears in the doorway to her bedroom.

"So," he says, "when are we going to see Mini Reed again?"

I try to stop myself from wringing his neck, instead patting Hads on the head and sending her out of the room. Nicolas takes this as an invitation to come further into the room, but I can see the hesitance in his step. He knows I'm not happy with him— knows he's not going to get away with saying things about Evie.

"What did you do to Bethany?" I ask instead of actually murdering him in cold blood.

He stalls, expression momentarily darkening. I've caught him off guard. Hit a nerve. He looks like he's choking on his words, sorting through memories.

"I don't know what you're talking about."

I push myself to my feet, forgetting all about Hadley in the room next door. "You son of a bitch." I blink. "You actually make me feel sick sometimes, you know?"

He looks hurt. Bastard. "That's nice, River, real nice."

"I don't care if I'm being *nice* to you, Nicolas, you *killed* my mother."

He flinches as if I've shot him or punched him or fatally wounded him or even all of the above.

I don't even care if this hurts him. I couldn't care less about his feelings.

"River, Hannah—"

"No." My voice is sharp and angular like the cut of his jaw, loud and piercing like the sound of a bullet ricocheting off trees and pressing itself into the tanned skin of Evie's stomach. I almost flinch away from it, away from the sound it makes that sounds so much like something that would never come from me. "You don't get to say her name, Nicolas. Not ever. You lost that right the second your fist hit her in the face."

*****

Nicolas doesn't come with us to Nana's. He lost *that* right when she kicked him out in December of 2017. One month after Aiden's death. I wonder if Aiden and Nicolas knew each other— if the reason he left was because of Aiden. I even let myself wonder for just a second if Nicolas killed Aiden, killed Bethany, Jackson, Nevae. Part of me is joyous with the thought of him behind bars for the rest of my life, but the rest of me thinks back bitterly *you're just as bad as him if you let yourself wish for such hellish things.*

"You alright, son?" Dad asks. He doesn't know about the fight I had with Nicolas, having only gotten home from work about ten minutes before we left.

I nod. "Yeah. Just a bit shaken up, you know,"

He nods understandingly. "Nevae Bradbury, yes. I knew her parents— Joan and Bruce. Nice folks. Hated each other in high school, though." A small chuckle escapes him, but he cuts it off like a dead leaf. "Nasty business in this town, River. I hope you're staying safe."

It's a warning. *I better not be seeing you in the woods, son.* He doesn't want me to be next. I could waste five minutes explaining to him why I definitely am not on the killer's hit list, but that would involve telling him about the psych project and the reason Evie came home from our "first date" crying and covered in her own blood.

"Don't worry, Dad. I ain't going anywhere, don't you worry,"

He nods to himself, as if yes yes he knew all along I was being safe, being a good boy, a good man. Keeping safe. It makes my chest ache, lying to him. I might not be the next victim, but I'm close enough to the whole thing to be caught in the crossfire.

I'm glad when he changes the subject.

"You treating Miss Evelyn Reed well, son? I wouldn't want old Nicole's wrath raining down on us all,"

I let out a dry chuckle. If only he knew.

"Yes, Dad, don't worry. We're not together though, so you don't need to worry at all, actually,"

He arches a brow. "You haven't asked her out on a proper date yet?"

"'Course not, Dad. She's just a friend,"

But saying it sounds weirdly wrong. Is Evie just my friend? We've been through enough together, spent enough time together, that "friend" doesn't quite feel like it works for us anymore. Best friends sounds too intimate, though. Too much like we should have known each other for more than a month.

Weirdly enough, partner sounds better to me.

Partners in solving crime.

I smile to myself.

"Look at you," Dad punches me lightly on the shoulder, "you're blushing and smiling like a goddamn gooey girl!"

"Oh, shut up," I swat his hand away.

He laughs. Deep, baritone, familiar. *Dad.*

33] FIANCE, DAUGHTER, FRIEND.

evelyn

FEBRUARY 20th, 2021, 2:09pm

I stand next to Henry Di Santis at the funeral.

He asked me if I would stand by his side the night before over the phone. He's phoned me a lot since she died. I'm not sure why— but he seems to find comfort in our late-night conversations, where he's tipsy on red wine and I'm sipping depressingly on a glass of cheaply bitter pinot grigio.

So I stand next to him in front of everyone, watching her white casket be lowered into the ground. The headstone hasn't been made yet and neither Henry nor Joan and Bruce Bradbury can afford to have it rushed, so for the next few months there's just a short, insignificant wooden cross to mark where *Nevae Bradbury: Fiancée, Daughter, Friend* is buried.

It's heartbreaking to watch Henry stand there, staring at her like she's going to come back and they can carry on living the life they wanted to live. They were supposed to get married in the summer, she was going to get pregnant and she'd told me a thousand times her plans for the townhouse they had their eyes on in Portland.

Now Henry has to go through her things and decide what to do with the engagement ring the funeral home gave back to him in a silk cloth, and the binder full of wedding inspiration and the wedding dress at the back of her closet.

The beautiful silk and lace floor-length gown she'd spent all her life savings on and gushed to me over for the past year.

It's funny how it only really hit me when she died that she probably stuck to me like an urchin because I was Bethany's other half. I was Bethany when Bethany wasn't there. I was Bethany enough for Nevae and in her grief she clung to me, used me as her best friend when her own left her.

It makes me tear up, and I have to bite my lip really really hard to stop from sobbing right there in front of her literal fiancé when he hasn't shed a tear since she died. It hasn't hit him yet. But it's hit me a million times over, and I don't even deserve to mourn her like Henry does.

Maybe *I* clung to *her* because she, too, was Bethany when Bethany wasn't there. She was the older sister that left me, the replacement delivered right to my doorstep when she returned from college.

Henry reaches across for my hand in the midst of the early warning of an incoming rainstorm, and his freezing fingers wrap around mine. I squeeze them. He's mourning the loss of the love of his life, and I don't know why but he's chosen me to cling onto like Nevae clung on to me. So I stand and I hold his hand.

*****

When I get home, there's an email waiting for me. It's become a habit to check my laptop every few hours for that horrible bold, black *new message* from that horrible, horrible killer. I wonder if Nevae got the emails too, like Bethany did and like I have. I wonder if she kept them a secret from Henry— or if he knew about them, and that's why he thought Nevae would be next. Maybe she kept them to herself in hopes they would go away— or maybe she even let it all happen because she knew what they meant and knew that she would die and hoped for it. Did nothing to stop it.

Maybe, after living in a world where both her best friends died and she couldn't get pregnant no matter how hard she tried, she thought it best to just let the killer get what they wanted and take her life.

Still, all of that speculation doesn't take back the fact that she's dead and I'm probably next and a three week break from killing instead of three years is terrifying. What happens if three weeks turns to three days?

This time next month, am I going to be dead?

I open the email, pulse leaping and jumping sporadically and painfully in my chest.

1 UNREAD MESSAGE

To: evelynareed2002@gmail.com

From: nodancer2119@gmail.com

R.E: 2119

The clock is ticking.

04.02.21

Please don't make me do this don't make me do this evie please don't make me do this.

I hope you miss nevae and i hope that she knows what she did.

I know you didn't help them do what they did but you know too much you're too close to the truth and i know that if i don't eliminate you soon you'll tell everyone and i've spent too much time running just to be dragged back here and paraded in front of everyone.

April.

 Second.

I'll be waiting.

Much love,

L

34] STOPWATCH

FEBRUARY 20th, 2021, 6:19pm

41 days until april 2nd

Evie is going to die.

I know this fact as well as I know the lines of my own hands.

I hate this fact as much as I hate Nicolas Lopez.

I hate that she has to live for the next forty one days knowing that she might not live to see graduation, that she *probably won't.*

I hate it I hate it I hate it I hate it.

"We just have to find the killer, River. We *just have to find him and kill him first.*" This is what she keeps saying to me, as if it's a definite solution, as if all she needs is to just believe this and it'll happen, as if sheer will is enough, maybe *more than enough* to keep the killer at bay, to keep his gun at his side, to keep his impulse where it belongs—anywhere but near Evie.

"It's not that easy, Evie." I say. Ever the pessimist.

"So you just want to *give up?*" She asks me. Outrage clings to her skin, to the lines of her face, to each individual tiny little pale freckle on her cheeks. "To let Bethany and Jackson and Nevae be forgotten by this goddamn town because we didn't think we *could?*"

I can't speak. This is too much. And yet too little— she's right, we need to do *something*. I want to shout at her *I don't care about Bethany and Jackson and Nevaeh, I care about you.* But I can't because it's inhumane. Of course I care that three (no, four) people died without any real reason, and of course I want the person responsible to rot in fucking hell, but Evie is my friend. My *partner*. I'm closer to her after one month than I ever was with anyone from New Brunswick even after living there for eighteen years.

She crumples then, face falling in on itself, knees going out from under her. I catch her, holding her, pressing an impulsive kiss to her head, pulling her to the couch, setting her down, holding her as she cries in big, heaving sobs.

"Just breathe, Evie, it's going to be okay." It's not, but I can still tell her lies; blissful, sweet lies. She gasps some more, huge wretched cries tearing free from her throat. Hadley watches from the floor, a doll in her mouth, looking scared shitless. As scared shitless as I feel right now, helping Evie through this panic attack because some psycho told her he's going to kill her in forty days.

"Shh," I say, "it's going to be okay."

But the lies sit heavy under my skin, weighing me down, making me feel sick of myself.

*****

Dad gets home about half an hour after I've gotten Evie to fall asleep on the couch, Hadley curled up against her chest, snoring loudly with a pacifier stuck tight in her mouth. In the quiet, I tidied up the whole house, put some tortellini and Bolognese on the stove, and told Mae about what happened with Evie, the panic attack (but not half the reason it happened, even though I want to), the way she's probably going to need a lot of emotional support now.

"I'm home!" Dad says, bustling through the door. I rush out into the hallway and shush him wildly, gesturing to the living room.

"Hadley and Evie are in there sleeping. Evie's been through a lot the past few days, so I thought I'd bring her here to get some sleep,"

He just about melts. "Oh, son, that's fine. I smell dinner— what are you cooking up?"

"Your favourite." I say, grinning.

Nicolas gets home a bit after that— he's been taking some community college courses, trying to at least behave enough to get some kind of useful degree so he can get a job and get off the couch. He's giddy when he finds out that Evie's staying for dinner (which I *almost* kill him for, but not quite).

We sit around the table like we did all those weeks ago, when we'd just found the text messages on the phone we found in Bethany's bedroom— when Evie went in there for the first time and took the first steps in getting over her grief. Five dishes of almost-cold tortellini, Hadley giggling away in the corner, talking to Evie through hand gestures and funny noises. Nicolas quietly talks to Dad about his day.

Normalcy.

That's what it is— an unfamiliar feeling in my gut, buried deep in my stomach. Normal. We haven't been normal for a very long time.

Dad lifts his glass of red wine to his lips and takes a drink, looking at Evie.

"So, Evie, do you have any plans for after high school?"

She sets her fork down politely, "I'd like to go to college in Bangor. Stay close to home, you know? I'm looking at studying photography, maybe getting an internship in Portland, and then coming back here and setting up my own studio."

This piques my interest. "I didn't know you were into photography," I say.

She sends a fleeting, deft wink my way, "I'll show you some of my pictures some time. Honestly, I haven't really been thinking about it as much recently— what with all that's been going on,"

"Oh, dear. Of course— you must be under so much stress," Dad empathises.

She nods through a mouthful of food. "Yeah. Yeah, it's been a bit hard. 'Specially since Bethany's come up again— it's been hard on my mom, you know?"

At the mention of Bethany, Nicolas' expression turns stony. I expect him to speak up, talk about how he knew Bethany— maybe offer some words of comfort, but he doesn't. Anger, bitter and acidic, stirs in my veins.

"Nicolas, you must have been here around the same time as Bethany, yes?" Dad says. The silence that follows is suffocating enough that I almost excuse myself to breathe somewhere else. Nicolas just nods.

Head up. Head down.

"Oh, did you know her well?" Evie says. She's taunting him. Teasing the truth out of him. I should stop this before it gets ugly, before Dad gets wrapped up in all of it as well, but I just sit there, finding myself unable to find the willpower to intervene. Something in me, something dark, wants to watch this play out.

"We were friends. Saw each other around school, you know." Nicolas says.

"Is that all? She mentioned you once or twice, now that I think about it,"

The sickly-sweet tone to her voice screams that she's lying, that this isn't going to end well, but poor oblivious Dad, just keen on making friends and good impressions, nods through his tortellini. Even Hadley has gone quiet, blinking long inky lashes, and frowning at her almost-empty plate.

"That's all." Nicolas sounds choked.

"Sure?" Evie reminds me of a cat playing with a mouse, just before striking the kill. I'm afraid of her, and for her. Dad just munches on happily. Mateo Lopez never was one for being particularly smart or attentive when it came to things like this.

"Why don't we go outside. You know, talk in private? I'd love to get to know the Bethany you knew, and I'm sure you'd love to hear some stories from when I knew her."

This makes Dad happier than he was on any of his wedding days. He claps gleefully. Hadley joins in, grinning widely. "Oh, that's a wonderful idea!"

Nicolas stands up, looking down at Evie. "You up for it?"

She nods, looking about ready to throttle him. I stand up with him, irritation peeling at my skin. No way am I letting them out there alone. "I'd like to come too."

"Oh, yes, you kids go outside— you could use some new friends, Nicolas," Dad chuckles to himself. He makes his way over to the sink and turns it on, humming a tune.

Evie, finally, stands up with us and we make a slow, hesitant path towards the door. Nicolas goes out first, leaving the door open behind him. I grab Evie's wrist, stilling her.

"You don't have to do this, you know." I say. "You really don't owe him anything."

"I want answers for myself, River. I want to sink my teeth into him and give him the pain that he caused me. He did a horrible thing to my sister, and I need him to pay, okay?" She says.

I nod. "What did he do?"

But she doesn't answer, instead pushing out onto the porch.

35] GRIN AND BEAR IT

evelyn

FEBRUARY 20th, 2021, 7:49pm

41 days until april 2nd

"We met at school." Nicolas says. "I said hi. She said hi. That night she walked past my house, and I invited her up to the porch for a beer. And then we were friends,"

"What day?"

"I don't know— sometime in September? Late September, probably. I don't remember a lot from the first few weeks that we knew each other." He says.

"Right. Okay. Um, what about her and Aiden? Do you remember a lot of that?"

He tenses. "Aiden was my best friend."

"He was? I never knew that. I, uh, I'm sorry."

He sends me a grim smile. "It's alright. Long time ago, you know?"

"Do you know how Bethany and Aiden came about? She never mentioned it to me, so I've been looking for someone who knows. I'd ask Nevae and Jackson but, yeah."

He nods. "Yeah, 'course. Uh— I saw them dancing at a party not too long after they met. I was a bit jealous, you know, but no hard feelings anymore. After that they just sort of started hanging around at school. She sort of drifted away from all of us and started hanging out with this group of girls from the college."

"Who?"

"God, now you're testing my memory. "He scratches his chin. "Mary? Maybe. Mary B something. And there was another girl. Poppie?"

"Marie Blaine?" I ask, my blood running cold. "She was friends with Marie Blaine?"

Nicolas scoffs. "That's a bit of an understatement— those three were attached at the hip."

So that just confirms it— I need to talk to Marie Blaine as soon as possible. If she was really this close to Bethany in the months before she died, then she could be the next victim— or she could have some valuable information. Either way, I'm going to need to find some way to contact her, sooner rather than later.

Hands trembling slightly, I wring them out behind my back, feeling the weight of the concern in River's frown on my back. He's angled behind me like some kind of guard dog. I don't know what he has against his brother or what he did to River, but I know what he did to me, so I kind of enjoy the reassurance of having him behind me. Of course, I can handle myself with Nicolas fucking Lopez, but his presence is comforting still.

"You know, Evie, I never meant to do what I did to Bethany." Nicolas says, almost on cue.

River tenses behind me, I can feel it. I tense myself, all over, suddenly motionless. Why would he bring it up? I thought we were trying to have a civilized conversation, but then he had to go and bring up the one thing that I hate him for.

Why?

"Yes, you did." I say, creeping one step closer to him without realizing. "How do you *accidentally* cast someone out of your life completely for no reason? How do you *accidentally* cause someone to come home screaming and crying in the middle of the night because they just lost one of their best friends? You turned *everyone* against her, Nicolas. *Everyone.* I will never forgive you for that, and I have no time or patience to listen to your excuses. I got what I wanted from you— which was another person to talk to about Bethany, so I don't need to waste my time talking to people, lowlifes, like *you*."

And, like a complete girl boss, I push past River and saunter into the house.

A little while later, River and I are curled up on my porch drinking hot chocolate wrapped up in thick winter coats watching the streetlights dance in the darkness. I've got my head on his shoulder, our elbows are touching.

It's nice and fluffy and warm.

"What did he do?" I find myself saying to the darkness. I feel River move his head, looking down at me. I stare across the road, at his house, at the dim lights in the windows where Nicolas is right now, probably helping his dad with the washing up.

"What?" River asks, voice thick and coarse with exhaustion. I wonder when the last time he got a good night of sleep was. I know I haven't slept well since this whole thing started. Since before we met.

God, has it really been that long?

"Nicolas. You hate him, and I know it's not just because I hate him— siblings don't work like that. What did he do to make you hate him?"

He goes still and quiet for so long that I don't think he's going to reply.

"You don't have to tell me," I defend, "I know that whatever it was must have been bad enough to drive you two apart and that makes it a big deal— you probably don't want to think about it anymore. I know I—"

"He killed my mom, Evie." His voice in the darkness is brutal, ruthless, stark. Loud in my ears, deafening against the night.

I don't know what to say to that. I sit there silently whilst his words sink in.

And then he starts speaking again, "I was seven years old when he beat my mother to a pulp right in front of me. I don't know why he did it. I assume it's because there's something wrong with his head— Aunt Carolyn always says he was born wrong. Something in his brain developed wrong— made him brutal and violent like that sometimes.

"He beat my mother— our mother— absolutely senseless. But that wasn't technically what killed her. What killed her was when she got piss drunk and drove off a cliff because she couldn't stand her own child hating her that much. Wanting to kill her. *Almost* killing her. So she did the job herself— made it easier for him. I've spent eleven years thinking about why she killed herself, and I think it was because she didn't want Nicolas to kill her— she didn't want him to have to live with the fact that he killed her mother, even though now she's gone I still blame him for it. And I think I *hope*, he blames himself."

River goes very quiet after that, as if he's spoken all of the words he knows and has run out of things to add. I reach an arm around his broad shoulders and squeeze— a silly half hug that probably does absolutely nothing for him. Tears are pricking against my eyes, but I push them down, force them back angrily because this isn't my story to cry about. This is his and he trusts me with it. That truth is enough to make a sob come to life in my throat, but I muffle it against the thick puff of the arm of my coat. He's too lost in his own thoughts to notice my emotion, so I force it all back down and put a lid on it and focus on him.

"I'm sorry about your mom." I say. "I really am."

He looks at me, and the glistening in his eyes makes my heart just about snap into two uneven, savaged pieces. "My Mom isn't the only person I've lost. Dad married twice after she died. Emma and Grace. Both of them died. Emma killed herself. They married when I was ten and she died when I was twelve. After her was Grace. Grace was the only woman who really felt like my mother other than my actual mother. She died three months ago."

"She's the reason you moved here? To get away?" I say when he goes quiet again. I'm trying to gently prod at him, to ease out the infection from the raw wounds he has because he must have kept all of this bottled up for too long.

"Yeah. Dad couldn't bear to live in that house anymore, in that *country*, knowing that it had seen so much loss— that I'd seen so much loss." A deep, exhausted sigh mars his chest in one heaving movement. "You know, before he showed up here, I honestly thought that we'd lost Nicolas for good. After what he did to Hannah, my mom, we sent him away to live with family. First it was my Aunt Carolyn in Quebec, then it was Aunt Louise and Uncle Larry in Toronto, then Grandma Laurie and Grandpa Poe in Texas, then Nana Lopez here, and then back to Aunt Carolyn for the last few months of high school. He ended up back in Texas for college, but he got kicked out and had the bright idea to come visit us here in Eastwood. He hasn't left, the son of a bitch."

I can't do anything but nod and squeeze him and nod as he struggles through the words, taking his time, leaving stretches between sentences as if the words have lived inside of him for so long that they don't know how to breathe on their own.

I sit there and I let my heart break for him.

This River I've been burdening with all my own problems, and he's here with all that inside him— it, well, I feel like a terrible person.

But then he leans his head, rests it on top of mine, and covers my hand with his, squeezing it, and I know he forgives me, I know he acknowledges my selfishness and accepts it because grief makes people selfish, makes them only see themselves, and he knows the truth of that fact far better I ever could.

*****

Benji is still sleeping on the couch. He doesn't tell me anymore about the reason he is here, about how long this has been going on— about how much he is hurting inside.

So I let him go on. I drive us to school together and he acts like we came from different places. Every time River comes over, Benji disappears to a different place. He is so afraid of people finding out that his step-father kicked him out. I know he is ashamed, and I wish that I could just make him know that he does not need to be ashamed, that the person who needs to be ashamed is his father.

I don't even know what part his mother has in this. Has she abused him as well? I do not think that Catheryn Hassan is capable of such monstrous behaviour, but apparently, I don't know the Hassans at all.

Catheryn is a lovely, small woman. She wears her hair in long braids intertwined with colourful thread and wears pretty dresses that go down to her ankles. Benji has her eyes— big, round, and woeful and a gorgeous shade of dark brown.

I don't know a lot about his family, but I do know that Benji's father died when he was six years old. Catheryn married Samael (a pot-bellied, red-faced trucker from New Jersey) when he was eight. Samael is a horrible monster of a human being (this I am sure of).

Benji gets back just after River leaves for the night. He sits next to me on the porch steps, and I hand him a bottle of cheap, too-sweet tea from the pack next to me. He takes it, and says, "My mother wants to go out for lunch with me."

Shocked into silence, I just gape at him.

"She says she doesn't want Samael's actions to affect our relationship,"

"That's bullshit." I say.

"Yeah," he says. "I'm gonna go."

"Does Cathryn know what that bastard's been doing to you? Did she even *try* to stop it?"

Benji looks at me then, and the lines of his face are hardened with anger. "Do *not* talk about my mother, Evie. Please. You don't know at all what's going on here."

My mouth is too big. I have too many words to say and none of them are right— all of them are hurtful. If I was a better human being, I wouldn't say anything at all. "So tell me, Benji. You do not have to go at this alone, in the dark. Let me be there for you. *Let me understand.*"

He goes very quiet. And then,

"The first time Samael hit my mother; I was twelve years old."

Everything seems to go quiet then. The cars in the distant, the breeze. All of it, quiet, as if the whole world is waiting for him to tell his story.

"I didn't really understand what he was doing at the time. I mean— I knew that Samael smelt of booze and cigarettes and public toilets, and that he was heavy handed with me and forceful with my mother. I assumed it was normal. It *was* normal in rural Maine. But when he struck my mother across the face, so drunk he almost missed her entirely, I thought that because they were married and because he showed up to the wedding with a freshly shaved face and styled hair and a nice suit and my mother was radiant, that love wouldn't allow them to fight.

"The second time he hit her, he wasn't drunk. And that was when I started standing up to him. I yelled at him— I told him to get out, that he didn't deserve my mother if he treated her like that. She was screaming and crying, Evie. She knew what was going to happen. She knew that Samael was the kind of man to turn his rage on anyone that made him feel the least bit inferior. So he started hitting me."

He takes a deep, shuddering breath. I just sit there and listen.

"It was once every couple of months. And then I turned fifteen, and people started saying I was a *man* now. And I think that made him more insecure. So he started hitting harder, more often. It was horrible— it *is* horrible, but I just kept telling myself *at least it's not my mother*. When he hit me the night that you found me on that bench— that was the anniversary of my father's death. Twelve years. And I just— I don't know, I felt like a failure, for letting Samael be my father— letting him stay in our lives when I'm strong enough now to hit him back."

I nod. "But he's white."

Benji looks down at his hands, lets out a dry, sickening chuckle. "Yeah, Lynny. He's white. And I'm Black."

It's so unfair.

Unfair feels too weak a word.

Benji doesn't cry. He just speaks, letting the words fill up the air around us, painting a picture of horror that I never knew about. Misery that I ignored.

Pain that I didn't— that I *refused*— to see.

Grief makes people selfish echoes in my mind. A stupid, silly, futile excuse for my blindness.

36] GHOSTS

river

FEBRUARY 22nd, 2021, 8:23am

39 days until april 2nd

Life goes on.

Evie's life has a clock on it, but life goes on like any other cold Monday morning in February. I drive through the rain to Cathy's and buy two lattes, and then get back in the truck to get to school and park by the entrance and meet Mae, Evie and Benji by their lockers. We smile and greet each other, and Evie and I exchange knowing looks. But Mae and Benji don't know about any of it, so we act normal. Life goes on.

In psychology, Evie works on her fact file for Nevae that she's been working on alongside ones for Bethany and Jackson. Again, we're not making very much progress on suspects and things, because we're concentrating on the history—gaining detailed insights into the lives of each of the victims. Aiden, Bethany, Jackson, Nevae. *Evie.* My stomach churns and protests my breakfast when I think about adding her name to the list.

I wonder if she's scared.

Of course she is— she's not mentally okay, but she's not insane. She knows to be scared when someone basically threatens her life like that. I hope so. Since I bared my soul to her on Friday night, I haven't seen her all weekend. I wondered briefly in fits of sleeplessness if it was a mistake— telling her all that spewing all my emotional baggage onto someone who really could do without the extra grief. But I've convinced myself that it was the right thing to do— that it's what friends do. Good friends. *Partners.*

I look at her now: bags under her eyes, no makeup except some old mascara that's probably been there since last week, hair pulled behind her head into a low bun, tied with a dark green frayed ribbon. Evelyn Reed. She's so surreal to me that I want to reach out and touch her to make sure I haven't imagined her.

This whole thing feels like a fever dream, but her especially so.

She catches me looking at her and winks, a smirk pulling at the corner of her mouth. I smile back, happy with the normality with it all. She's not in a constant state of panic and depression like me, and that's enough.

"What are you looking at, Lopez?"

"I'm wondering how you're still in one piece, honestly." I say.

"*You're* wondering how *I'm* still in one piece?" She asks, incredulous. I nod, because, yes, that is what I said, and she lets out an exasperated chuckle. "River, my pain is nothing compared to yours. If I'm in more than one piece, then you're shattered across the floor— and we're both still here having this conversation, so we must be pretty strong."

I don't say anything to that, because she's said it all. Yeah, I guess we are pretty strong.

The library is mostly empty except for us and a few freshmen I'm pretty sure are trying to skip class, but they're very obviously hiding out in the back of the room, chatting noisily. I doubt they'll get away with it.

"Do you miss New Brunswick?" Evie asks a moment later.

I'm surprised— she's never asked me about my old home before.

"I guess, a bit. I mean, I don't miss being constantly reminded of what we've lost— there were memories stuck to everything over there. It felt like every street sign, every restaurant, every cafe had some kind of memory attached to it associated with Grace, Hannah, or Emma."

"Did you have many friends? Anyone you still talk to?"

"One." Ophelia. I haven't thought about her for a long while. "This girl, Ophelia? We hung out sometimes— we worked together, so it was just nice to have someone to talk to there, I guess."

"No one else?" She sounds shocked. I guess I never really realised before how content I was with my own company.

"No, I guess not. I wasn't particularly popular, no one really went out of their way to talk to me. I was kind of a freak show back then. A little bit like you, actually. You know— the whole no one knows how to deal with the kids that have lost someone type of fear. No one wanted to risk saying the wrong thing, even though I was literally kind of desperate."

That weird feeling in the bottom of my stomach comes back. I'm not usually the type to spill my guts like this, but the emotions just keep bubbling to the surface, the words too.

"I'm sorry, River. I am. Even though Eastwood's such a shithole, I guess it's good that you've got me and Mae and Benji, yeah?"

"Yeah." I say. "Yeah, it is."

She looks like she's going to say something else, but stays quiet, instead going back to concentrating on her work.

*****

It's calorie Monday, which means we meet at Cathy's at around seven. I'm not that hungry, but I show up because after psychology I've realized that I've got good friends here, and I need to keep them. I've also become extra grateful that Evie and I have found each other in the midst of all of that pain, because we're in the same boat, a boat on a sea of grief, and hopelessness, but we know how it feels to be on this boat on a sea of grief, and we're sailing along it together.

We take our usual booth at the back of the diner, Hailey, with the bigger than life smile and constellations of freckles, sauntering over and embracing Mae, the two sharing a sweet, chaste kiss before she flutters back to collect a dish from the kitchen. It's surprisingly busy for a Monday evening, so the diner is a little less than half full. Considering most of the time it's almost empty, the low buzz of noise is strange, off putting, almost. I order what I always do— latte and a pancake stack with extra maple syrup (I'm Canadian, obviously).

Hailey smiles and chats for the few minutes that she finds spare in her shift and it's nice. Familiar. Makes me feel like I really do have friends, which is a wonderful, sweet feeling.

"So, you two have been sneaking off a lot together recently." Mae says, with a wink. I tense. Evie made me promise not to tell her or Benji about the danger she's in. Which is probably a really bad thing to agree to, but I'm so desperate for friends that I've been keeping my mouth shut around them to keep Evie happy. It's not like there's much they can do anyway. I mean, Mae will tell the Sheriff and— and maybe the Sheriff can help. The thought hits me suddenly, and I realise that in all of my desperation to be close to Evie I've ignored the blatant truth right in front of me.

There is no way we can handle this alone. If Evie wants to live, and I definitely want her to live, then we're probably going to have to get the Sheriff involved.

I need to tell Mae.

I know that she will always do what's best for Evie, and she'll help me decide whether telling the Sheriff is the right way forward or not.

Yeah, I'll do that. I'll ask her at school tomorrow.

Yeah.

"Earth to Lopez?" Evie is waving a hand in front of my face. I snap out of the daze, blinking.

"Huh? Sorry."

My latte's arrived. Hailey sends me a small, sympathetic smile that tells me she's seen the bags under my eyes, and someone's dropped hints to her that we're all struggling around here right now. I thank her and wrap my hands around it, ignoring the bitter, scalding burn that inflicts itself upon my skin.

I need something to keep me awake, to keep me in this conversation, and not in my mind. I've been spending an awful lot of time in my head recently, and I'm pretty sure that's just as a result of everything that's been going on, but it could also be because all of this death, watching Evie go through all of this grief— it reminds me of myself

Grief makes people selfish, right?

Then why am I so goddamn worried about her and not about me?

"We've just been working on the project— that's all." Evie says in answer to Mae's question, which feels like it was asked centuries ago but was probably just a few moments.

Mae nods, but winks conspiratorially. Benji looks between us, a small smile on his face.

"Sure. River, it's been more than a month since you moved— is this place getting any more interesting? Or, you know, less shitty?" He asks.

I give an attempt at a tired, lopsided grin. "Yeah, thanks. It's not so bad. Just very, you know, rainy."

Mae sighs dramatically. "Oh, don't get me started on the *rain*,"

Benji rolls his eyes, sipping noisily on the little bit left in his milkshake. "Here we go again— Mae, your hair looks *fine* when that horrible drizzly sort of rain comes about. Lynny— tell her. You're a girl, y'all must be able to, like, relate to each other somehow."

Evie's nose crinkles in reply. "Benji, what have we told you about trying to convince girls of things they're already absolutely certain of— it is *impossible*. And the sooner you realise that the sooner you'll stop getting into such petty fights with poor Ivy."

"Poor *Ivy*? Poor *me*."

And I sit there, watching them squabble, drinking my latte, and just enjoying the company of my *friends*.

3 7] T O B E H U M A N

evelyn

FEBRUARY 23rd, 2021, 5:17pm

38 days until april 2nd

I've decided to go for a run.

The air is nice and cool on my face and though my nose is cold and numb from the chill, my cheeks are warm, and my legs hurt.

The stitches in my stomach are pulling, I can feel them tugging on my skin.

It is a good pain.

Pain is better than nothing at all.

Pain is a reminder that I am still human. I am still Evelyn Reed. I am still the person I was before all of this. I am not dead yet.

And the *yet* is probably the scariest part in all of it.

I push harder. I'm sprinting the length of Morning Road and soon I will swing a hard left onto Forest Road. My feet are slapping the asphalt of the sidewalk hard, sending pinpricks of pain up my legs that reverberate in my shins. My stomach is heaving with each manic breath.

My lungs are shuddering with the effort. My running sneakers are too small, so my feet hurt, too.

Everything hurts.

From my feet to my head to my lungs to my brain, my mind, my exhausted mind.

I push even harder.

The unfairness of everything serves as a driving force, keeping me moving forwards. One foot in front of the other. I start to count the steps under my feet.

One, two, three.

Another shuddering breath. This one hurt more than the others. I know I should stop, but I don't.

Four, five, six.

A stitch blossoms in my side. Sharp pain in my stomach.

Seven, eight.

There's something warm on my stomach now. Sweat, probably.

Nine.

I am forced to slow down, anger seeping into my veins. The pain is too much.

Ten.

I press my hands against my stomach, bending over at the waist to try and dispel the ache. A metallic taste springs on my tongue.

My hands come away bloody.

I look down properly, and there— a bloodstain the size of both of my hands has spread across my abdomen. The patterned green fabric of my shirt is ruined.

Gasping, I lift up the material.

The messy, mismatched stitches have been pulled from where they thread into my skin. The area around the open gash is bright red and stinging. I grit my teeth.

I hate this.

I hate this *weakness* I have. I hate myself for being so *fucking weak*.

Tears burn the backs of my eyes. I can't even wipe them away, because then I'll have blood on my face as well as my hands.

All of the rage I've been holding in since the moment Bethany died starts to make its way up my throat. And it's directed at one person.

Arnold Windsor.

He's the one that shot me. He's the one that found Bethany— that didn't save her.

He's the one that caused all of this weakness and all of these horrible, horrible feelings inside of me that make me despise the person I see in the mirror.

His house is just up the road. I can see it from here— with its brown brick exterior, sitting smugly overlooking the forest and the river beyond.

I hate Arnold Windsor, so I start to run again.

The pain is horrible and acidic, and hate is so rampant in my body that the word no longer has any meaning— it is just *normality*.

It takes just over a minute to run up the hill and come to a stop outside of his front door. Hailey's car is in the driveway, and I'm confused until I remember that Hailey is Arnold's daughter.

Hailey Windsor.

Arnold Windsor.

I've known this since Mae and Hailey met, but I haven't fully *realized* it before.

Is she going to be in there?

Am I going to run in there, angry, and bloody, and is she going to see me and immediately report back to Mae?

At that moment, I don't care.

I just want Arnold Windsor to know what he did to me.

I want him to know that I hate him for not saving Bethany.

So I raise a hand to the door and knock loudly once. And then again. The whole door shakes, just like my body, just like my bloody hands.

A second passes, and then the door opens and there is Arnold Windsor, standing right in front of the door.

Usually, I keep to myself in this town. Usually, I give people no reason to believe the lies that people like Izzy Beaumont spread about me.

But not today. Today, all I see is *hate* and all I feel is red hot anger and the bitter stench of weakness.

"Evelyn? I—" he says.

I cut him off. I walk through the door and I back him into the hallway. I don't even register how opulent the room is until I've backed the old man against the ornate wallpaper.

"Shut *up*." I grit out. "Shut *up*."

He looks too shocked to say anything.

So I do all the talking. "Why did you shoot me, in the forest? Hey? Why did you do it?"

Quiet. He looks stricken. But there's no protest, no defence— it *was* him. Confirmed.

Arnold sputters and coughs.

I realize I have my hand around his throat. I realize that I'm going to kill him. I let him go, stepping back.

I stare at my bloody hand and the faint blood stains around his throat. *I was going to kill him.*

I feel sick to my stomach.

"Evelyn, I know you must be very angry. Rightfully so. Call the police."

No reply comes out of my mouth. Of all the hours I've spent thinking about hate, I have nothing to say to him now. He shot me.

Arnold Windsor shot me and now I'm here, in his house, bleeding on his fancy floor and I've put blood around his throat. I am disgusted with myself.

"Call the police." He says again. Quieter, this time. "Please."

He sounds broken. I know the sound of a broken voice too well.

"Evelyn, I am sorry," he says.

I blink. It's like I've woken up from a dream— like I've sleepwalked into Arnold Windsor's giant house and held him by the throat and then let go, woken up, become myself again.

"No, I—" I start.

"Please, can you just let me explain?" He says. His voice is worn thin, tinny and small in the monstrous room.

I step backwards, towards the door, towards escape from the person that I have become.

He steps forward, mirroring my movements, coming closer and closer and then I'm pressed against the door and he's a few feet away from me.

I can see the lines under his eyes and on his cheeks and the desperation in his face.

"You shot me." I say, this time quietly. There's no accusation there, just realization, just a prompt for him to explain why. Why I'm here and bleeding all over his expensive rug.

And then I hear footsteps on the stairs and a small gasp, and I look up and there is Hailey. She's looking between me and her father with a hand over her mouth. Her hair is in messy waves down her back and she's in one of Mae's hoodies.

"Evie? What are you doing here?" She asks me, hurrying down the stairs. And then she catches sight of the bright red stain on my shirt and gingerly lifts it up to see what's happened.

"Oh my. Are you okay? What happened? What are you doing here?" Her voice is panicked, but still sweet and kind.

"I—" I start, but how do I tell her that her dad shot me?

How do I tell her that River and I were in the woods at night not even a week after Jackson's death?

"I shot her." Arnold speaks up.

Hailey freezes. I look at her face, and she's gone ashen. I don't think she can speak. So I do.

"It was an accident." I say. "I swear— I was in the woods, um, running, and he thought I was a deer."

"It's illegal to shoot in Eastwood Forest." Hailey says. "It's protected land, Dad. You know that,"

I can't tell what she's thinking from her voice— I've never heard bright lovely Hailey talk with such a cold, detached tone. She wraps an arm around my shoulders and leads me out of the hallway, leaving her dad behind on the fancy bloodstained carpet.

She leads me into a spacious, ornate bathroom and I get Deja vu as she helps me hop up onto the counter. "I know you don't have health insurance, Evie. I'll just stitch you up,"

"Just like sewing." I say.

She nods, a small smile on her face. "Just like sewing."

"I'm sorry." I say. "I'm sorry for coming here, I just—"

"When did it happen? There are already stitches here, Evie, but you pulled them. When did you get shot?"

I swallow hard, hesitant to tell her. I know that this is going to find its way to Mae and she's going to be so disappointed in me, but right now Hailey's hands are gentle as she dabs a wet cloth to clear up the blood and I'm tired from blood loss and my inhibitions are all the way down.

"Just over a month ago." I say. "Just under a week after Jackson died."

"Oh, Evie." She says in a sigh. "Did you stitch it up yourself?"

She doesn't seem to want to know the details about how it happened, or maybe she doesn't want me to have to explain what I was doing. I am overwhelmingly grateful for it.

"I didn't, actually. River did. I was with him at the time. He took me to his house and stitched me up,"

"And you've been close friends ever since?" She asks, a teasing lilt to her tone.

I can't help but smile. "Yeah, I guess."

Hailey leans in closer, inspecting the ruined stitches. "Looks like he did a good job. I'll just go and get the sewing kit."

In the moment I'm alone, I have to force a sob back down into my throat. I'm alone in Arnold Windsor's bathroom bleeding everywhere. I keep barging into people's lives and ruining their fancy things and making them worry and making them stitch me up. I am such a burden.

Even after all the theatrics, I still don't know why Arnold shot me.

And I still don't know what the nagging feeling about him, and Richard Wells is. But something is still telling me that they're hiding something big and important. I secretly hope that it's to do with the case, because I don't know where to look next.

At that moment, Hailey reappears with a sewing kit and a first aid kit along with a change of clothes. I desperately do not want to endure the pain of stitches without any kind of numbing cream, but I would rather go through half an hour of agony than die of blood loss without even finishing the investigation.

So I sit there and let her stitch me up.

38] IT RAINS
(SOMETIMES)

FEBRUARY 24th, 2021, 6:29pm

37 days until april 2nd

Dad has gone out for dinner with some of his work friends.

I've invited Evie over, not to work on the case, but to actually spend time together as friends instead of partners for once. We're babysitting Hadley, and she's currently in the living room demolishing a plate of lukewarm Dino nuggets and baked beans. Her face is sticky and red and so are her fingers.

The air in the house is warm and stuffy with the scent of two-year-old and beige food, and yet it's easy to breathe. Breathing doesn't hurt here, living in this house is not difficult when Nicolas isn't here, and when Evie and I aren't in front of laptop screens researching the death and horror in this town.

In fact, Evie is smiling easily over her mug of coffee. We're in the kitchen, leaning against the countertops and making light conversation about school.

She wasn't at school today and has yet to tell me why.

So I ask her, instead. "Why weren't you at school today?"

She freezes, as if caught doing something she shouldn't be. "I— I was ill."

"Oh," I say, not believing her for a second and wondering vaguely why she's choosing to lie to me. "Then maybe you should go home—"

"No— I— not that kind of ill, really. I— you see— yesterday I, erm, pulled my stitches."

I had a feeling this was going to happen at some point— Evie is determined and stubborn and is notorious for pushing too hard too soon.

"How?" I ask instead, mildly amused. She's okay. She's in front of me drinking coffee and upright so she must be okay.

"I went for a run."

"Oh, Reed, you goose. Who stitched you back up again?"

Her face falls when I say that. She squeezes her eyes shut and sets the half-empty mug of coffee on the counter, and I take a step forward, setting a hand on her arm.

She opens her eyes and looks at me and the hazel color is full of regret.

"Do you want to sit down?" I ask.

She nods, and her bottom lip gets caught by her teeth. It goes white as she bites down and probably draws blood. My heart clenches. Can this girl ever catch a break?

We go into the living room, and Hadley sets her plate on the table. I prompt her to go and play in her room and she pouts but obliges.

"Are you going to start kissing?" She asks, tilting her head at us on her way out of the room. "Niccy said that's what you two do."

Evie and I both turn several shades redder. She lets out a small giggle. I'm stuck between anger and amusement. *Niccy?* Way to reduce Nicolas into someone who sounds completely harmless. But why has he been talking to Hadley about me and Evie?

"Just go to your room, Hads, okay?" I say, voice pitchy and embarrassingly squeaky.

She nods and toddles off, ever oblivious to what she just did.

Evie settles on the couch, tucking her legs under her like she always does. I sit opposite her.

She brings a hand down and hooks her fingers around the hem of her shirt. She lifts it up and I'm confused and dumbfounded and very much alarmed until she reveals the wound.

It's red and angry looking again, but the new stitches are even and much better looking than mine. It'll be a nicer scar.

Maybe her pulling the original ones out was a blessing in disguise.

"Hailey did them," she says. "I was running up Forest Road and pulled them not far from her house, and she saw me."

"Hailey lives on Forest Road?" From what I can remember, Forest Road is full of manor houses and definitely not a place I imagined Hailey, who works at a diner and is still in college, to be living.

"Oh, yeah, she lives there with her dad. He's, um, Arnold Windsor."

My stomach flips. I did not know this, and it surprises me. "Grumpy old Arnold Windsor is Hailey's dad? The same Hailey who is literally the nicest person ever?"

Evie nods, a small smile on her face. "Yep."

"Was he there? Did he see you?"

"That's the thing, River," she says, "I almost killed him."

My stomach drops as she tells me about what she was doing last night— going to his house bleeding and vengeful, wrapping her hand around his throat.

"I'm still totally sure he's hiding something." She says when she's explained everything and I'm too shocked to speak. "I think we should go there and search his things."

"You're kidding." I say. The moment those words left her mouth, I was completely knocked out of my stupor.

She sighs heavily, leaning towards me. She has her puppy eyes on. They're very effective.

"Evie, we can't." I say. "That's illegal."

"I think we're past legalities at this point." She says. She's Evelyn freaking Reed. I know she's not going to back down, but that doesn't make me like it anymore.

"Can we talk about this another time?" I say. "I invited you over here because I want to talk to you about things that aren't the case."

She nods, but that determined flash is still bright in her eyes. "What do you want to talk about, Lopez?"

"What happens after the case?" I say. "Do we keep being friends? Do we stay in touch at college?"

Evie frowns. "Well, we're friends, aren't we?"

I nod. Of course we are.

"Then yes, River, we'll stay in touch after high school. I'll come and see you in New Brunswick and you can come and see me wherever I am. We'll go to high school reunions and Mae and Hailey's wedding *and* Benji and Ivy's." She smiles. "I'm not going to let you go that easily,"

Her promise echoes around me warmly. *I'm not going to let you go that easily.* The mention of New Brunswick reminds me that my plan has always been to escape Eastwood and go back to Saint John as soon as possible. Run back to Ophelia and hope she'll be my kind-of friend like she was before. But then I look to my phone on the coffee table, and its silence. Ophelia hasn't texted me for weeks. The only person that's actually made any effort to contact me outside of school recently is Evie. And she's the one here now, making me feel like this.

Is there anything left for me in New Brunswick?

A large, empty house with a thousand memories, a sprawling gray city, miles, and miles of sea. Winters full of snow and Ophelia.

"Where are you going for college?" I ask her. "What are you going to study?"

"Law, probably." She says. "Nothing makes me feel as alive as solving crime and fighting for things I believe in, like Bethany and Jackson and, erm, Nevae."

Nevae's name joining the list of victims strikes a painful cord in me.

Nevae who served me coffee and teased Evie and me and poor Henry, who she left behind.

I swallow back tears that aren't mine to cry and nod. "You'd be a great lawyer."

One side of her lip quirks up. "What about you? What are you going to study in New Brunswick?"

"I don't know, actually." I say. "I don't even know if I'm going back to Saint John."

She arches her brow. "Really? But— you miss it, and God knows Maine isn't exactly a university hotspot."

I let out a small laugh at that. "Yeah, you're right, but— I don't know, I guess NB isn't really my home anymore. I don't think it has been for a while,"

"So you're going to stay here? With me?"

"I don't know." I say with a sigh. "I'm sorry, I just don't know what my future looks like,"

Evie doesn't even bat an eyelid; she just keeps on half-smiling. "I can imagine you doing something in psychology,"

"That's just because it's basically the only lesson we have together,"

"Yeah, but I can tell you love it— people's minds, and you're a good listener. Therapist, maybe?"

All this talk of my future is making me sweat, so I laugh and shake my head good-naturedly.

This I think as I watch Evie drink her coffee and go off about all the potential colleges in Maine and even New York that I could study psychology at. *This is where I want to be.* With her, where talking is easy and even through all of the darkness we can talk about normal things as normal people and smile and laugh.

This.

39] CONCERNED

evelyn

FEBRUARY 25th, 2021, 6:12am

36 days until april 2nd

It's six am and someone is screaming.

It takes my eyes a second to adjust to the near-darkness, streetlights bleeding through the window and the sound of a cry from the living room.

I know who it is before I even get out of bed: Benji.

He's had nightmares here before, but he's never screamed quite this bad. My heart is breaking for him, knowing that there's nothing I can do. Or, if there is something I can do, I'm not putting enough effort in to help him.

I feel completely and utterly useless.

Rubbing my eyes, I swing my legs out of bed and stand up, stretching. The screaming stops for a second and then starts up again. I hurry down the stairs and into the living room and shake Benji awake. His skin is slick with sweat and his face is contorted with agony.

"Benji, wake up. It's okay. You're safe," I say.

His eyes flicker open and then he's hugging me and I'm hugging him back and trying not to cry.

My best friend is in so much pain and I can't do anything to help him. Except hold him and talk the demons away.

I reach out a hand and flick on the old lamp next to the couch and it lights up the room with a soft glow. Mom is standing in the doorway, looking solemn and concerned and mildly annoyed. I look away from her and back to Benji, whose breathing has slowed. He's calming down, but his forehead is still creased, and tears are still leaking from his eyes.

I sigh into his shoulder. What am I going to do?

Benji is my best friend, and I can't just leave him like this— I can't let him live in my house and have nightmares and not do anything about his stepdad, sitting at home with his mother acting like nothing is wrong.

I clench my jaw. The injustice of it all is horrible and exhausting and I just don't know what to do.

If I could, I would tell Mae— she's level headed and she's the smartest one out of all of us.

Benji lifts his head from my shoulder, and I release him from the tight hug.

He wipes some stray tears from his wet eyes and brings his knees to his chest, hugging them to him like a life vest.

"Are you okay?" I ask him.

He nods, even though he cannot possibly be alright. "Just tired. Sorry if I woke you up,"

I shake my head. "Don't be sorry, I'll go and make us some coffee,"

Standing up from the couch, I pad quietly into the kitchen. Mom is standing by the coffee maker, staring down into her mug. When I walk in, she looks up and forces a smile.

"Hi, dear. How's Benji? Poor kid."

I nod, "He's alright. Shaken, but okay,"

"Evie, I hate to get in the way of all that he's going through, but when exactly do you think he'll be going home?"

"Hopefully, he'll never go home, Mom." I say. "But I don't know when he'll be moving out— probably not too much longer. I just— I just don't know what to do,"

Mom's face softens, and she sets the mug on the side and comes a step closer to me. I swallow hard.

"You don't need to fix everyone, Evie."

Except I do. "Benji is my best friend, and he's lost and in no position, really, to be making big decisions,"

"So you're going to make them for him?"

"No, I just—" I falter. His next steps do need to be his decision, but I can't let him do it alone.

"Let him take his time, Evie. Let Benji decide what he wants to do, okay? You just stand by his side and be a shoulder to lean on when he needs it, okay?"

I nod. My eyes are welling up, because this is the first piece of motherly advice, she's given me since Bethany carved a hole inside of her and left her hollow.

My mom is coming back to me.

*****

After school, I find myself with nothing to do.

Benji is at practice, River is busy with Hads so doesn't have time for a couple of hours at the library working on the project, and Mom is at work, as usual. I decide to catch up on some schoolwork, since my grades have been slowly slipping since I stopped focusing on homework and tests and started focusing on my sister's murder. I make a big mug of coffee and sit at the kitchen table with a pile of notebooks and my favorite pen. Music through my headphones, and the rain coming down outside.

It's peaceful, and normal.

Until there's a knock at the door an hour later.

I get up and put the empty mug in the sink before wandering to the front door, not pausing to see who it is.

When I open the door, Mae is standing on the doorstep. She is wearing a sweater with the hood up to protect from the rain, which has waned in last half hour or so. Her hair falls in its usual collarbone-length blond waves, and she's not wearing any makeup.

Her mouth curves into a smile when she sees me, and a warm feeling blooms in me.

"Hi," she says.

"Hi," I say. "What are you doing here?"

"Hailey told me about what happened on Tuesday. You know, with her dad and all that."

My stomach turns. Of course Hailey told Mae.

Of course I now have to make up a whole elaborate lie in front of my best friend. I suddenly feel sick, the old taste of coffee bitter and gross in my mouth.

"I'm sorry, Mae, that I didn't tell you, I— how much did Hailey tell you?"

"That you showed up to her house all bloodied and had a shouting match with her father, and then ran out."

So Hailey didn't mention the whole getting shot by her father thing. Great. How am I supposed to explain *that* in a way that makes sense without spilling about the investigation?

I let myself imagine, just for a moment, what it would be like to tell her. It would lift a huge weight off my shoulders and make it a whole lot easier to breathe around her, but she would tell her father. And Mohamed would make me stop doing the whole thing and I'd feel so horrifically useless.

"I don't really want to talk about it, Mae." I go to shut the door, but she shoves a single bruised Vans clad foot between the door and the frame and sticks her puppy-dog eyed face through the gap.

"Please. Evie, please talk to me. You've become a stranger recently and I— I want my best friend back. Please, just talk to me."

I look to my feet, too cowardly to meet her eyes. "Fine." I say with a sigh.

Mae pulls back her foot and tugs the door open again, since my grip on the handle has gone slack. "Come on then, saddo. We're going to Echo Hill,"

I get in the passenger seat of Mae's bright blue VW Bug, and she takes off in the direction of Echo Hill and, I can't get it out of my head, Deepwater. Richard Wells' little wooden house sitting there, full of answers I don't know how to ask for.

My head leant back against the headrest of the leather seat, I close my eyes and just feel the bumps of the road under us.

My best friend is less than a foot away from me, but I've never felt further away from her.

Twenty minutes later, we're sat elbows touching at the top of Echo Hill, overlooking the Clerwood as it winds its way towards Eastwood and the sprawl of green that makes up Loye Valley, Eastwood, and Redwood as well as the highway that takes you south to Bangor and a few hours east to New Brunswick. All the world, so tiny at our feet.

"I miss you." She says to the cold, damp air. There is no wind, so her quiet voice carries well across the tiny distance between us.

"We see each other every day."

"I know," Mae says, "but I miss you and me how we were before all of this started— before River moved, before everything."

She adopts that sympathetic look again, and I have to look away. Tears are pricking at my eyes, sharp and unwelcome. I am sick of crying.

"God, I'm sorry." I say. "I can't stop crying, or thinking about crying,"

She lets out a light laugh, and it's like we're crouched down at the Clerwood, aged twelve, whispering about the meaning behind Devil's Pathway. The thought of making up stories about ghosts surrounding that place makes me sick now— poor Aiden Islington, his memory erased from this place so much and so thoroughly.

Devil's Pathway.

Aiden wasn't the Devil.

God, he was anything but.

"Has your mom been holding up well?" Mae asks.

I nod. "Yeah, alright. She's taken on a load more shifts at the bar, though, so I haven't been seeing her much."

"Maybe you should check up on her."

I nod, because yes, I should— yes, a good daughter would have done that.

"Have you spoken to Henry much?" She asks, deft fingers playing with a frayed hem on her sweater. "Is he doing alright?"

"Yeah, he's been calling me quite a bit— talking about her, talking about what he wished they could have done. God, it's horrible." A bird squawks loudly in the distance, its cry agonizing and yet beautiful. "He's not doing great— but I'm pretty sure that's normal."

She nods. "Yeah. This is so— God, I hate all of this. I hate that you're hurting like this, I hate that we don't hang out anymore, I hate that there's not a darn thing I can do about any of it!"

And it hurts even more when I realize she doesn't even know River and I are investigating the case— I made him promise not to tell either her or Benji, because she would have to tell her father and both of them wouldn't rest until I stopped. But they don't get it— they don't understand that working to find the killer makes me feel useful and it stops me from spending all of my time at home wallowing and crying because everyone is dead.

And then there's the emails and the fact that I'm next.

The ticking clock— the days scratched off from the calendar.

How many days are left?

Forty, I think, maybe less.

That's just over a month until I die.

Until I'm murdered. At least if I kick the bucket on April 2nd, River will know that it was murder and River will be able to give the police everything we have. I'll die for the right reason— to give them more evidence, another crime scene to analyze, another chance for the killer to trip up.

"What about you and River?" She asks me, a teasing smile on her face. "You two spend a lot of time together,"

And I *blush*. God. That's embarrassing.

"We're literally just friends, okay? You can tease me about it all you want but the answer will always be the same. His story isn't mine to tell, but he's lost people too— so it's just nice to have someone around to understand what it's like, you know? We're friends."

She smiles sadly and nods, "It's okay. I understand."

My phone chooses that moment to ring, buzzing in the pocket of my jeans. I silence it and decline the call. I won't let Mae and I's first moment alone together like best friends for months be ruined.

"I am sorry I've not been hanging out with you as much, Mae."

"Don't be sorry. I know you've been going through stuff— what with all the shit from the past coming back and literally everyone talking down your ear about Bethany and Nevae and Jackson and what the hell is wrong with this town."

"How're things with Hailey? You two still going to get married and ride into the sunset together?"

Mae laughs, a blush on her cheeks. "As far as I'm aware, yeah. I'm happy with her, Evie. I am."

"Trust me, I know."

We lose the last bit of light then, slipping away behind the hill at our backs, and I have to blink to make out the outline of Mae in the dark, but she's there— slender shoulders, long torso, longer legs clad in yoga pants and her favorite pair of battered Vans on her feet, which are kicking against the log.

"You want to stop being so pitiful, right?" She asks me.

I blink. "Yeah."

"Why don't you dig that cello out of your closet?"

My heart skips. My cello. I haven't played it since Bethany died— but maybe Mae is right. Maybe it would be nice to go back to something normal like that. Having a hobby other than sitting around and moping and trying to solve murders that definitely don't want to be solved.

"Maybe I will." I say. And she smiles.

"Evie?"

"Yeah?"

"Promise me you'll talk to me more often? Promise me you won't slip away,"

I nod vigorously. "Yeah, yeah, of course."

"Promise me."

"I promise, Mae. I promise I won't slip away again."

"I love you."

"I love you too."

We fall into silence, and even though the conversation feels like it's over I'm so tired of silence between us.

"I was shot." I say to the darkness.

There is no reply.

And then, "Evie." It's spoken in a breath, something so light that it just sits on the air, hovering over us.

"I'm sorry I didn't tell you before, but I didn't want you to worry, and—"

"When? How? Are you okay? Is that why you were bleeding all over Hailey's floor?"

I take a deep breath that pulls on my stitches with a little pinprick of pain. "I'm okay. It was back in January, not long after River moved to town."

"What happened?"

"We were in the forest. I, erm, I was showing him Bethany's spot. And someone shot me. We thought, maybe, at the time it could have been the killer. But then I thought it was probably Arnold— with the big gun and bad aim and, yeah."

"So you, what, pulled your stitches on Tuesday and went to his house for... revenge?" Mae asks.

Nodding stiffly, I turn to look at her, barely making out two vivid blue eyes in the hazy dim light. "Yeah, I guess. I went for a run, and I ripped the stitches out and I got so, so angry that he had made me weak and I just broke, I guess,"

"I'm glad Hailey was there to help you," she says.

"Me too." I say, "Me too."

I feel a hand wrap around mine, warm despite the definite chill in the black night air.

Mae squeezes my hand, and whispers, so quietly I have to strain my ears to hear it, "Don't be a stranger, Evie."

She drives us home, navigating the dark roads expertly, like someone who has lived in these woods for all her life. Like someone who has never known the stretches of flat, empty land that lie beyond this state. She pulls into her driveway, and we get out, but before she can walk back to her house, I put a hand on her arm to still her.

"Mae, why don't you come to my house? We could eat ice cream and watch a film, if you want,"

Her smile is lit up gold by the glow of the security light on the front of her house.

She nods. "Yes, I'd love to,"

Inside my house, the light in the living room is on. The TV is on, playing some rerun of a show from the nineties. Benji is curled up on the couch, eyes fixed to the screen. There's an empty glass on the coffee table and a pile of schoolbooks on his lap.

He looks up when we walk in, and Mae stills.

"Benji?" She asks, a confused smile on her face, "What are you doing here?"

"Hi, Mae." He says. He looks sad. His eyes flick to mine and I don't know what he's thinking. Until he clears his throat and sets the books on the coffee table and scoots up, making room for us next to him. "I need to tell you something,"

Mae and I sit down on the couch and sink into its comfort, whilst Benji tells Mae about his stepdad and the abuse.

I'm so proud of him as he tells the story of how I found out and how he was kicked out of his own home, left by himself in a world so cruel. She is tense and pulled as taut as a string and I can see the tears in her eyes, but she doesn't let a single one fall.

This is not our story to cry about.

This is Benji's story, and it is his pain.

Finally, when he comes to a tentative, shaky end, Mae launches herself at him and hugs him for centuries. I watch, playing with my phone and the tarnished alloy ring on my middle finger.

They're only forced to pull apart when Benji's phone starts to ring, and we all look over at the sudden noise, the shrill ringer echoing in the room.

The name written in bold text at the top of the screen makes my heart drop into my stomach.

Mama

40] HEY MA, IT'S ME

evelyn

FEBRUARY 25th, 2021, 8:29pm

36 days until april 2nd

Benji answers the call with a stony expression, only the faintest traces of emotion seeping through the narrow cracks in his facade.

Mae and I stay completely silent.

"Ma?" He says.

There's a stretch where she's speaking and then Benji's voice rings out again, "I miss you too."

He looks up at us and then turns the phone onto speaker— Mae and I shake our heads, because this is a private conversation that we don't need to hear, but Benji doesn't waver.

His ma's voice is crackly and distant through the crappy phone speaker, but we can make out her words clear as day and sharp as a knife.

"Benji, my boy, why don't you come home? Why do you stay away like this? Samael says he is sorry. We want you home,"

"Samael kicked me out." His voice is raw and stern.

An exasperated sigh floats through the line. "I miss you, my boy,"

"I know. I miss you too, Ma. But I can't come home." Benji turns away from us, but I can see the wetness in his eyes, "He'll hurt me again."

"You need to come home and talk to us, Benji. You're hurting me by staying away,"

"Well, I'm not beating you up and kicking you out, am I? That's what he did to me, Ma. That is what he did to *me*."

"Samael didn't mean it, dear." Ma says. "Stop being childish and come home. Be a man,"

And she hangs up.

Benji's head falls to his hands and his shoulders shake with tension. Mae rubs his back with a pale hand of long fingers, and I feel so utterly powerless.

"Samael is the son of a bitch." I say, because it's true.

Benji looks up at me and shakes his head. "Evie, no. He's not. He's— he's just doing what he thinks is right,"

I swallow hard. "Why are you defending him? He gave you bruises and kicked you out of your own home!"

He's silent, but Mae sends me a look that's like *don't*.

"Tomorrow I'll go and talk to them," Benji says.

"You don't owe him anything," I say.

"I owe my mother a goodbye, at least. I'm not going back there again, but I need my things and— and I need to say goodbye, okay?"

I nod. "Yeah, sure, of course."

"Will you come with me?" He asks.

Mae and Benji both look to me, their eyes drilling into mine. I start to sweat a little under the collar of my jacket.

"I— um, sure. But isn't this something you should do alone?"

"If you're there, then maybe my step-dad won't freak out so much and he won't, you know,"

I nod silently, furious up and down movements. "Yeah, yeah, of course. I'll be there. After school tomorrow?"

*****

It feels strange going through a whole day knowing that Mae and Benji and I all know a huge thing that River doesn't, and he makes his way through the day cheerily like he always does, chatting about gossip and funny things his sister has done whilst we watch him with strained smiles that are almost painful, knowing what's going to happen once the final bell rings at three-thirty.

I spend psychology going over more factsheets with River and thinking about when I'm going to be able to speak to Marie Blaine and track down Poppie Masters. Nevae's death has definitely left a gaping hole where my information is coming from, and a similar sized one in my heart. My second big sister is gone, and I've been working myself to the bone with the case and Benji to the point where I have barely taken a second to just grieve for her.

But there is no time to get upset now, because Benji needs me.

Once the final bell does ring and my AP Mathematics class is dismissed into the grimy math corridor, I gravitate towards the parking lot with a sense of urgency and a pit of dread brewing in my stomach.

Benji is going to confront his stepdad. In two hours, it could all be over— Benji could be free from the abuse, *finally* after God knows how many years.

His long, broad figure is leant against the Volvo when I approach it near the back of the lot, under the shade of some dead-looking pines. He smiles when he sees me, even though he can't be in a smiling mood.

"Are you okay?" I ask.

He shakes his head. "Not really, but I'm going to do this,"

"I'm really proud of you,"

"I know. Thank you. I just— I'm so scared, and I don't know why. I'm literally twice the size of the guy,"

"It's okay to be scared— you just have to be strong enough to overcome your fear, too."

Benji gets into the passenger side of the Volvo, and I get into the driver's seat, turning the key in the ignition.

His house is on the other side of town, and when I pull up outside Benji is shaking.

I place my hand on his shoulder and squeeze. "Are you okay? We don't have to do this— you could just walk away, and I'll drive you to the Sheriff's station."

"I want to do this, Evie. I need to tell him to his face that I'm done playing this sick game,"

So we get out of the car and march up the porch steps and Benji's knocking on the door loudly and Samael Logan, the red-faced, chubby-cheeked man at least two inches shorter than Benji opens the door.

He smiles when he sees us. "Finally, son, you're back,"

Benji grits out, "I'm not your son," and pushes into the house.

I follow him like a lost puppy. I can't remember the last time I came here, saw the lavender-painted walls, the warmth in the honey-coloured floors and the small rooms filled with earth-toned decor. Benji walks to the kitchen, where his Ma is standing by the sink, peeling potatoes. When he walks in, she turns and gasps and hugs her little arms around him tightly.

Her hair is swept up in a patterned scarf and her smile is big but strained. I sort of just stand there awkwardly and watch, feeling wildly out of place but not planning on going anywhere until Benji has done what he needs to do.

Samael stands not more than two feet from me, and I can smell the thick stench of whiskey coming off him in waves.

"Son, why don't you introduce me to your friend here," Samael says.

I know for a fact that we've met before, years ago, but I'm not surprised he doesn't remember. He doesn't seem to be a man that cares to learn much about his stepson. Benji steps back from his Ma and looks at me apologetically.

"This is Evelyn. She's my friend, and she's here to help me pack my things," he says. I'm proud of the strength in his voice— the unwavering quality to it.

"You're leaving?" Samael asks, eyebrows high.

"Yes," Benji has his hands stuffed in his pockets, his wide stance accusatory and ready to fight.

"I— son— I'm sorry for whatever I did to you, I am. You're not surely going to move out and leave us, are you?"

"*Whatever you did to me?* You hit me, you kicked me, you threw glass bottles at my *head!* You're an abusive piece of shit, that's what you did to me,"

"Benji, son, you're being a bit dramatic, don't you think? You're really going to leave your poor mother behind without her son? Think about what you're doing,"

And, horribly, Benji does seem to think for a second.

For a second, I think he's going to stay. He opens his mouth to speak but nothing comes out, like the fight has just drained out of him.

I reach out a hand and close it around his, squeezing and trying to give him some more of that strength he was waving around a second ago. His eyes squeeze shut and its decades until he's opened them again and he speaks.

"I'm going, whether you like it or not." He says.

Samael looks stricken and his Ma looks vaguely injured.

Benji lets go of my hand and nudges me towards the kitchen door. I take the hint and hurry out of the room and up the stairs, going by memory to find Benji's room.

It's a mess.

There's a broken bottle outside the door, and the wooden panel has been kicked from its hinges. What happened the day he was kicked out? My heart breaks for him as I step over the glass and into the room. It smells like old whiskey and the bitterness of stale coffee. I navigate the trashed remains of his belongings and haul a suitcase from the open closet, throwing it open on the bed. I grab his pillow, thinking it would be useful to make the couch a bit comfier. And then I go through his drawers and pack underwear, socks, the two pairs of matching pyjamas in the bottom of his closet and the clothes I've seen him in a lot— his favourites, hopefully.

There's a stuffed animal on his bed, one I recognise from long ago sleepovers, which I press into the top of the suitcase. In the bathroom adjoining his bedroom, I scoop up a handful of toiletries that look like they were used recently and a neon pink shower pouf that makes me laugh on the side of the shower.

By the time Benji's heavy steps come up the stairs and he appears in the doorway with a tearstained but determined face, I've zipped up a suitcase of his belongings and am hauling away from the carnage and towards the door, to freedom, to a world where he can be free from his pain.

I let the handle of the suitcase go and a moment later I'm hugging him to me, my face buried in his neck and him sobbing into my shoulder. I'm sure his Ma can hear from downstairs, but a sick part of me wants her to hear, wants Samael, too, to know the pain that he is in.

"You did so good." I say. "I am so, so proud of you,"

*****

The Sheriff's station looks formidable and large in the early evening light.

Benji is by my side, and we're going to go in and he's going to tell someone about his stepdad and it'll all, finally, be over.

Finally.

We walk in the front door and Benji goes to the reception desk, where Tia is working, and with his hand tightly in mine he tells her with a shaking voice that he'd like to report domestic abuse.

I am so proud of him that it hurts.

An hour later, Benji has written a statement and spoken to Tia and Deputy Cabot about what happened, and I've given my statement as a witness, having seen him beaten and bruised twice.

They say that they can't guarantee anything will happen for a while, but that they will try their very hardest to get Samael the punishment he deserves. Benji is exhausted and so am I, but there's a happy glint to the heavy mood across us.

Benji has been through hell, but he has come out alive.

On our way out of the Sheriff's station, someone's calling my name.

"Evie!" It's Henry Di Santis, and he's jogging from the corridor of interview rooms right up to us. When he stops, I see how frantic he looks.

"What's going on, Henry? Are you okay?" I'm asking him but he's just shaking his head.

"Evie, they've brought in the FBI."

"What?"

"For the case— for— for the murders. They've brought in the FBI, and they're going to solve the case, Evie. They're the big guns, right? They can do anything, right? They're brilliant."

"I— yeah, that's good." I say, but I'm still slightly in shock. The FBI? I guess this isn't really just small-town thing anymore.

"They're going to solve the murders. Nevae is finally going to get some justice. Bethany too. And Jackson, of course,"

I don't have the heart to tell Henry that the FBI may be good, but there's still no guarantee of catching L.

But I can at least pretend to have a little faith, right?

Hoping never hurt anyone.

42] WHAT'S LEFT UNTOLD

FEBRUARY 27th, 2021, 12:13pm

34 days until april 2nd

Saturday afternoon, I'm helping Dad cook pasta in Nana's kitchen. The rain is coming down in harsh, heavy rivets outside— the streets are flooding, the Clerwood burst its banks hours ago, and most of the roads surrounding the town are shut (including the bridge into Loye Valley). So the town is confined to its houses for the day, and we decided to come and keep Nana company. She's got Hads on her knee in the living room, catching up on two years' worth of lost time.

"Why did you move away?" I don't expect an answer— because any reason that resulted in him not coming back for twenty years probably means it's a sensitive subject, not one for a day like this in Nana's house.

"Mom made me." Dad says.

I'm quiet for a second, seeing the pinched look on his face— as if the mere memory of it is difficult for him to endure. "Oh?"

"Yeah— I'll tell you the whole thing one day, son, but now— I guess it's really not the time. But you deserve to know, I think, why you never met your grandma until now."

I nod, going back to the cooking, mind whirring. What happened here twenty years ago?

*

Lunch finished, stomachs full, we sit around Nana's small, oak table, the rain still going strong and heavy outside. Nana looks to me, smiling over the pot of flowers in the center of the table.

"So, River, have you decided where you're going once you've finished high school?"

I haven't been thinking too much about after all this is over— *if* it's ever over, so I resort back to what I say to everyone. "I'm going to go back to St John and maybe study psychology? I've applied for a conditional place in their human studies college, so fingers crossed."

She smiles. "Psychology. That's exciting. A Lopez man finishing college will be something to behold. Your father never finished college, and neither did your grandfather. I'm proud of you,"

I smile and nod. "Did you go to college?"

"Yes, I did. The women in this family have always been more useful than the men." She chuckles at that, patting the top of Hadley's head. "I went to nursing school in New York— worked as a nurse for forty years, I did."

"Wow," I say, because yes— wow.

"Do you think you'll stay in touch with Evie when you both go to college? You'll miss her all the way back in Canada." Dad says.

I can't help the furious blush. It's disgustingly embarrassing. "Probably."

Nana's eyes crinkle around a smile. "Nothing's happened between you and her yet, then?"

"Not yet, Mom." Dad says, "But they do spend an awful lot of time together."

"Is that where you always are, instead of visiting your Nana? You should bring her over some time— I haven't seen the Reed girls in years. God, it really is horrible what happened to Bethany, isn't it?"

"Did you see much of her?" I ask, before I can stop myself. "She was friends with Nicolas, did you see much of her when he lived down here?"

Nana blinks, taken aback by the offhand mention of Nicolas— who is sat at home by himself, moping like he's so good at doing. "Oh, um, yes possibly. He never really brought people around, but a couple of times he took drinks out onto the porch, and I heard talking. Could have been anyone, really."

Dad clears his throat, pushing to stand up from the table. "River? Will you come and help me with the dishes?"

4 3] R O L L T H E D I C E

evelyn

FEBRUARY 27th, 2021, 8:14pm

***34** days until april 2nd*

1 UNREAD MESSAGE
To: **evelynareed2002@gmail.com**
From: **nodancer2119@gmail.com**
R.E: **secrets**
Have you really not figured out what they did?

Really?

Fine, I'll give you a hint— maybe it'll make you understand and make you *stop*.

Bethany had a lot of secrets, but the biggest one was the one that Poppie and Marie knew about. And me, but I can't tell you what it is because I swore never to speak about it again.

Much love,
L

Poppie and Marie.

Poppie? I don't know a Poppie. But Marie— I know her, and I can talk to her. I know where she works, and in a town as small and remote as Loye Valley, how many employees can a tiny coffee shop have? The chances she's working at least tomorrow morning are pretty high. River told me it was the Coffee Cubby on the northern edge of Loye Valley where he saw her, and I do recognise the name. The majority of Eastwood's residents know that Cathy's is the place to get coffee around here, but I've been to Loye Valley with middle school friends before, ending up in one of the booths at Coffee Cubby on multiple occasions. I remember it being small and quaint and cheap, and I wonder if Bethany spent a lot of time there. I wonder a lot of things about her, and it makes me realize, once again, that I hardly even knew her at all.

****

The next morning, the rain has stopped and the Clerwood floodwater quickly, efficiently drained. The bridge to Loye Valley is open so I park the Volvo in the parking lot for Coffee Cubby and sit there, staring at the squat little building. Am I really going to do this? Why am I even so sure that she's going to be in there, working? What makes me think she's actually going to want to talk to me?

To procrastinate, I go through my voicemails. The phone call I declined the other day when I was with Mae has popped up in the voicemail box. It was from Hailey. She never calls me unless it's an emergency— I probably should have answered it at the time.

I let the voicemail play.

"Emails, Evie. I found emails that show— oh my god, emails between my dad and— and Richard Wells. They were hunting illegally in Eastwood Forest. They have been for— God, these go back for years." Her voice sounds panicky and shaky, and adrenaline is running through my veins. Richard and

Arnold had been illegally hunting in Eastwood Forest? For *years?* It doesn't really surprise me, but it does piss me off. That must have been what Arnold was doing when he shot me. He thought I was a deer or something.

I think back to that night, how the bullet missed hitting anything important. Well, he's not a very *good* hunter.

"I need to talk to you, Evie. Please. Call me back when you get this, okay?"

I'm itching to call her now, but I know it'll end in another rabbit hole and there's something more important on my mind now. I force my focus back to the task at hand. Marie Blaine and what the hell she was doing with my sister for all those months.

Eventually, when my heart is racing a bit too fast, I snap myself out of this unproductive haze and throw open the door, stepping out into the cold, dull light. My thick knit cardigan does little to keep the bitter chill out, so I pull it closer to my body, wrapping the fabric tight around my abdomen, wincing when my hand brushes the still-healing bullet wound there.

There are hardly any people hanging around this part of town, so the shop is empty when I push open the door, the shrill ring of the bell stark and shocking against the silence of the cafe, broken only by the dull, quiet drone of the radio.

Marie Blaine is standing behind the counter. I recognise her face. I remember seeing her now, around school, once she was standing on our porch, talking to Beth. Her name tag reads *Marie* in short, staccato font. She smiles at me from over the counter, but when her eyes fix on mine, she freezes.

Her hair is down, and although it's the same platinum blonde as it was the last time I saw her, there are streaks of blue woven in with the bright blonde.

I step further into the shop, letting the door close softly behind me.

"Hi, Marie."

"Are you Bethany's sister?" She says, voice wavering.

"Yeah," I say, taking a step towards her, " yeah, I am."

"Why are you here?"

She sounds scared. Anxious. Almost like she's afraid I know something I'm not supposed to. Or I'm here to confront her? For what?

Is she afraid I know something— something like *she* killed Bethany? No. Stop jumping from conclusions. The adrenaline in my blood is warping my common sense. Still, I stay wary of her as she steps around the counter, but still leaves three meters between us.

"You look just like her," she says, "well, I mean you are— um, were— sisters and everything, so,"

"Yeah," I say.

"Yeah," she says, looking down at her feet. "Can I get you a coffee, or?"

"I'm good, actually, thank you."

Marie looks right in my eyes then, without blinking. "What are you doing here, then? I have nothing to say about Beth— I didn't know her that well at all."

She's lying. She must be. "'Course. I didn't mean to impose or anything, I just— I want answers, Marie, the truth about why she was friends with you. I mean, no offense, but you were in college when she knew you, and as soon as she started hanging around with you, she got all closed off and weird and distant."

"Who told you I was here?"

"My friend— River? He came here a few weeks ago,"

"I remember him. Nice guy— bit nosy, though."

"Yeah, that was kind of my fault."

"I'm sorry, but I really can't help you." Marie turns to go back behind the counter, the conversation clearly finished, but I'm not done yet.

"Do you remember Nicolas Lopez?" My voice cuts across the stillness of the room, disturbing dust, and dead skin cells, playing with the temperature, making it drop several degrees. Marie stops. Turns. Looks at me again, her gaze piercing.

"Don't talk about him, *please*."

"So you do remember him? If you don't know anything about Bethany— then let's talk about him."

Marie looks desperate. "Please, I'm at work, I—"

"There's no one else here, Marie. Please. My sister is dead and you and him and Poppie Masters are the only people alive who knew what Bethany was doing in the months leading up to her death."

"Why do you want to know? The truth will ruin the way that you see her and remember her." Her eyes go sad, wistful, gooey. "Don't you want to remember Bethany as your sister? The one who loved you more than she loved anything, who smiled and was *happy*?"

"My sister was never happy, Marie." Those words stab at my heart, but I know they're true, however much I hate the idea of them. "I'm here because I want to know why, and I want to know whose fault it was and then I want to find out who killed her, and you're one of the only people who can tell me, so *please*. For Bethany, tell me everything that you know."

So she tells me.

About the drugs, the night they met. She makes me a strong cappuccino and sits at a table with me, telling me with a cracking voice about the amphetamines, the blurry nights spent behind the wheel of the Volvo, singing and shouting, and she tells me about Aiden and Nicolas and how they had an unbreakable friendship with Bethany in the middle of it. How Nevae and Jackson hated it— they wouldn't leave Marie and Poppie alone, cursing them out of existence for stealing their best friend away from them.

An hour later, she gets to the month of Aiden's death, and she stops.

"There you go." She says. "That's all of it."

"Marie— you only made it to November. What happened next?"

She blinks, swallows, looks down at the bottle of water gripped between her trembling fingers. I reach out a hand and cover them, stilling her hands. She looks up at me again.

"November— was the month Aiden died. It was the month that it got really bad— Beth stopped hanging out with even us. She spent all her time with Aiden in the forest, getting high every day, getting distant from us, I'm not even sure she went home most nights. I just— do you really want to know?"

"Yes."

"God, okay. She hated her family. I don't even know your name! She never spoke about any of you. I don't know what you did, but I don't think I want to know."

This truth, this *hurts*. I feel the tears stinging the back of my throat, and swallow hard. "It's none of your business." I say this despite the fact that I don't know what we did. I don't know anything.

I hate that.

There is nothing more heartbreaking than realizing that you know nothing about the person you thought was your everything.

She knew everything about me. What did I do?

Is it my fault that she turned to drugs? Is it my fault that she died?

Maybe the issue wasn't that I went monumentally wrong somewhere.

Maybe the issue was that I never asked.

"Do you know what happened to Aiden?" I ask.

"What?" I've caught her off guard.

"Do you know what happened on the eighteenth of November? Why was he in the forest? Where was Bethany? Was she there?"

"All I know is what I told the police when it happened. Bethany told me she was going to meet him there, they had a date or something, and then when she showed up, he was dead."

"Wait," I say, "Bethany found his body?"

Marie nods. "Yeah, yeah, she did."

"And she didn't tell anyone else that she was going to be there?"

"No, I don't think so,"

I stand up suddenly, my heart racing and my stomach roiling. A memory has come to me, from the first time we searched Bethany's room. I need to go home, and I need to go home now.

"Thank you so much, Marie." I say, slapping a ten dollar note on the table. "You've been a massive help— keep the change, I need to get home."

"You're welcome. I hope I could help— let me know if you ever need anything, yeah?"

I nod, forcing a tight smile as she stands up and hugs me loosely. "Thanks again, see you soon."

I head to the door, push it open, but before I step outside, I turn back around. "Marie?"

"Yeah?" She calls from behind the counter.

"Evelyn. My name is Evelyn, but you can call me Evie."

She smiles. "Bye, Evie. It was nice to meet you."

44] HONEY, IT'S OKAY

river

FEBRUARY 28th, 2021, 3:32pm

33 *days until april 2nd*

"River, I really need to get home." Evie's voice crackles over the fuzzy phone line. I run a hand through my hair.

"Please, Evie. Can you meet me at Cathy's?"

There's a sigh that could also have been an awfully convenient gust of wind, and then, "Sure. Yeah, I'll be there in ten minutes."

I can't help the smile that reaches my face. "Thanks. See you then."

Dad looks up at me from his pile of papers on the table. "Everything alright?"

"Yeah," I say with a tight-lipped smile. "Yeah, everything's fine."

"You just desperate to see her?" He teases, grinning. "Why don't you just take her out on a real date? You know— the ones that girls like, instead of taking her to Cathy's?"

I look down to my feet, cheeks warm. "How many times do I have to tell you it's not like that? We're just friends." Besides, I'm pretty sure that coffee at Cathy's is the kind of date that Evie would love.

*****

Hailey is working the shift at Cathy's when I walk through the door. She smiles at me from behind the counter, and I smile back, scanning the room for Evie. She's sat at our usual booth, a glass of water on the table in front of her and a latte opposite her, in front of an empty seat.

"Hey," I say, walking over, "anyone sitting here?"

She looks up at me, smiling despite the weariness in her face and pallor of her skin. "Hi, Lopez."

I sit opposite her, wrapping my cold hands around the warm mug.

"You want me to tell you what Marie said?"

"Yeah, I do." I say. "If that's alright. Why were you in such a hurry on the phone?"

"Something she told me, I— I think there might be something in Beth's room that leads us closer to the killer. Well, Aiden's killer."

"You think he was killed by someone else?"

"Think about it— the M.O there doesn't fit with the rest of them. I mean, it would be so easy to assume that we're only looking for one person, but if I'm right— then there's a second killer. But I'm not sure we'll have to worry about the second one,"

"But there isn't really an M.O, is there? The signature is polonium-210 poisoning, but Bethany was drowned, Jackson shot, Nevae choked. Nothing matches except the polonium. We've never seen Aiden's autopsy. We don't know how he died."

"So maybe we shouldn't be sitting here drinking coffee, Lopez. Maybe I should go back home and look through Beth's things and find what I'm looking for, and you should start drafting a plan to break into the Sheriff's station and get the autopsy."

I genuinely can't tell if she's joking or not. "What?"

A pause.

"I'm being serious, River."

"That's insane! We can't break into the sheriff's station! It's, like, the most protected building in Eastwood,"

"It also has a lot of windows, which I'm pretty sure aren't locked most of the time. Besides, you only have to sneak in the back entrance and get into the evidence locker, which Mae knows the code for."

"And how do we ask Mae for the code without telling her what we're doing?"

She looks me dead in the eye, then. "You have to figure that out. But whatever you do, *do not* tell her why."

Something has changed with Evie.

She's got a new kind of motivation in her. She's asking for us to split up, which is a tremendously stupid idea. She's becoming reckless, suggesting breaking into the Sheriff's station and *stealing* from them.

What did Marie tell her? Whatever it was, it was enough to push her into making a plan that's reckless and probably won't work. But if it does— then we can confirm that we're looking for two killers, and not just one.

"What did Marie tell you?"

Evie blinks, swallows, looks to her hands, which are wrapped around the glass of water. "She told me that the only person that knew Aiden would be in the forest was Bethany, and it reminded me of something I saw in her room when we looked."

"What?"

She flicks her eyes around the half-empty diner, leaning closer. "I can't tell you. Not here. But I need to go home and find it."

"And you want me to break into the Sheriff's station? Today?"

"If you're scared, I'll come with you,"

I consider accepting her offer, but then I think of my own plan— the plan I've been forming in my head for a while. One I think will make Evie hate me but will make her better off in the long run. "No, thanks, Reed. I'm not scared,"

One corner of her mouth lifts into a teasing half-smile. "Yeah, whatever."

Having polished off the latte, I slide Evie a five-dollar bill, which she pushes back to me. She gets up with me and we say goodbye to Hailey before pushing open the squeaky door and stepping outside. We pause in the parking lot between the Volvo and the truck, and she hugs me tightly without warning.

When she steps back, there's tears in her eyes. I fight the urge to reach up and wipe them away.

"You okay?" I say.

She looks down. Nods. Looks back up at me. "Are you?"

"Yeah."

"River?"

"Yeah?"

"Thank you. For this. For everything."

"Hey," I say, "we're partners. You and me."

She laughs weakly. "Yeah. Partners."

Evie takes another step back, fiddling with her car keys. "I'll see you later?"

"See you later. Good luck."

"And you, Lopez. Good luck."

She gets in the Volvo, and I get in the truck. When she pulls out of the parking lot, I dig my phone from my pocket. I dial Mae's number, which I asked for during the week. I didn't tell her why I needed it, but it was for times like this— I need to talk to her.

"Hello? Who is this?" Her sweet, airy voice drifts through the phone on the fourth ring.

"Hi, Mae. It's River— I need to talk to you." I swallow thickly. This is it. "It's about Evie."

A pause. And then, "Oh. Is she okay? Where are you?"

"No— no, it's not urgent. Well, not really. She asked me not to tell you this, but do you know about the psychology project?"

"The one about murderers— yeah, I've heard some kids talking about it. Why?"

"Evie and I, we're working together. And we're studying the Eastwood murders."

"What, like Bethany, Jackson and Nevae?" Her voice sounds empty, void of emotion. On the verge of panic.

"Yeah. We're trying to solve the murders."

"*That's* what you two have been sneaking around doing for the past two months?"

"Yeah,"

"And she asked you not to tell me?"

"Yeah,"

"Oh, God. River— I— thanks for calling me. But why now?"

"Because she just asked me to get the code for the evidence locker at the Sheriff's station from you and break in to steal Aiden Islington's autopsy."

The silence then is so long that I have to check she hasn't just hung up on me.

"Oh," she says. Her voice is small.

"Yeah."

"What does Aiden Islington have to do with it?"

"We think he was killed by the same person as Bethany, Jackson and Nevae."

"Oh shit, River."

"Erm, yeah. She asked me not to tell you and Benji because she knew you'd try and stop her. But, Mae, I think she's really going a bit far now." I pause, and then take the plunge. "The killer has been sending her emails, and the most recent one implies that she's the next victim, and she's going to die in thirty-two days."

A choked sob. A fractured breath. "*Oh my god.*"

"I'm sorry I didn't call you sooner, I—"

"How long has this been going on for?" She asks, voice pitchy and incredulous.

"She got the first email three days after Jackson was killed."

There is a pause, a stretch of silence, which goes on for what feels like days. I can hear breathing that sounds panicked, and I wonder if I should have waited to tell her this in person, but then she speaks up again.

"River, I could sit here for hours and scream at you for not telling me sooner, but that's a waste of time. I'm going to give you the code for the evidence locker and help you break in, and we're going to find Aiden Islington's autopsy and you're going to go back to her like nothing happened, okay?"

"Okay," I say, because she has left no room for argument.

"And then tomorrow me and Benji are going to talk to her. I'm not going to let her die, River."

"Are you going to tell your dad about this?"

"I should, River. I really should."

"Tell him, Mae. Tell him. I don't want her to get hurt, okay? So you do everything you can to keep her safe."

"And you, River. Please,"

"'Course."

"And she's going to hate you for this, River, you know. When she finds out that you told us, it's not going to be pretty."

"I know." I say, even though it's hard. "I just— I'd rather her be safe and hate me than in danger and my friend, you know?"

"Oh, River. You are fucking golden. Promise me that if she forgives you, you'll take her out on a date and make her happy? You two are brilliant together."

That makes me blush, and I rush to finish the call. "Right, okay. I can come to your house in ten minutes, if you want. And we'll go to the station from there?"

"Yep. I'll be waiting!"

4 5] I N M Y D R E A M S

evelyn

FEBRUARY 28th, 2021, 4:55pm

33 days until april 2nd

Every time I step into this room, it's difficult. It steals the breath from my lungs, leaves my hands shuddering by my sides.

In this room, Bethany is still alive. And it terrifies me, breaks me, snaps me right in two.

I know what I'm looking for. I reach a hand under her bed, pull free the plastic box under there. It's full of papers— the same papers I rifled through the first time we came in here. The one I need is sat right on top.

Reggie's Garage,

12 Gretchen Road
Eastwood
Ashwell County,
Maine.

BILL TO		**INVOICE #**	100
Miss Bethany Reed,		**INVOICE DATE**	20/11/2017
16 Hastings Road,			
Eastwood,			
Ashwell County,			
Maine.			

Invoice Total $321.90

DESCRIPTION	**AMOUNT**
Extensive repairs done to car's exterior after collision with foreign body. Cosmetic repairs: painting, new bonnet. Internal repairs: replacements of internal bodies.	321.90

R. Arnolds

TERMS & CONDITIONS

Payment is due within 15 days

46] ALL THESE THOUGHTS

river

FEBRUARY 28th, 2021, 4:20pm

33 days until april 2nd

PHONE CALL TRANSCRIPT
PRIVATE NO.
TO SHERIFF'S STATION
02/28/21: 4:18PM
ANON: Hello?
Dep. Tia: Hi, this is Eastwood Sheriff's Station, how can I help?
ANON: I found a body.
DT: Sorry?
A: A dead body. In the forest. Help.
DT: Sir, where are you? Can I get your location? You're using a private number.
A: Be quick.
End of Call.
PHONE CALL TRANSCRIPT
PRIVATE NO.
TO SHERIFF'S STATION

02/28/21: 4:20PM

ANON: Hello.

Dep. Cabot: This is Eastwood Sheriff's Station; how can I help?

A: There's a bomb inside that building. You might want to leave.

DC: What? Sorry?

A: Get. Out. There is a bomb in the building. Get out, or die.

DC: Ma'am—

End of Call

Two fake phone calls to the Sheriff's station later, the building has been evacuated and two of the four police cruisers deployed holding three of the best deputies. With an empty station, Mae and I creep around the side of the building. It's old and weathered, so the windows on the back wall probably don't lock anyway. They give up on the first try, and I help Mae through the small gap before climbing through myself, my shoulders bruising as they squeeze through the narrow gap.

And then we're in a small room with a desk in one corner and a haphazard, wonky bookshelf against another wall, littered with photographs of a gap-toothed, young Mae and her sisters. Sheriff Whittle's office, then.

I trust Mae knows where she's going and follow her out into the deserted hallway before watching her put in the code for what must be the evidence locker.

"Aren't there security cameras?" I ask as a sudden, stomach-dropping thought hits me.

"No. They broke a few months ago and the state won't give them the money to get new ones. Don't tell anyone, though, they're pretending they still work so people won't do things like what we're doing right now."

She sends me a sly smirk and then pushes the door open, the lock releasing with a shudder. The evidence locker is narrow, long, and smells pungently of damp and what is likely to be mold.

"Lovely." I say, scrunching up my nose. Mae rolls her eyes and leads me towards one of the shelves nearest to us.

"Oh, stop being a princess. I used to organize all this stuff on weekends for a bit of extra cash. Aiden's box is somewhere near here."

I follow her like a lost puppy, watching as her eyes flick across every box, not touching, afraid to disturb the dust patterns and leave behind a minute sign that we've been in here. Finally, she finds the one she's looking for and slides it out from the shelf it's on. It looks exactly like all the other gray cardboard boxes, but it's the one that'll decide whether we were wrong this whole time or not.

I clench my hands into tight fists as Mae carefully lifts the lid of the box off and places it next to the shelf. I can hear, faintly the echo of sirens in the distance—people are arriving to help with the "bomb" situation.

We have to hurry.

Mae rifles through the pile of papers in the box and then finally comes up with one, handing it to me.

"Here,"

I scan the document, barely absorbing any of the figures and long names I don't recognise or can even begin to understand. I dig my phone from my pocket and take a photo of the whole thing to send to Evie, and try not to shake too hard:

AUTOPSY REPORT

Ashwell County Hospital, Elworth, Maine
Deceased:
Name: AIDEN ISLINGTON
Age: 18
Race: WHITE
Sex: MALE
Rigor: ABSENT
Livor: PURPLE
Weight: 180lbs
Eyes: BLUE
Hair: BROWN
Length: 80 INCHES
Attending physician: DR. RICHARD THORNTON M.D.
Apparent cause of death: BLUNT FORCE TRAUMA TO ABDOMEN/CHEST
Clothing:
1. **Gray t-shirt with *Atlantis* graphic on the front. Blood-stained and well-worn.**
2. **Black jeans, blood-stained, cut where first responders removed them to better access leg injuries.**
3. **Black belt**
4. **White underwear briefs**
5. **Blue and white striped socks**
6. **White Adidas sneakers**
Pathologist description of injuries:
Bruise outlining the round parking light and headlight on left thigh. Diameters: 24cm parking light and 35cm headlight. Primary impact injuries appear to include a spiral fracture of the left

shin and compound fracture of the right tibia, and eight rib fractures (4 vertebrosternal and 4 vertebrochondral). The fracture of the true rib pairs appears to have caused significant damage to the sternum/put excessive strain on the bone.

Pathological Diagnoses:
1. **A. impact injuries to legs**
   0. **Spiral fracture to left fibula**
   1. **Compound fracture to right femur**
   2. **Shattered left first, second and third tarsals**
2. **Impact head injuries**
   0. **Depressed skull fracture, parietal bone**
3. **Rib fractures**
   0. **Ribs 4-9 traumatic displaced rib fractures**
   1. **Pulmonary laceration and massive hemothorax caused by displaced 5th rib**
   2. **Ribs 1-3 traumatic displaced rib fractures**
   3. **Brachial plexus avulsion**
   4. **Flail chest**

CAUSE OF DEATH:
Massive hemothorax caused by pulmonary laceration from displaced 5th rib.

OTHER LAB PROCEDURES:
Toxicology

"It's not on here." I say. "The autopsy— it doesn't say about the polonium. Does that mean it wasn't there?"

Mae sighs and goes back to the box. "It means that you need the toxicology report, stupid."

She hands me another sheet of paper, this one single-sided and even more confusing than the autopsy.

LOYE VALLEY
TOXICOLOGY LABORATORIES
PATIENT RESULTS: ISLINGTON, AIDEN.
Post-mortem Toxicology Report

Analytes Found	Lab Result (Qualitative)	Lab Result (ng/mL)
Ritalin	POSITIVE	>50
Adderall	POSITIVE	>20
Ibuprofen	POSITIVE	>10

Mae is looking over my shoulder. "The kid was on amphetamines, River. If that's what you were looking for."

"I was looking to see if he was poisoned. By Polonium-210."

Mae gives me a knowing, vaguely sympathetic look. "Then no. No, he wasn't poisoned by Polonium-210."

I barely have time to register what that means when the door bangs open. Bright lights flood into the space.

"FBI, hands over your heads, get down on the ground."

We've been caught.

By the FBI.

4 7] N O T M Y S I S T E R

evelyn

FEBRUARY 28th, 2021, 6:10pm

33 days until april 2nd

I feel sick. The overhead light in the room suddenly feels too bright, the room too small, too constricting, everything inside of it breathing down my neck.

She hit something.

With her car.

She went to the garage two days after Aiden died, having hit something— maybe a deer, a bird, or maybe— maybe a person.

Could she have really done it? Really killed Aiden? She wouldn't have done it on purpose, of course not. But it's easy to believe that if she was high or drunk and was going to meet him that she couldn't see where she was going and swerved and

hit him.

And killed him.

Oh, God.

At that moment, my phone rings next to me. It's River. I pick it up, holding it to my ear.

"Hello?" I say. "River? Did you get the autopsy?"

"I did." He says, sounding out of breath. "Yeah, I did."

"And?"

"And Aiden Islington had no polonium-210 in his system, Evie. He wasn't killed by the same person as the other three."

"Oh god." I say. "Oh god, oh god oh god."

"Evie— Mae and me, we got caught. We're in custody— they let me call someone, and I called you. So could you please get your ass down here with my father. What did you find out?"

The adrenaline doesn't allow me to properly digest the full calamity of what he's just told me.

"I think— I think Bethany killed Aiden, River. I think she hit him with her car and— and *killed him*."

4 8] J A I L B I R D

FEBRUARY 28th, 2021, 6:23pm

33 days until april 2nd

INTERVIEW ROOM 01 is a small, stale room with linoleum floors and no heating. From the dark color of the walls to the metal legs of the table and the metallic screech every time I even think of moving my chair, everything is designed to put you on edge.

And, boy, is it succeeding.

Despite the chill in the room, sweat sits on my neck and under my shirt. There is no one in here, yet. They don't think I killed Bethany, Nevae, and Jackson, do they?

No, of course they don't.

They *can't*. I have an alibi— they've been through this with me before. Is Mae still in custody as well? Surely, she can't— her dad is the *Sheriff*.

A horrible, nagging thought pinches at my mind. *The Sheriff has no power anymore*. If the FBI are here, then what power does Mohamed Whittle have? None. That is terrifying. He was my only hope that we would get out of this swiftly.

Evie is on her way. I keep telling myself this, when everything seems impossible. Evie and my dad are on their way. He'll call a lawyer and—

The door opens.

It screeches horrible against the floor— *metal, everything is metal in here.*

A woman steps in, tall and muscled. Her hair is dark and pinned up behind her head, and that paired with her tailored dress pants and pristine, fitted t-shirt give her a distinctive air of authority. Despite being sure that I'll be out of this place soon, a tiny bullet of fear impales itself in my heart. This woman looks like she could ruin my whole entire life with just a phone call.

Talk about intimidating.

She pulls out the chair opposite mine and sits down. One side of her mouth lifts in a chilling, uncomforting smile. "Hi, River."

How does she know my name? "How do you know my name?"

"I know a lot about you,"

"When are you going to let me go?"

"When you tell me why you wanted Aiden Islington's autopsy report." Her voice holds such a definite tone to it that I don't feel like I should say anything else.

"Who are you?" I say, stupidly. I don't care what this woman's name is, I care about getting out of here and making sure Mae and Evie are still in one piece.

"I'm Supervisory Special Agent Amy Cosette. I'm the head of the Violent Crimes Unit of the FBI, and I'm here to talk to you about Evelyn Reed."

My throat goes dry. What? That is not at all what I thought this was going to be about. Do they think Evie did it?

Oh, God.

"What?" I say, because right now it's about the only thing that I'm *able* to say.

"I need you to tell me about what Evelyn Reed has been doing since January 9th, 2021."

"Like— everything? What do you mean?"

Cosette leans forward on one hand. "Maevellah told us everything."

Maevellah. I've never heard anyone use her full name before. This is official. I'm a little bit terrified.

I guess I wanted Mae to tell them everything, I just didn't want Evie to go down for it.

"Is Evie in trouble?"

"Evelyn is fine. We have her in custody next door."

They probably got her coming into the station. God, why did I tell her to come here?

"She didn't kill any of them." I say. "She didn't."

Her face softens. "Oh, River. I'm not saying she did."

"Then why do you want to know? Why am I handcuffed to a table in an interrogation room? Why is she in *custody*?"

"April 2nd is thirty-two days away."

She says it loudly. It echoes. It stands, stagnant, above both of our heads. It infiltrates every bone in my body. We're both quiet, letting the statement make a home in the walls.

I know what she's saying. Evie is in danger. She needs to be kept safe. She can't be alone. *I can't protect her.*

"I know." I say. Quietly. It doesn't feel enough. *I know*. And? How does that help?

"Then let us keep her safe. And you."

"Me?"

"You're close to her, River. Close to this investigation— you're going to get caught in the crossfire."

"So you're going to keep us here? For a month?"

"No." Cosette blinks. Sighs. This job is tiring, I can tell. "We're going to let you go. If the killer senses something is off— something has changed, someone knows something they shouldn't, then it will only accelerate the clock."

"So you're going to let her walk around like nothing is wrong? Like she *doesn't* have a giant ass target on her back?"

She looks down, at the table. "Yes, River. That is exactly what we're going to do."

"So why did you bring her into custody at all?"

"Because someone is next door, telling her the details of the 24-hour protective guard she'll have, and the guards stationed around her house, hidden, at all hours of the night. We're going to trap this son of a bitch,"

She says that last bit with so much defiance and anger that I understand completely. Amy Cosette has studied this case for hours— she has spoken to Mae: she knows the stakes; she knows how much has gone wrong and still *could* go wrong.

She wants it to end.

We have the same goal, so I should let her help. I'm going to let her help. I'm going to be helpful.

So I tell her everything.

From the moment we found her in the road to the moment I called her ten minutes ago.

Every detail, every interaction that I can remember—every email and when she got them. What they said. What the emails to Bethany said.

I know Evie will never forgive me, but if she dies then I will never forgive myself. At least now I can tell myself that I tried to save her. I tried my absolute best, and it better be enough.

49] I CAN'T SAVE US

evelyn

FEBRUARY 28th, 2021, 7:44pm

33 days until april 2nd

As soon as Deputy Tia, who is the only one left in the interrogation room, tells me I'm free to go, I'm up and sprinting out of the door.

River is signing paperwork on the reception desk.

This hot, angry, acidic feeling in my blood infiltrating my veins— it's betrayal. It's nasty, it's painful, but it's there and it is vivid, and I am in

shock.

I can barely even bring myself to meet his eyes, and yet here I am, staring straight into the dark, dark brown and getting lost in a confusion of emotions. I am horribly, disastrously angry at him for spilling our horrible, beautiful secret— and yet how do I be angry at River Lopez?

The River Lopez who scooped me off the road in January and delivered me here, to the Sheriff's station? The River Lopez who held me, who hugged me when no one else would?

How do I hate *him*?

I can't.

But I try. Oh, do I try.

My hands are flying around my face and even though I'm not speaking, I'm almost screaming.

"Evie." Mohamed says, from behind River. It feels like there's sides— with Agent Cosette, Tia, Mohamed, even Cabot, all of them behind River and nothing behind me except for the street outside, rainy and wet through the stained windows. The isolation feels all too familiar.

"Evie." Mohamed says again. "Evie, look at me."

But I can't move my eyes away from River.

Oh, beautiful, heartbreaking River.

From the corner of my eye, Mohamed steps forward an inch. He's cautious. Like I'm an unexploded bomb. Maybe I am— maybe that's all I've been for three years, and this is what they've all been waiting for. For me to explode, and for all of the shrapnel to hit them.

"Evie, listen to me. Do not blame River for this, okay? We made him tell us the truth. About your project and what you're trying to do. And the emails, Evie. The emails you've been getting from L?"

Hearing it all out loud, spoken softly from his mouth— it breaks me.

I stand still, silent. Waiting quietly for his next move.

But it's River that speaks next. His eyes don't leave mine, but his mouth is suddenly moving. "I'm sorry, Evie. I'm sorry that I broke your trust and I understand if you never forgive me for this. But ever since I met you, even before you told me who you are— who your sister is— I could tell that something had broken you. You have been broken many times, destroyed by this town, eaten up and spat out by the people that live here.

"You must feel so lonely and so isolated. Benji and Mae are wonderful friends, I know. But they are not the whole town. They do not represent the world that rejected your grief and judged you for feeling what is literally completely normal."

He's quiet for a beat.

I breathe.

And then he's going again. "The thing that you need to understand now is that us, standing here, surrounding you, are here to save *you*. Because you are worth saving, and you are not alone anymore. You hear me? *You are not alone,* Evie."

I have to close my eyes then, against the desperation and the *love* in his.

You are not alone.

The words fill me with a warmth so potent that I tear up a little. I am not alone. Really? *Really?* I have been relying on my sister these past few months. Using her and Jackson and Nevae as an excuse to be upset. I have been using the case as a shield— as a distraction from what I'm really feeling.

Could this horrible, bottomless despair have been loneliness?

Could the solution to my grief be the people in front of me right now?

Could I really let them help?

"You are not alone," River says again. It's more a whisper— letting the words take to the air, fly over to me, and settle in my heart in my bones in my blood. The room suddenly feels vastly constricting, like there isn't room for all the emotion seeping from our pores and filling the empty air between us. I turn and push open the clear glass door, stepping into the muted wintry light outside.

The fresh air is a blessing, and I fill my lungs with it over and over.

"Evie." River's voice is quiet but clear. "I'm sorry."

"Why did you do it?" I say.

He doesn't hesitate. "Because I like you, Evie. Because I care about you, and because I don't want you to die."

"If you cared about me at all you would have kept my secret, and kept the police out of it— they couldn't even figure out that Bethany didn't kill herself, so what makes you think they're going to be able to find the bastard that did it?"

"I— they can protect you, Evie. Better than I can, and better than you can protect yourself."

Anger is a living, writhing thing under my skin and it pushes me forward a step, legs unsteady against the uneven asphalt. "Are you calling me weak? Do I need to be *saved* by a bunch of men in uniforms?"

I'm hurting. I'm hurting and I'm lashing out at him, twisting his words into monsters that they're not, and using them against him like swords.

"No." he says, after a long sustained moment. "I'm saying that we don't have guns and protective custody and witness protection and shit like that, Evie. I'm saying that I need you to understand that I only broke your promise because I'd rather you be safe and hate me than in danger and like me."

I step forward, closer to him. He steps, too, and then we're close enough to touch.

"You are not alone." The words are carried on a breath that touches my cheek. Warm. He smells of coffee and firewood and vanilla shampoo.

Everything else goes quiet— muffled, muted.

It's just us.

I reach up a hand. Shaking, of course. My bones always shudder in his presence. My hand comes to rest on the soft, smooth skin of his cheek. My thumb reaches and traces the rounded lines of his chin. He is beautiful.

"You are not alone," he breathes, again.

And then I kiss him.

And I am not alone anymore.

5 0] I W O U L D G O

evelyn

FEBRUARY 28th, 2021, 7:50pm

33 days until april 2nd

I don't really know why I do it. I don't know why I reach up on my tiptoes and place a tentative hand on his chest and press my lips to his. I don't know anything at that moment.

All I know is that he cares about me, and I care about him, no matter how hard I hate him right now. I know that I don't hate River Lopez, the kind, doe-eyed boy who pulled me out of the middle of the road three months ago and invited me to his house to meet his family and has brought me coffee every morning since we met. I hate what he has done to my dignity.

But dignity is repairable, I can build it up again. Relationships with people like him only come around once in a lifetime, and when they do you have to snatch them up and never let go. So I snatch him up, with no intention of letting him go.

****

The next morning, I wake up and the sun is just on the cusp of rising.

My cheeks are flushed, and my covers are soft on my skin and there's a fluttery, blissful feeling in my stomach. *Happiness*, I realize. This is what happiness feels like. The police know everything, and River and my friends betrayed me, but even though the bitterness of anger and betrayal still occupies a part of me, I'm choosing the happier option instead. I'm choosing forgiveness, I'm choosing to not just see the worst in people anymore.

I decide to go for a run, because I've woken up an hour earlier than normal.

On my way to the kitchen to get a morning cup of coffee, I see Benji awake on the couch. He's got his laptop open on his lap and is scrolling through a real estate website.

Of course. When he turns eighteen in no more than three months, he's moving out to an apartment somewhere in Loye Valley, probably.

It's going to be strange not having him around the house. It's been like a month of sleepovers, and I'm not sure I'm ready for it to end. But him moving on is a good thing. It means he's free from his stepfather's wrath and is getting the justice he deserves. Since we both testified, there's been no word from the police, but we're patient.

He says good morning to me when I sit on the couch opposite him, scrolling through my phone whilst drinking a mug of hot, bitter coffee. It wakes me up even more, and I feel surprisingly airy and productive when I stand up again.

The air outside on the long, straight stretch of Hastings Road is cold and seeps under my jacket like freezing water. But it's a good cold. A refreshing cold.

I take off running down the asphalt, each foot hitting the concrete hard, letting out a bit of energy and pent-up emotion.

I feel free, sprinting down Hastings and then swerving up Morning Road and onto Forest.

I slow down to a walk near the manors of Forest Road, casting a look over the Beaumont house with its brown brick exterior and swooping arcs and curves of impressive, old architecture. And then I hear it.

Sirens, wailing up the road.

Police sirens.

As I come to the top of the hill and Eastwood Forest spans out beneath me with the sun hovering in the horizon, I can make out dim blue light echoing up the road.

Two police cruisers, parked outside of Arnold Windsor's house.

On instinct, I pick up to a run again and sprint down to where Arnold Windsor is being escorted into the back of a police cruiser, handcuffed wrists behind his back, looking solemn but accepting.

Hailey's phone call comes back to me.

Emails, Evie. I found emails that show— oh my god, emails between my dad and— and Richard Wells. They were hunting illegally in Eastwood Forest. They have been for— God, these go back for years.

Arnold Windsor has been caught.

A smile spreads across my face as I watch him be stuffed into the back of the car. Cabot is at his side, and he catches my eye over the black and white shiny vehicle. He raises his hand in a wave, which I return.

Hailey is standing on the doorstep of the house, looking upset. I walk towards the house, towards the few neighbors standing on opposite doorsteps wrapped in expensive looking robes sipping from sleek white mugs and whispering in each other's ears conspiratorially.

"Hailey, hey, what's going on?" I ask her when I'm within earshot.

She looks over to me and she looks deflated and tired, in her pyjamas on the ornate doorstep. "Oh, Evie, thank God you're here. They've arrested him for illegally hunting on protected land."

"Did you tell the police what he did to… me?" I don't know what I want her answer to be.

"Oh, no, I didn't. Sorry— I just— I don't know,"

I find myself relieved. At least I have just one part of this investigation that is still mine to keep.

"Oh, it's okay. I don't really want them to know. It was an accident, anyway. If your dad gets tried for shooting me as well as illegal hunting he'll probably be away for a while,"

"I'll miss him. We'll have to sell the house, which honestly, I'm a bit glad about,"

"It is a bit, well, monstrous," I say, looking over the towering building. She laughs lightly.

"Yeah, it is kind of ugly. Maybe I'll get a little house near you, and Mae."

"I'd love that." I say.

Hailey smiles. "Yeah— maybe Benji can move in with me until he finds a place of his own,"

"Mae told you?"

"Yeah, she did." Hailey says. "I feel so horrible for Benji, but at least he's, well, okay now. Kind of."

Nodding, I lean down to tighten my laces. "Yeah. He's doing better. Looking for apartments, distracting himself with school,"

"Well, send him my love when you get home," she says.

I check my phone for the time. Nearly six. I stand back up again and give Hailey a quick goodbye hug.

"I'll see you at Cathy's later?" I say.

Hailey nods. "Yep. I'll probably have to take some time off work whilst I sort this mess out, but I'll be there tonight to give Benji a big bear hug in person,"

As I start making my way away from the sirens and back towards the center of town, there's an air of finality over everything.

Arnold and Richard have been caught.

The man that shot me and caused me a whole month's worth of pain, which still annoys me even now, has been caught.

It makes my day even better.

51] IN MY HEAD

MARCH 2nd, 8:01am

31 days until april 2nd

Evie hasn't shown up to school.

I wonder briefly if it's because of our kiss, the one that ended with bright pink cheeks and rushed goodbyes and then, later in the day, a visit to my house with muffins and apologies. She doesn't forgive me— I'm not sure if she ever will— but for now, we are still friends. Still Evelyn and River. Just now, Mae has told her father, the Sheriff, about the danger that Evie is in, and Evie has agreed to send copies of the emails to him and the agents from the violent crimes unit working on the case.

Nothing else, though. She hasn't told him anything else. She is still bruised and battered inside, fed up with all of the theatrics and the waiting around whilst nothing is actually happening. But she doesn't hate me, and she's going to be kept safe, and that is enough for now.

But she isn't here now.

Part of me holds a horrible, sour fear that something has happened to her, that she's run off or been found by the killer or—

No. The other, larger, part of me says. She's probably just gone to the station to be questioned and be told what the way forward is going to be, how they're going to solve this monumental disaster.

How they're going to save her life.

She doesn't show up to where we usually meet in the mornings with Mae and Benji, by her locker. Benji and Mae also don't know anything.

In first period business, I get about halfway through the task on the board when there's a knock on the door. It's loud and harsh and strangely ominous. Mr Harrison ambles over to the door in that lopsided way of his and the whole class goes silent as a series of hushed whispers ensue.

Mr Harrison steps back from the door and a Sheriff's deputy steps in. I recognise her loosely as Deputy Tia, with the tight bun and sparkly earrings. New is the engagement ring on her finger. She looks concerned yet harsh as she surveys all of our wide eyes.

"River Lopez? Can you come with me, please?"

5 2] H O L D O N

evelyn

MARCH 2nd, 2021, 8:30am

31 days until april 2nd

They have me in an interview room, Mohamed, and Deputy Cabot opposite me. Two men staring me in the eyes and asking me questions I don't know the answers to. Behind them is Agent Cosette. She doesn't say anything. She lets them do the talking. I don't care to know why.

Mohamed is a nice, familiar face, but his voice is unfamiliar— his work voice. All work, no room for hugs and softness. There are lives at stake. Well, *life*. Me.

I'm at stake. It's both heart-warming and very guilt-inducing that so much effort appears to be going into saving my life. Safe houses, witness protection, a plethora of other things. Round the clock guards outside of my house. When they started discussing that with me, I shook my head politely and said *no, no*. I'm not worth the trouble.

Really.

When I leave high school, it'll be a miracle if I get into college. And if I do, then there is no way I'll actually make it through the law course I want to do. I answer their questions because they have a duty to protect and I have a duty to follow what I'm being told to do. So I nod, and I tell as much of the truth as I can bear.

"When did you get the first email?" 2 days after Bethany's anniversary.

"Who knows your email address?" School. My family. A couple of friends that I try my best to name.

"Is your email address public anywhere?" No.

"Has anyone been following you? Have you noticed any unfamiliar vehicles around your house recently?" No.

"Have you been contacted anywhere else?" No.

"Is there anyone who might want to hurt you?" I don't know. I don't think so. I've tried to make myself likable, but everyone in this town stays away from me like I'm crazy or something.

"Did your sister ever say anyone was acting strange towards her? Hostile? Any ex-boyfriends?" I don't think so. She never spoke to me about that sort of thing. *Except Nicolas.*

"What about her friends? Did you overhear any conversations?" No. They didn't come over closer to, you know, the end.

It goes round and round in circles like that until Mohamed claps his hands together in a way that feels final. I'm exhausted, even though it's only been an hour and a half according to the big digital clock on the wall that may or may not be correct.

"That's great, Evie. Thank you for coming in, and thanks for talking to us." He says, kindly.

I nod and smile. "It's no problem, really. I just, you know, I want you to catch this bastard."

He smiles politely. "We will, rest assured."

I'm escorted out of the room, and as I pass through the waiting area I feel a hand on my wrist, stilling me. It's cold and soft. I look up. Agent Cosette. She looks like she could be a kind woman if she stopped taking things so seriously.

"Evelyn, hello."

"Um, hi? Are there more questions, or?"

She shakes her head, "Oh, no, nothing like that. I just wanted you to know— that I'm not going to rest until this sick bastard is caught."

And I smile, "Me too."

She lets me go with one last kind look and turns, walking back towards the offices and interview rooms. I step out of the door, letting the chill overtake my body and the gray sky darken the whole street.

When did this place lose its life?

What else have we stolen from it?

1 UNREAD MESSAGE
To: evelynareed2002@gmail.com
From: nodancer2119@gmail.com
R.E: enough
You're getting there. I know you know what she did. Well done. Now you know why I did what I did. Congrats, or whatever.

But you told the people I didn't want you to tell.

For that, you get punished.

Much love,

L

53] TO PULL IT DOWN

MARCH 16th, 2021, 4:19pm

17 days until april 2nd

Two weeks after the interviews, nothing has changed. On my way home, I look over Eastwood and I think, *God I hate this place.* But I can't quite say the same about the people in it. Evie and I haven't spoken properly about the first kiss, but we have done it a few more times, on a long walk in the woods over the weekend, in my bedroom, in her bedroom. It's blissful, living in a dazed kind of beautiful ignorance.

We haven't done anything else for the case, but we did hand in the last email she got. It was a worrying one, but Mohamed assured us that we didn't have to worry, that if the son of a bitch tried anything, then they wouldn't get away with it. It was a loose, untrustworthy statement, but it settled our nerves enough to allow us to relax, if only for two weeks.

When I turn into Hastings Road, my heart shudders.

There's a police car outside of my house. As I approach the house, I tell myself that they're just here to talk, that nothing has happened. That they just want more information— that they have a lead.

But as soon as I park the truck and climb out, an officer steps onto the porch and I know something is wrong.

"River Lopez?" He says. It's Deputy Cabot, from the station. "Could you come in, please?"

It's fucking weird to be invited into my own house, but I'm too nervous to say anything. I just go inside, and I almost turn right around and go back out again. Dad is on the couch, staring into nothing whilst Mohamed Whittle sits across from him, consoling him. Agent Cosette and one of her roadies are standing by them, looking stony. The first thing I think is *where is Nicolas*. And the second thing I think is *where is Hadley*.

"What's going on?" I ask, stepping into the house. It smells like people that don't live here, and the indescribable stench of danger and fear.

Agent Cosette stands up when she sees me. "River. Hi. it's nice to see you, I just wish it was under different circumstances. Why don't you take a seat?"

I sit on the couch, feeling all jittery and anxious. "What's going on?" I ask again, like a broken record forced to repeat the same question over and over again until someone puts me out of my misery. "What's going on?"

Dad looks at me then, and the look in his eye is familiar. It's the same look that came across him when he found out about Hannah, Grace and Emma. It's a look of grief, of loss.

319

"River," Cosette says, "there is no easy way to say this, but your sister, Hadley, has gone missing."

I hate this town.

54] SHAKING GROUND

MARCH 16th, 2021, 4:44pm

17 days until april 2nd

My father, Mateo Lopez, dropped her off at day-care at nine am. He picked her up at 3 and took her home. On the way home, he stopped at the grocery store in Loye Valley to get some ingredients for dinner. When he got back to the car, she was gone.

He drove straight to the Sheriff's station and filed a missing person's report. Because of this town's history and my recently discovered connection to this case (that I've been interfering with since January), Hadley was deemed a high-risk victim. So they immediately put out an amber alert state-wide to all the Sheriff's stations. They sent her picture to all the patrols around the borders.

Mohamed and Cabot are trying to convince me that she's going to be fine, that the best is working her case, but all I can think about is a statistic I read a few weeks ago whilst I was knee deep in research for the case.

76% of abducted children die within the first three hours.

88.5% of abducted children die within the first twenty-four hours.

"River, I can assure you— Hadley is going to be safe, okay?"

76% of abducted children die within the first three hours.

"I understand this is hard, but the whole state has their best people on it, okay?"

88.5% of abducted children die within the first twenty-four hours.

By the time seven pm rolls around, there is only a 24% chance that my baby sister is still alive.

55] STRANGER THAN MOST

evelyn

MARCH 17th, 2021, 6:40am

16 days until april 2nd

It's on the news.

2-YEAR-OLD ABDUCTED: POSSIBLY RELATED TO THE EASTWOOD MURDERS.

Hadley has been reduced to sharp, bold black writing, *2-year-old*. No, her name is Hadley, and she is wonderful and beautiful and she is going to live the long, incredible life that she deserves.

River hasn't spoken to me since it happened, and that is okay. He's with his family, they are hurting together. I didn't sleep at all last night, so now I sit on the porch watching their house, as if she's going to come toddling out of the door like she does sometimes, grinning and waving at everyone that walks past.

It hurts. It's agonizing, to look at their house and how still and empty it is. It reminds me, suddenly, of what it looked like before the Lopezes moved in: lifeless and sad.

It's horrible to the point that anger replaces sadness. Hot, acidic anger that seeps into every vein, every artery, infecting infecting infecting infecting.

I stand up. I turn around, and I go back inside of my house, refusing to sit there and torture myself by staring at their house. Mom's at work like always, so I stomp noisily and angrily up the stairs and fling myself into my room, refusing to cry because these tears aren't mine to dish out. Instead, I open my laptop and log into my email account.

I haven't deleted the emails, no matter how many times Mohamed asked me to, and I promised that I would. I click on the most recent one, the one that, now I think about it, probably was hinting at Hadley's kidnapping. I wonder if she's still alive.

I hate to think about it, but she probably isn't. This is a murderer, not a kidnap-and-use-for-a-later-date-er.

How do you do that? How do you look into the eyes of a two-year-old girl and kidnap her? How do you look into the eyes of a two-year-old girl and kill her?

L.

L is the killer.

Who is L? L for loser?

My mouse drifts across the screen, and hits *reply*.

My heart is racing, but the anger is still there, threatening to boil over if I don't turn the heat down soon.

MESSAGE DRAFT:

To: nodancer2119@gmail.com

From: evelynareed2002@gmail.com

R.E: please

You do not deserve to take everything from this town, L. Stop this. Give Hadley back, and you can have me. I'm Bethany's sister. We look the same, we act the same. If you kill me, it will be just like killing Bethany— and I know you would like to relive that moment again and again.

Give back Hadley, and you can take me and do whatever you want to me.

No love at all,

Evelyn.

It's probably not going to work, but I press send anyway.

Three minutes later, the reply appears.

NEW MESSAGE

To: evelynareed2002@gmail.com

From: nodancer2119@gmail.com

R.E: please

I will have you when I want to, Evie. And I want you on April 2nd. The clock is ticking.

I appreciate the enthusiasm, but I want to enjoy our time together for a little longer. Please don't reply to one

of my emails again, or someone else will
suffer.

In fact, why don't you and River meet
me down at the river on the 19th? 6pm. To
show him what happens when you get
involved with things that have NOTHING TO
DO WITH YOU.

Much love, see you soon,

L.

And my anger comes back like a tsunami.

PART 4

DEAR

GIRL,

WHAT

ARE

YOU

DOING

TO

YOURSELF?

56] JUST A CHILD

evelyn

MARCH 19th, 2021, 5:50pm

14 days until april 2nd

I have never seen River drive so fast. I didn't even know that his ancient cherry red truck could go past forty. But here we are, barreling down Forest Road at fifty-six miles per hour towards the forest, which looms large and green in the distance. It's getting dark, the sun slipping through the sky, barely holding on to the last few pieces of light. We're going to be early, but at least we're not late.

Hadley.

That's the only thing that this can be about, right? Hadley.

He has Hadley. L has Hadley, and we're going to get her.

If she's still alive. I grip the seat under me tightly, so tightly it hurts, because I'd much rather have a physical pain than the horrible, horrible ache that comes with thinking about Hadley dying. Young, innocent Hadley who never did anything to anyone— she never did anything to become wound up in this.

It's my fault.

Of course it is. I never should have roped River into this, knowing he was probably going to get hurt. But I guess I never thought Hadley would become involved.

That's my problem— I never think. I am so unbelievably selfish.

The truck swings a hard right into Devil's Pathway and finally River slows a bit. Eastwood Forest is a huge place, but our best bet to finding Hadley is probably either Bethany's spot, or the place where Jackson and Nevae died.

Bethany drowned.

I really, really hope Hads isn't in the river.

He parks at the bottom of Devil's Pathway, the truck scratched and horrible silver gauges in its previously perfect paintwork. River takes off running without saying anything to me, sprinting down the track. His blue sweater is nothing but a dim indigo in the evening light. He is a rabbit in a sea of spears.

I take off after him, my jeans quickly caked with mud.

River disappears behind some trees, and I know he's made it to the spot.

A cry echoes through the empty air, then.

It is raw and loud, and it is no more a cry than a scream, full of so much emotion that I almost fall to my knees at its agony.

My heart

Drops.

My legs pick up, running faster and faster until I barrel through the thicket of trees and the clearing opens up in front of me. There is a slumped figure in the center of the grass, illuminated by the bleeding sun in an orange glow. River is hunched over, and I can see his shoulders shaking.

Quietly, cautiously, I make my way over to where he is until I can see his face, and Hadley.

Hadley's small, fragile body is in his arms.

She's still alive. Her eyes are open, seas of warm brown, but even from here I can see the fear in them.

She's bleeding from her nose and her mouth, and I don't want to know what L did to her.

So I just watch as River rocks her backwards and forwards and I can see his hand wrapped around hers, which is impossibly small.

Two years old.

She is two years old, and she is fighting for her life in her brother's arms.

"Hads, can you hear me?" His voice is quiet and rough. I feel like an imposter, but I can't look away.

"River?" Hadley replies. She sounds terrified.

"I'm going to get you out of here, okay?"

"River? Don't let the bad man get me, please. I've had enough." Her voice is high and shaking and all the words are trembling and soft.

Tears are pouring down River's cheeks and when he goes to speak a choked sob comes out instead.

"I won't let the bad man get you, I promise." He says. "I won't let anyone hurt you anymore,"

"It doesn't really hurt."

He nods. "That's good." We both know it's very very bad but I, too, am relieved that she can't feel the pain. That she isn't suffering.

"Who was the bad man?" River asks.

Hadley's next breath comes shakily and frightfully slowly. She lets out a little whine. "I don't know, I sorry. The bad— the bad man was wearing a— a black thing,"

A mask? Why?

River is shaking so violently I'm afraid he'll fall apart. "I love you, Hads, you know?"

"Eww," she says.

He lets out a sound that's half-sob and half-laugh. "I love you so much."

"I'm scared, River."

"You'll be okay."

"I sorry, River." She says. "I sorry I let the bad man take me,"

"Don't be sorry, Hads. Please, you have nothing to be sorry for. This is not your fault,"

"Am I going to die?" She says.

"Where did you learn that word, you silly goose?"
He's going to fall apart in a second. I can feel it in the air. Blood starts running out of Hadley's nose at an alarming rate. River reaches up a hand, his sweater pulled around his fist, and rubs the blood away.

They don't have much time.

"Am I?" She asks.

River shakes his head. "No, Hads. You aren't going to die. But you're so brave, you know? You are so, so brave."

"What does that mean?" Her voice is sluggish, her eyes drooping.

"It means you're an amazing girl, you know that? It means you're wonderful and no bad man can ever take you down,"

"I'm— I'm amazing?"

The air in the clearing is so quiet and empty and it's like it's just those two in the universe, like time has stilled.

"You are the most amazing person in the whole world,"

Hads smiles.

And then she closes her eyes.

"I love you, big bro," she says so quietly I almost miss it.

And then River breaks.

His head falls forward, and he's pulling Hadley to his chest, and I can hear the sobs so clearly, so loudly, so heartbreakingly tender and deafening at the same time.

My knees don't want to hold me up anymore, so I fall to the ground just a few feet from them.

She was a baby.

She was just a baby.

Hadley. He's screaming. *Hadley, please.*

When he loses his voice, he just starts sobbing, crying, weeping, begging to anyone that will listen.

She was just a baby.

And now she's dead.

Hadley is dead, because of me.

57] YOU ARE NOT LIVING

MARCH 19th, 2021, 6:45pm

14 days until april 2nd

I have lost four people now.

Hannah Lopez.

Grace Amy.

Emma Garcia.

Hadley.

Hads is my sister, but she is also just another name added to the list of loss.

I can't speak anymore. I can't do anything except nod and stare and hold myself together.

I am angry. I am disbelieving. I want to go to sleep. I want to never wake up again.

I want to stop breathing.

But I cannot do any of those things, because my father has just lost his daughter.

And I need to make sure that I don't lose him.

But Nicolas, the monumental fuck up, is already gone. I don't see him when Cabot takes me home from the woods, from the *crime scene*. I allow myself to hope, distantly, that he has moved out, but I don't have much room in my mind for any other thinking. I walk in the front door and sit with Dad as he howls and weeps and sobs and hits me and scratches my arms like a vicious, nasty cat.

I take it all.

And when it's over, when he's tired and falls asleep on the couch, I pull my shoes on and step into the night.

Evie meets me on her porch steps. It is ten pm, but Evie is wide awake and so am I.

She doesn't ask me if I'm okay, she just sits on the ground and lets me lie across her, head in her lap. She strokes my hair, hums in my ear, and lets me cry.

It's at that moment that I think *I love this girl.*

But I also think *I hate this girl,* because if Evie had never inserted herself into my life, then I would still have a little sister.

5 8] L U N G S

evelyn

MARCH 26th, 2021, 6:13pm

7 days until april 2nd

They found Hadley's body by the river one week ago. Seven days. River is not back at school, will not be for a while, but he is spending a lot of time with me, coming up with a plan to take this bastard down.

We have spent hours and hours crawling through all of Bethany's followers on Instagram, and Nevae's, Jackson's. Aiden's.

Nothing.

Only two people were following all three:

Nicolas Lopez, and Lauren Beaumont.

I'm starting to think that Lauren Beaumont had something to do with it, because the initial signed at the end of every email is a stark *L* and Lauren seemed to have injected herself into their lives and never left. Then again, she wasn't close to any of them, nor did she have any association with Aiden Islington.

But she's my only lead. So I step out into the chilly afternoon in a practiced fashion. How many times have I done this, marched into the cold convinced that *this person* or *that person* will give me all the answers? It's getting tiring and feels futile because no matter how many times I do it, people still die. Hadley died. She was just a baby.

The Beaumonts still live in the big house on Forest Road. I walk there, taking fifteen minutes to breathe in the fresh air and think about what I'm going to say to her (if she's even there).

The Beaumont house is large and looming, and I can spot it even through the fog that sits dense and heavy over the forest. I falter on the front steps. Could Lauren Beaumont really know anything? What if she *is* the killer? What if I walk in there and she shoots me, and I die?

I guess there's only one way to know.

I raise a hand to the knocker and let it fall loudly against the large wooden door once. Twice. Three times.

Silence.

I stand there, hands in the pocket of my jacket, contemplating backing down off the porch and running back home. Why am I doing this?

Lauren opens the door. She looks older than the last time I saw her, at Bethany's funeral. Wearier, too. I wonder if she gets as much shit at college as she did at high school. She may have thrown the best parties, but she was the only Black girl in her grade. And small towns are unforgiving to people who don't have rural Maine pale skin.

She takes me in with wide, pretty dark eyes. "Are you Bethany's sister?"

I swallow thickly. "Yeah."

"What are you doing here?"

"I want to talk to you about Bethany,"

She goes stony. "I don't have anything to say about her."

"Do you know what she did?" I don't know why I ask her that, there's no way she could possibly know—

"You mean what she did to Aiden? Yeah, Evelyn. I know what that two-faced bitch did to my boyfriend."

Stomach shuddering and protesting, I step closer to her. Lauren Beaumont knows something, whether she wants to admit it or not. "Can I come in?"

She looks over her shoulder, as if trying to find an excuse— a reason to object, but then sighs and opens the heavy oak door further. "Whatever."

Inside the Beaumont's house, the floors are checkered marble, and all the doors are dark oak, looming and haunting and also very intimidating.

"Why did you come here, Evelyn?" She asks me as she leads me into a sitting room. One of many, I assume.

"You can call me Evie. You know, if you want."

"I don't believe that Bethany's kid sister would come here to try and make friends with the girl who kept trying to steal her boyfriend,"

"You liked Aiden?"

Lauren pins me with a gaze so strong and frightening that I'm forced to sit, not moving. "I never stopped liking him, Evie. Why do you think I'm still here? In this house? In this fucking town? I can't *move on from him.*"

"But— he's not coming back."

"I know." She says. It's not angry, or even indignant. It's just a statement. She knows he's not coming back, but still she sits here— waiting.

"How do you know the truth about what happened to him? *Who* did it to him?" I ask. I have a million questions for this girl who knew Aiden much better than anyone else.

"Because, Evie, I was there."

"What, in the car?"

"No, in the trees. Watching. I knew he would be there that night. Bethany was supposed to be meeting him so they could meet their drug dealer in the woods and hand over the money they owed him."

So it's true then. She *was* a drug addict. Somehow, the confirmation stings more than any of the speculation.

"Oh." I say. "Why? How did you know they would be there?"

"I kept tabs on him, Evie. On Aiden. I hate myself for it— but I was *obsessed*. I hated that Bethany got to have him and I didn't. So I made him my whole life. It was horrible— I would never rely on a man like that now, but at the time I— I don't know. Teenagers, eh?"

I think of River's lips on mine, of the comforting weight of his arms around me. "Yeah."

"Do you remember when Nicolas and Bethany fell out? Do you know why that happened?"

This piques my interest. "No. I know he was half the reason she was so miserable that everyone believed she could kill herself, but I don't know any details."

Lauren suddenly looks so, so sad. "It was me. It was my fault. I asked Nicolas to keep Bethany away from Aiden— to drive a wedge between them. He wanted Bethany, you see? Not romantically, I don't think. But he wanted her to himself. No one was really happy about Bethany and Aiden other than Bethany and Aiden themselves."

"And what— she found out what he had done?"

"Yeah. She was furious. She thought Nicolas wanted her to be miserable— so it's almost like she went off and pretended that she could be miserable all by herself,"

"And then he moved away." I say.

"And then he moved away." She confirms. "Left Bethany behind, miserable as ever. No one was a winner."

"Especially not Aiden." I say. "God, he really didn't deserve what happened to him."

"Killed by the girl he loves? That's a fate *worse* than death,"

And I only have to nod. And then I remember something else that Nevae told me. "Aiden and Nicolas, they were friends though? Nicolas didn't hate Aiden,"

Lauren sighs. "Nicolas and Aiden's relationship was a complicated one. I think it might have even been romantic, in a way. Yes, it's true that they couldn't get enough of each other. But they also seemed to destroy each other at the same time."

59] MANIPULATED

MARCH 28th, 2021, 1:16pm

5 days until april 2nd

I have spent a lot of time at Evie's house recently. I have tried to be there for my father, but he doesn't want me to be near him. He doesn't know a lot about why Hadley died, why she was a target in the first place, but he knows that it has something to do with me and my actions and he hasn't forgiven me yet.

Evie is sitting against the arm of the couch with my head in her lap, and Benji is on the other side, his legs draped over mine. We're a tangle of bodies and friends and watching a monotonous film on the TV. My eyes are heavy with sleep that I haven't gotten much of recently, and Evie's hand is running through the dark curls on my head, massaging my scalp and sending me into a woozy, tired haze. Everything is warm and lovely from the rain coming down outside to the blankets draped over our bodies to the steam rising from half-drunk mugs of coffee on the table.

I'm just about to succumb to sleep when there's a loud, pounding knock on the door that's so powerful the door rattles in its frame. Evie sighs and I lift my head off her lap so she can get up and go out into the hall.

The door creaks on its hinges as she swings it open and then quiet for a second. And then the yelling starts.

"You bitch! You complete bitch!"

I recognise the nasally, high-pitched wail immediately. Izzy Beaumont.

Through the living room door, I watch Evie back up towards the stairs and a second later Izzy comes into view, finger pointing at Evie's face and sharp nails waving like weapons.

Izzy is a mess.

She's wearing ratty sweatpants with a t-shirt that I think has some holes in, and her laces are untied.

Benji leaps up from the couch and hurries into the hallway and I brush off the thin remains of exhaustion to follow.

Izzy's eyes barely leave Evie's for a moment to look at us before she's backing Evie against the wall again, hands waving and voice shouting.

"You bitch!" Over and over again with, "How could you?" and "You're just like your sister."

"Hey, hey, calm down." Benji says, pulling Izzy away from Evie. Evie looks at me, and her eyes are wide and her hands in anxious fists by her sides. She does that when she's scared, I've noticed.

Benji is directing Izzy out of the door, and Evie watches them leave with a look of half-horror and half-confusion on her face. Eyes wide, mouth agape, unmoving.

I feel completely useless, so I follow them out onto the porch.

Izzy is writhing in Benji's strong grip, his muscles flexing under his t-shirt with the strain it takes to keep Izzy from charging back in there after Evie.

"Take a breath." He says. "Breathe for a second, Izzy, and tell us why you're here and what Evie did."

"She is just like her sister." Izzy spits at us. "Bethany killed Aiden and made loads of people *miserable*. Evie told the police about what she's been doing at school like a *fucking creep* for months, and what happened? Hadley died. *She killed someone, too.* Just like her murderer sister."

Whatever I was expecting Izzy to say, it definitely wasn't that.

Evie killed Hadley? How does Izzy even know that Beth killed Aiden?

How does she know what Evie and I have been doing? And that we told the police?

A million things aren't adding up, but I look back at Evie, and she looks ill. Her cheeks are pale, and her mouth is pursed in a tight frown. Her eyes are glossy, and I don't think she's really focusing on anything except what's in her head. Which can't be anything nice.

I know what she's going to take from this. She's going to take on even more of the blame for my sister's death and she's not going to let anyone tell her otherwise.

My hatred for Izzy reaches a crescendo, and I want her off Evie's porch.

"Izzy, where did you get all that information?" Benji is asking. He's the only calm one in this scenario. I'm glad he's here.

Izzy lets out an animalistic screech, shaking her head. "He doesn't want me to tell you. I can't tell you. I just know that Evie is a murderer, just like her sister,"

He doesn't want me to tell you.

Something is very, very wrong here.

Does Izzy know the killer?

Does she know L?

Has L told her all of this, and set her rampant on Evie for all these years? Has she been manipulated into thinking these horrible thoughts and getting upset and angry with Evie for no reason?

"Who? Who doesn't want you to tell us?" I ask her.

Izzy just shakes her head. Her breathing gets faster and faster and she looks so tired. "He told me not to tell you. I can't tell you."

She sounds like a broken record.

She sounds like a broken *girl*.

And just like that, Izzy takes off running down the road. Gone, leaving us behind as confused as ever.

But one thing's for sure: Izzy knows something that we need.

And it would be helpful if we could figure it out before April 2nd.

60] THE LAST TIME

evelyn

MARCH 30th, 2021, 7:15pm

3 days until april 2nd

It's on a cold, dreary Tuesday evening before the start of spring break that I get the final email.

NEW MESSAGE
To: evelynareed2002@gmail.com
From: nodancer2119@gmail.com
R.E: excited
Meet me in the woods, Evie. Do it or someone else dies. You don't want any more bloodshed, right? Do as I say, and we can end this. All that suffering—gone. Just like that.
Meet me in her spot.
Much love, see you soon,
L.

The message makes me, rather psychopathically, excited. Excited in the way that new deputies get when someone is killed, or something very big and very bad happens— finally, the moment I've been waiting for. The end to a week of monotony, of nothing happening at all.

On April 2nd, I'll meet this bastard in the woods and end it.

It all sounds so epically simple.

So wonderfully inevitable.

The end is so close that I can feel it with the tips of my fingers, just there, out of reach, a little further along in the calendar. On the horizon.

In a week, it'll be over. The thought makes me feel giddy, blissful.

River regards me over the top of his black coffee. We're holed up in Cathy's, as we always are, a brownie each and a black coffee to nurse us through to late at night.

"What?"

I show him the email, and he frowns.

"Is it really that easy? You just show up, they take what they want, and bam— it's over?"

I nod eagerly. "Yes. Yes— that's it." I don't mention that the likelihood is that what they want is my life, because he already knows this.

"I'll show up, and you can come, and call the police, and—"

"Wait. You're *going*?"

"Of course,"

"Right. And do you want me to stand and watch L kill you? Evie—"

"No, no, of course not you goose." I lean my chin on my hand and lower my voice, wary of the thin evening crowd. "You're going to call the police, and tell them that we're there, that if they go to the forest, they'll find the killer."

"And what if you get shot or something before they get there?"

"Then I die for a good cause,"

River still doesn't look completely convinced, but he nods anyway. He knows me well enough to know that I won't be backing down.

He takes a sip of his coffee, "Where do you think Izzy Beaumont fits into this?"

His question surprises me. I'd almost forgotten about the incident with her the other day.

I'd gathered from the whole thing that she knows the killer, and L is manipulating her into believing things that aren't real. Radicalizing her. Making her see L's views and take them in as her own.

Textbook manipulator.

But I've been taking Mr Black's psychology class for four years. I know that if she's been this heavily threatened and made to think these extremist thoughts, then there's no way of getting it out of her without a big ol' fight and a lot of trust-building.

Which we're not going to be able to do in time.

"I don't know, River. But I don't think that she's our way into knowing the truth, honestly. I don't think she's going to be able to tell us anything. Even if we hammer into her all night and all day,"

He nods solemnly, as if he knew that was the answer to his question even before he asked it.

"I just wish we had some kind of idea of what you're walking into," he says.

I reach out my hand and place it over his, squeezing gently. "I know. Me too. But we tried our hardest. We know a lot more than we did in January. We know L's weaknesses."

"Aiden." He says.

"And me." I say. "If they saw me as important enough to send me all those emails and kill someone when we started to get too close, then I mean something to L, to this whole investigation. Think about it— all the victims revolved around my sister, and going after Hadley— it was an attack through me,"

River is still and quiet. He knows I'm right.

He knows how important it is that I do this alone.

No matter how much he wants me to be safe.

61] G R O W I N G   P A I N S

evelyn

APRIL 2nd, 2021, 8:15pm

0 days until april 2nd

I make tortellini for dinner. Mom's home for once, so she hands me a glass of white wine whilst I dish up the steaming pasta and peppery sauce. It smells delicious, and I'm proud of myself for not burning the kitchen down for once. Mom looks tired as she sits opposite me at the table, and by the time we finish eating she's excusing herself to bed. Grateful to not have to make up an excuse as to why I'm leaving, I quietly wash up and put everything away and grab a jacket from my room. My hands are shaking as I fumble with my Converse, the laces slippery between my fingers.

By nine pm, I'm out on the porch, sitting on the top step in the dark, waiting for River. I told him I would drive us in the Volvo because I'm certain that I'll be able to drive us back again. I'm not going to die tonight. God can have me eventually, but not now, not in the same way as

Bethany. I don't think Mom would be able to cope if she lost her other daughter.

River appears then, a tall, slim figure under the yellow glow of the streetlights. He holds his hand up in a wave before crossing the street, and I can see even from several feet away the outline of a small smirk on his face. He's hurting inside, but he still manages to put on a brave face for me, to try and keep my nerves at bay.

"Hey," he says.

I smile. "Hey yourself,"

"Are you ready to end this?"

I nod. Nod and nod and nod. "Yes. Absolutely."

The killer sent me an email earlier today— we're too meet at Bethany's spot at quarter past nine. Just me, alone. Of course, that's not quite the case— River will be in the trees, waiting for my signal. If something goes wrong, he calls the police. If I signal, he calls the police. If something as much as feels wrong, he can call the police.

They are our safety net, but I'm almost completely sure that they won't be able to do anything anyway. Mae and Benji don't know about our plan, and I'm pretty sure that if they did, they would do everything in their power to stop it from happening. But I am too close to answers now to care that much anyway.

River reaches out a hand. I take it, hoping he can't tell that my hands are sweating, that I'm far more nervous than I'm letting on. If he knew how much I was terrified out of my mind to do this, he'd never let it happen.

*****

The walk through the forest to Bethany's spot is painstaking. It takes us centuries to find Devil's Pathway in the thick darkness. It takes us another few decades to amble over the uneven terrain. When we're in the grove of trees closest to the spot, I place a hand on River's chest.

"You have to stay here." I say.

He lets out a breath. I can see it dancing in the moonlight. "I know."

"If I die—"

"You're not going to die, Evie." He says. His voice wavers, like he's trying really hard not to cry. I try not to think about that, because River crying is enough to set me off as well.

He presses a long kiss to my forehead. I close my eyes, still my breath, let everything sink in. I'm going to end it. And I am not going to die.

"I'm gonna get this bastard." I say to the narrow gap between my forehead and his chest. River chuckles against my head, chest shuddering.

"Yeah, 'course you are, Reed. Of course you are."

There's a quiet resignation to his voice. He knows I'm going to march into the clearing and kick ass no matter how much he wants me not to.

"Remember our signal?" He whispers.

"I remember." I whisper back.

And he hugs me. One of those big River bear hugs. "I love you."

I almost lose it then. And then I find the words. "I love you, too." *Love*. Is that what this fluttery feeling in my chest is? This ache that's there whenever we're apart?

In light of so much darkness, I'm glad we've found a light.

"You'll be okay, right?" I say. "Alone, in the dark."

He chuckles again. Quietly. "I'm not afraid of the dark, Lopez."

No. He's afraid of what's in it.

I go up on my tiptoes and kiss him on the cheek. On the sharp stubble that's grown longer and darker since Hadley died and he stopped taking care of himself. "I'll be okay. You'll be okay. We'll both be okay. Tomorrow, we'll be wrapped up in blankets drinking coffee talking about how well this went, and how this bastard is in prison now."

He nods. Smiles. "Go get 'em, Reed."

So I squeeze his hand once and let go of the warmth. I'm going to avenge Bethany's death.

And Nevae. And Jackson. And Hadley.

All people that were lights in the dark. All people that left loved ones behind. All people that deserve *justice*. So I'm damn well going to give it to them.

I take a step away from River and into the thick of the trees. Here, the moonlight doesn't reach me. Here, I am between two people. Here, I am alone, and I am in the dark.

I close my eyes. *Who did it?*

Lauren Beaumont told me that she was there the night Aiden died. That Nicolas had helped her separate Aiden and Bethany.

That Nicolas made Bethany miserable enough that people believed her capable of suicide.

Nevae Bradbury told me that Bethany admired me. That she was jealous enough of me that she stepped into the arms of Nicolas, Marie and Poppie to get away from it all through drugs.

Marie Blaine told me that Nicolas and Aiden had an unbreakable friendship. That Nevae and Jackson hated how distant Bethany had become.

L told me that it was revenge.

I force myself to think through the haze of emotion that has blinded me for months.

Who had motive? Who had reason to want revenge?

And I only come up with one name. Someone who was close to the investigation, close to its parts, close to the people involved.

A figure steps into my field of vision. I can taste the fear that suddenly races up my body.

"Evie. You came."

Nicolas Lopez.

Oh my *god*. Nicolas Lopez killed my sister. He killed Bethany, and he killed Nevae, and he killed Jackson and he killed Hadley, who was only two years old.

And all I seem to be able to think is, *this is going to break River.*

I follow him out of the trees to the clearing. Where Eastwood meets its end, where the town gives way to the Clerwood. The place where my sister died. The place where Nicolas Lopez killed her.

"Surprise." He says. "You didn't figure it out, did you? Even after all those clues I gave you, the smarter Reed sister couldn't even work it out. Even when the answer was right in front of you."

"You sick son of a bitch." I say.

"You're calling *me* sick?" He becomes enraged quickly. Like the flick of a switch. "Your sister killed my best friend, Evie. And you call *me* the sick one? She stole a life from me, so I'm going to steal a life from her."

An excerpt from one of his emails comes back to me, then.

Give me back what she stole.

That's it. He wants to kill me, he's *going* to kill me, because Bethany killed Aiden, and for that he's going to take away the person that Bethany loved the most.

Aiden and Nicolas were closer to each other than I ever knew.

Grief makes people selfish.

In Nicolas, the grief manifested itself as violence.

"Why the three-year gap, Nicolas?" I ask. It's mostly irrelevant, but it's been bugging me since the investigation started.

He takes a step towards me then. "I was shipped off to another family member for three years, Evie. I was under such strict supervision to make sure I didn't relapse with the drugs that I couldn't get back here to finish the job until much later. Until I graduated high school and got kicked out of college. But don't worry, it was just three years that I got to spend getting angrier, and angrier that Bethany stole the only person who ever saw me as *me*. She loved Nevae and Jackson, Evie. And she loved you. So I'm going to take it all away."

And there is no regret in his eyes.

None at all.

And that— that is *terrifying*.

He backs me up against the river's edge. And something cold and metal presses against my stomach. I gulp. I close my eyes.

And he pulls the trigger.

62] THE PIECES

APRIL 2nd, 2021, 7:19pm

0 days until april 2nd

Panic.

Pure, untainted panic flowing as freely as the blood in my veins. Hands shaking, knees trembling, whole body weak with the stench of fear and its menacing presence. Evie could be dead. I keep telling myself that she's alive, that the gunshot I just heard was fired by her, or at the very least it hit her leg or another extremity that won't lead to her death. Begging to a God, any God, that there's something I can do— that I'm not losing another person I love.

I love.

Do I really love her? Is this love? Or is this just circumstance, heartache, and emotion stitching our hearts together so that they beat, practically, as one?

There's no time for thinking about this.

I'm tripping, flailing over roots and rocks and the low bows of trees in my way. One foot in front of the other.

All the exhaustion I've felt recently is gone, replaced by the sharp sting of adrenaline and the lightness of my lungs in my chest as everything, every pain in my legs from running for so long, every pain in my heart from beating too fast and for too long, is gone and replaced by new fear, new panic, new adrenaline. There's no room for sadness here.

So I keep running.

I keep leaping over tree roots, ducking under branches, wondering when this world will get bored of torturing us.

I reach the bottom of Devil's Pathway in time to hear the muffled sound of something hitting the water. My heart

drops.

So I speed up, trying my best to stick to the shadows and by the trees.

In the clearing, my brother stands by the river, looking into its depths like it's going to reveal to him some big secret. Evie is nowhere to be found. Evie must be in the river.

Drowning.

Just like her sister.

MY BROTHER IS A SERIAL KILLER. This thought is loud and intrusive. Loud. Loud. So loud. *When will the world give me a break? When will my family stop leaving me?*

Adrenaline leaves no room for questions.

"You bastard!" I find myself yelling, screaming into the pale dusk light. Nicolas turns, slowly.

I have heard the people close to serial killers say that when they see the person after killing someone, they look unfamiliar, strange, nothing like the person they know.

That's not true for me.

The person looking back at me is Nicolas Lopez, my brother, my mother's killer, my sister's killer, the girl I love's killer. No. Not *killer*. She's not dead.

Evelyn is not dead.

EVELYN IS NOT DEAD.

This is a fact that I am absolutely certain of.

"River." He says. His voice carving out the word like he's never said it before. I blink, all the fight suddenly draining out of me.

"You're a killer." I say, deflated. It's the truth, and yet it doesn't feel real. There was always something *wrong* with him— something ill and unnatural and violent, but I never quite believed he would be capable of something like this. I guess that's the point, right? We never see it coming until it's too late.

"Please, River. You're my brother, don't—"

"Shut *up!*" I find myself shouting, screaming. The words rip themselves free from my throat painfully, leaving it raw and bleeding and agonizing.

Nicolas takes a step back, shocked at the volume of my words.

"You are not my brother, Nicolas. Not anymore." I step forward, towards him, towards Evie, who is probably running out of air, and if she isn't struggling, isn't visible under the water, then—

No. She is *alive*.

There is no way that she can make it this far and not survive to see tomorrow.

No way.

I won't let it happen.

I take another step forwards, approaching Nicolas. He points to the water.

"She's not going to make it." He says, voice gravelly. "I shot her."

"You're a killer."

"I am not. They all got what they deserve. Bethany, Jackson, Nevae, Evelyn. All of them had something to do with Aiden's death— so they deserved to die for what they did."

"What did Evelyn do? Hadley?" I'm wasting time, but I *need to know.*

"Evelyn was her sister, and she kept sticking her nose into my business. And she was the reason Bethany felt bad enough about herself to turn to me, to the drugs, to the things which drove her to kill Aiden."

"And Hadley? She was just a baby, Nicolas."

"I needed to get rid of Hadley before she saw how horrible the world is. She doesn't deserve to live in a world so grimy and horrible and violent. You know that better than anyone."

I'm breathing heavily but not breathing at all.

My hands are shaking but I'm completely still.

The clearing is vast and empty, but claustrophobia is gnawing at me.

"You loved him, didn't you? Aiden?" I say.

Nicolas looks defeated. Head slumped; legs weak. The gun in his hand is slack and pointed towards the floor.

"Please don't talk about him, River."

"Look at me."

He does. His eyes are blue and piercing and terrifying and *home*. "Aiden was my home. He was my everything. We never would have been happy together, though."

"Why not?"

"Aiden was wonderful. Broken, just like me. And wonderful."

Nicolas starts to cry. The first sob rips from his throat and he's screaming at me, at the river, at the people that lost their lives here, at the people he killed and the reasons why.

It hurts to watch. Even though I hate him, even though he isn't my brother anymore. The sound is so agonizing that it almost brings me to my knees. Almost.

He turns back out towards the river again, and whilst he's looking the other way I bend down and wrap my hands around a rock, a big one. I swing my arm back, aiming for his head. It hits its mark, and he goes down, tumbling head first into the river.

My legs carry me to the bank, and I desperately search for a body. And there she is— hair reaching up in tendrils around the surface, she's resting just under the water, face down, the red tint of blood surrounding her. A voice in me screams that she must be dead, there's no way she's alive, but I reach down and pull her out anyway, tugging her body onto the bank, and then I'm pushing the heavy wet hair out of her face and leaning over her, ear over her mouth, feeling for breath and scrabbling with my hand to find a pulse against her wrist.

At first, nothing.

And then,

A breath.

I waste no time. "Evie! Evelyn, can you hear me?"

Another shallow, hesitant breath.

"Evie!" I'm shouting now. "Evie! For god's sakes, *wake up!*"

Another breath which turns into a gasp which turns into a cough and then her eyes are open and she's coughing and spluttering and breathing and *alive*.

One of my hands smooths the hair away from her forehead and the other searches for the place all the blood is coming from. Her stomach. It's coming from her stomach. I lift up the sweater she's wearing— and find it. Just under the jagged, horrible scar from where she was shot all those months ago, there's a hole closer to her ribcage that's pulsing weakly with blood. I rip the sweater off that I'm wearing, and press it to the wound, holding it tightly whilst she gasps for breath.

"You're okay." I say. "You're okay."

"River?" Her voice comes out in a breath, raw and weak. "It— Nicolas— I— I'm sorry."

"Shh. It's okay. It's over. It's over now, Evie."

"I'm tired."

"I need you to stay awake, yeah?"

She huffs out a breath. "Don't you tell me what to do, Lopez."

And I let out a breath, because *she's going to be okay.*

Whilst she grips onto my hand, tightly, I pull my phone from my pocket and dial the Sheriff's station.

"Hello? Eastwood Sheriff's Station, how can I help?" Deputy Cabot's deep, smooth voice drifts through the speaker. I am ridiculously happy to hear him.

"Cabot— I, it's River. Evie— I, *we found the killer.* Evie's here, she's been shot, we need an ambulance. I killed him, Cabot. Shit, I killed my brother."

"River— where are you?"

"On the bank of the Clerwood. In the forest, at the bottom of Devil's Pathway. Tell them— tell Whittle and Cosette that the killer is Nicolas Lopez and he's lying at the bottom of the Clerwood and call an ambulance."

And then I hang up.

It's over.

"It's over," I say to Evie, not really believing the words myself. "It's okay— it's over. We did it."

******

I spend two hours being questioned. More time spent in this tiny, horrible room being stared down by strange, cold faces. Whittle is at the hospital, waiting for Evie to get out of surgery. The paramedics say she should be fine, because it looks like the bullet nicked an artery, which requires surgery to repair, but it doesn't look like it caused any other damage.

When they release me, I stand in reception and turn my phone on for the first time since I called the Sheriff's station after it happened.

I have, surprisingly, held it together pretty well— but I'm sure it'll all hit me later. The calamity of what's happened, and what I've done.

I killed my brother.

No, that bastard was not my brother.

Nicolas Lopez was not my brother.

He's dead. And everyone's better off that way.

I focus my eyes on the lock screen of my phone, scanning for important messages. I have six messages from Mae, two missed calls from my dad and eighteen missed calls from Benji.

I go to Benji first, because *eighteen missed calls*? Has he found out what's happened that quickly?

Dialling his number, I press the phone up to my ear. He answers on the first ring.

"River— I— can you come to Amber Park, please?" He sounds pained. Something's wrong.

"Uh, sure. Yeah. I'll be there in a second," I hang up and run out of the front door of the place, quickly realizing I have no ride. "Shit."

So I start running.

I run over wet, rain-soaked streets, Eastwood illuminated by streetlights and the weak glow of the moon overhead. I run and I run, until my already weak legs are weaker, and my heart is completely fed up and tired of beating.

It's not over yet, apparently. Could Nicolas have a sidekick? Someone who's gone after Benji? But why— Benji has no place in this.

I run for ten minutes, until my legs are jelly, and my heart is millimeters from giving way completely. Amber Park appears in the distance, illuminated by the streetlights and their glow. A figure is hunched over in the center of the park, and I vault over the locked gate, sprinting towards Benji, who is sprawled on the floor.

His head is bleeding.

His mouth is bleeding.

There is a gash across his forehead.

"Oh my god," I say, pulling him up. He blinks through the blood, and I pull off my shirt, using it to dab at the blood. He winces.

"River. You came."

"Of course I did, Benji." I hold him upright, reaching over to my phone to call an ambulance. "Who did this to you? What happened?"

He takes a large gulp of air. "My step-father did this to me, River."

I freeze. "What?"

"I'll tell you the whole story later, but he's an abusive asshole and he came to Evie's house and wouldn't stop shouting so I went out to try and talk to him and he was drunk, and he hit me and I didn't know where to go so I came here,"

I can't seem to find the right words.

"I'm so sorry." I say.

"Evie knew." He says. "I was living at her house. For the past few weeks since I got kicked out, I've been sleeping on her couch. She came with me to confront my stepdad a week ago. I made her not tell any of you. I— God, I would have called her, but she wasn't picking up, and— where is she, anyway? I just assumed you two would be together,"

"Benji, do you know what today is?" I say.

"No," he shakes his head, and then winces.

"April 2nd."

He freezes. "No. Is she—"

"She's okay. I think she's in the hospital— the killer, he shot her,"

"Do you know who it is?"

I nod, gritting my teeth. "The killer was my brother, Benji. I killed him, and he shot Evie in the stomach."

"But she's going to be okay?"

I nod.

"Shit, I'm sorry, man. That's— God, that's horrible. I feel silly now for dragging you all the way out here for me,"

"No, shut up. I'm proud of you, man, for standing up for your dad like that— that takes a hell of a lot of courage, you know."

He smiles sadly. "Yeah. I just— I wish our lives could be easier."

"Hey, if you don't have anywhere to stay, then I'll ask my dad if you can stay with us. We have a spare room now, and all,"

"Bro, I don't have to move in with you— that room, I— no one should intrude like that."

I think back to Bethany's room, and how no one could bear to step foot in there. I shake my head. "No, it'll be good to move on. Come on, I'll take you to the hospital and then I'll talk to my dad, when some of this has blown over, okay?"

Benji nods. "Yeah, alright, man."

6 3] M O V I N G   O N

evelyn

APRIL 9th, 2021, 2:50pm

7 days since april 2nd

Today, Benji is officially moving in with River.

His dad, Mateo, as he's started demanding I call him, was all for it— he desperately didn't want such an empty house. I guess that's how he's grieving, by leaving no room for sadness to take over. That's where me and Mom went wrong when Beth died— we let the grief take over. We let it ravage us until there was nothing left.

I got out of the hospital this morning, just in time to "help" Benji move his stuff into Hadley's old bedroom. In reality, it'll probably just be me sitting on his bed whilst everyone else puts effort in. I can't risk pulling any stitches (I've learnt my lesson). Mae and Benji have spent the past few days stripping everything away and moving some of Hadley's things into the attic. It's the first week of spring break, so River has spent most of his time either with his dad, healing, or at the hospital with me.

From what I've heard, they dragged the river for Nicolas's body the morning after it all happened. It didn't take them long to find it, just a few hundred feet downstream caught on a rock. River isn't being charged with anything— it was self-defence, and Whittle twisted some of his words to make it impossible to press any kind of charge.

Nicolas was buried yesterday, and River went to the small, modest burial for peace of mind. To get over the loss of his brother.

He's starting therapy next week, to deal properly with the loss of his sister and his brother. Both of his siblings, gone. Just like that.

In the space of a month.

Two more lost family members. It's horrible. I'm still waiting for it to all hit him, for him to fall apart.

"What are you thinking about?" River. He's here now, leaning against the doorframe. I'm on the couch in his living room, staring into the distance. He's smiling. "It's nice to have you back here."

"Thanks. I'm thinking about how shitty everything is, was, and how weird it is— how much has changed so quickly."

He comes closer, sitting next to me on the couch. "How are you feeling?"

"Fine. Better." There is an incessant pain in my stomach, but I think it'll be there for a while. Battle scars. I have two nasty scars now, one on top of the other, jagged and gnarly on my stomach.

"I'm glad you're alive," River says.

"Thanks, me too,"

"Genuinely— I thought I'd lost you for a second,"

I let out a laugh, wincing at the tug on my stomach. "I'm not going anywhere anytime soon,"

He's positively grinning now, "Can I ask you something, Evie?"

"Of course,"

"Will you go on a date with me?"

And I'm grinning as well. "Yes, of course, you silly oaf."

For the first time in months, pure happiness springs alive in my chest. It's the best feeling in the world.

64] THE ENIGMATIC END

evelyn

JUNE 11th, 2021, 2:01pm

70 days since april 2nd

On our last day of high school, it's sunny.

Bright blue sky, cotton wisps of cloud. The perfect day.

The front of Elizabeth Gingham Memorial High School is littered with students saying their goodbyes, taking pictures with their favorite teachers and getting teary-eyed. I'm not exactly sad about leaving Eastwood, but there's something bittersweet about losing a familiarity that has been such a steady presence in your life for so long.

We all put an effort in to come in today.

Mae, pulling us all together. River, by my side, hand in mine, putting on a bright face for us. Benji, bruises fully healed, smiling and laughing. Me, a permanent unsteady, uneven quality to my gait now, wandering around like nothing ever happened.

Our parents are outside on the grass in front of school, celebrating our achievements. Even Benji's Nonna is here, with her new girlfriend—the iconic Ellie-May that she's been crushing on for months.

A real reminder that pining works, sometimes.

We're leaving in a few minutes, but River and I have something to take care of first. We walk through the empty corridors side by side, a notebook tucked under my arm. When we get to E3, River lifts a hand and knocks on the door. Once. Twice.

"Come in!" A bright but tired voice calls from inside. River pushes open the door and Mr Black looks up at us, a smile wrinkling his eyes.

"Oh, hello you two. How are you doing? Miss Reed— it's been a while since you came to one of my classes."

"We're all right, thanks Mr Black." I say. "Actually, we wanted to give you this,"

I hand over the notebook under my arms and he accepts it carefully like he's afraid he might break it. When he reads the title written across the top, his smile turns sad. He flips through it and then sets it down on his desk.

"Oh, Evelyn— River, both of you, you didn't need to do this. I passed you both— I figured that you've learnt far more than this topic could have taught you,"

"We thought, why let all this work go to waste?" I say, "I got bored in the hospital for a week, so I thought I might as well finish it,"

He nods, and then stands up from behind the desk. "I won't read it. It's private, of course, but I appreciate your determination to finish it— and I admire you, both of you for the strength you've shown these past six months."

He hugs me and then smacks River on the shoulder in that strange manly way that men do and shakes both our hands.

"Thanks for being such a great teacher all those years," I say.

River nods. "Yeah— those six months were six months of the best psychology lessons I've ever had."

Mr Black laughs heartily. "You're welcome, you two. Now, you should get outside— you've spent enough time in this classroom. Best of luck to you both, and I know you'll make us all very proud wherever you end up next."

We thank him again and head out of the room, but before we do I spend one more second looking at the notebook. Pages and pages of evidence and transcripts and fact files and thoughts and everything we squeezed out of the case.

And the title, which I wrote across the front of the book six months ago.

The Enigmatic End to Bethany Reed.

*****

At the end of the day, when the last bell rings, Nonna comes up to me. She looks somehow younger since the last time I saw her three years ago, and Ellie-May is by her side. She looks radiant as she pulls me in for a hug.

Nonna smells like cookies and home.

"Oh, Evie." She says. Her accent twangs warmly in my ears.

"Hi, Nonna." I say. "How are you?"

She pulls back, cupping my cheek with her hand, adorned with rings of various shapes and sizes. "Ah should be asking you that. Ah'm doing wonderfully dear. just wanted to come and say thank you for lookin' after my boy. It breaks ma heart, seeing what that horrible man did to him. But he said you were there for him, and ah can never thank you enough."

Her words make me tear up, but I can't cry in front of Nonna. "Benji's my best friend, Nonna. Honestly, I'm just glad he's okay,"

Nonna smiles. "Yes, me too,"

She hugs me one more time and then waves goodbye, making her way back over to where Benji and Ivy are taking pictures.

I spot someone I've been looking for since we arrived this morning.

Izzy Beaumont is standing towards the back of the crowd of people outside school, her hair pulled back in a tight ponytail and her face paler than I remember.

I haven't seen her in a while— not since April 2nd, I don't think.

I nudge River in the side. When he looks at me questioningly, I nod over to Izzy. "I'm going to go and talk to her. See if Nicolas was the person, you know, manipulating her and radicalizing her."

River looks concerned and cautious, but he nods, albeit reluctantly. "Be careful, okay?"

"Always," I say, leaning up to peck him on the cheek. He smiles and lets go of my hand. "Be back in a second,"

My legs are weak as I make my way towards her. My Converse sink into the moist ground and Izzy doesn't see me until I'm standing right in front of her.

And then her eyes meet mine and she tears up a bit, bringing a hand to her mouth to stifle the sobs. I put an arm around her and steer her away from the crowd.

We end up around the back of school, in the shade, where there's no one around but us and a few birds cawing twenty feet away.

"Evie, I—" she starts, "I'm so sorry."

"It's okay," I say.

"No, it's not. I was so, so horrible to you. I didn't realise until after he died what I had done to you. It was only when the whole story came out that I realized what he'd done to me,"

"Nicolas, you mean? Nicolas was the one who wouldn't let you tell us anything? The one who made you hate me?"

She nods, looking to the sky and taking several deep breaths. Gaining her composure— her dignity— back.

"I was in love with him." She says. "Nicolas. I thought he was the love of my life. The best thing that ever happened to me."

"Oh, Izzy."

"I guess— I guess I was so desperate to find someone to love me that as soon as he came along with his beautiful eyes and charming smile a year ago I was like putty. He molded me into a horrible person who was angry at you for making him angry."

"Did he ever hurt you?"

"No. God, no. He wasn't physically abusive, really. He just manipulated me into believing every single lie he fed to me. About you being the one that killed Hadley and Bethany being the one that killed Aiden just to spite him."

"I'm the one that gave him your email address, Evie." She says after I don't say anything for a while. Just digesting everything she's telling me. "I'm the one that found out everything you were doing in psychology. I stole your notebook in February and logged into your school account and read all the documents you typed up. I told Nicolas everything you were doing. It was like— I would do anything for someone to love me, and as long as I kept him happy by doing that, he— he was pleased."

"Izzy, I'm so sorry."

"It's okay. I— we only met in January, when he moved back to Eastwood. Before that he'd contacted me online last year, when he was living in Texas, and got to talking to me. I think he found me on Facebook, saw that I was following you, and started to use me to get to you. You want to know the worst part? Sometimes I miss him. I miss the way he would make me smile and the way he made me feel, when he wasn't angry at you and Bethany."

"That's okay, Izzy. It's okay to miss him. It'll probably be a long time before you can get over him properly,"

She nods, sniffling. She looks so broken. And now that I know why she hated me all this time, I just feel sorry. Sorry that I didn't try to get to the bottom of it sooner.

"But I'm also glad he's gone. I'm glad I realized what he was doing to me, and I'm glad that you don't hate me."

She gives me a watery smile.

I give her one back. "I don't hate you, Izzy. I don't think we'll ever be friends, but I'm glad that you're okay. I wish you all the best. Really. You deserve happiness."

Izzy lets out a weak laugh. "Thank you, Evie. That means a lot. You should probably get back to River and your friends. I think the speeches are starting,"

I nod, looking back towards where everyone else is. River is looking at me. He grins. I smile back.

"See you around?" I say to Izzy.

She nods, "See you around. Good luck wherever you end up,"

65] IT ECHOES

evelyn

JUNE 11th, 2021, 4:12pm

70 days since april 2nd

Much of Eastwood Forest has been sectioned off by the police so they can keep onlookers and news people away from the place Nicolas died, but they have left Bethany's spot alone. So I walk to the forest. It takes almost an hour to make it to the bottom of Devil's Pathway, but my legs are numb.

The sun is streaming through the trees and the late afternoon air is warm but there's still the threat of a breeze, the chill that sits everywhere in Eastwood now. The momentous weight on the town has lifted at last, but there will always be a bit of Nicolas Lopez everywhere. You cannot erase darkness entirely.

Wildflowers have begun to grow in the clearing by the river where Bethany spent so many hours, and where Hadley died. It's as if her body dispersed seeds across the clearing and now, she lives on through the flowers. White daisies with bright yellow centers and green stems reaching to purple petals. It's so beautiful.

But what I came here to see wasn't the beautiful flowers. It's the plaque sitting idly on the river's edge, watching over the waters to make sure no one else falls in.

It reads,

In loving memory of Bethany Reed, Jackson Miller, Nevae Bradbury and Hadley Lopez-Amy. All were too young, taken too soon from a world too dark.

Of course, the committee that put together the memorial didn't know that Aiden, too, was a victim of this town's darkness. Nicolas may not have taken Aiden's life, but it was a consequence of his actions. His love.

In the months since his death, I have read and reread the emails hundreds of times. Each one marked *L* for Lopez. Each one filled with words that bite at my heels and will haunt me until I die. I have read the emails and written them out across my mind, said them aloud, seen them in my dreams.

Hadley has spoken them through dry, bloodstained lips and Nevae has whispered them in my ear with bruises around her throat. Bethany has read them aloud from my laptop in her lilting, rhythmic voice. Jackson has wheezed them out, bleeding from his chest.

I take a deep breath of the fresh air, tinged with the scent of flowers and the salty air of the Clerwood.

This is exactly where I was standing one hundred and fifty-three days ago when Nicolas fired the bullets that killed Jackson Miller. This is exactly where I was standing when my entire life changed.

I have changed so much.

I can smile freely now. I don't feel guilty every time I think of Bethany and her freckled cheeks heavy with a frown. I have spoken to my mother without awkwardness, and it almost feels like we are returning to normal.

This spot, right here by the river, with the plaque and the ghosts and the wildflowers, is where I was standing the night I met River and Mateo and Hadley.

This is where I was standing when Nicolas decided to keep avenging his best friend.

This is where I was standing when the enigma started to unravel.

EPILOGUE: BETHANY REED

bethany

JANUARY 9th, 2018, 7:00pm

It's funny— how some people's stories end.

Mine began as Bethany Reed, aged eighteen, monumental disappointment but overall a good person. I was kind, I was understanding, I had friends that loved me.

I loved my friends.

And then I met Nicolas Lopez, and everything changed, and my story ended with violence and tragedy and something I should have seen coming from the moment I sat down with Marie and Poppie and Nicolas at Lauren's party five months ago.

But the most important thing— the thing I want you to remember— is that I was happy. When I was with Aiden, with Nicolas, Poppie and Marie, I was *happy*. Happier than I have ever been. It may have been a short-lived happiness, but it was a happiness that *lived*.

And that is enough for me.

AUTHOR'S NOTE

The purpose of this novel was not only to entertain and tell the thrilling story of a small-town mystery. This novel was also an exploration into grief and the way it manifests itself into different people. It was a character study of Evie, River, Benji and Nicolas and the vastly differing ways that they dealt with losing someone they love.

I wrote this as an example that sadness does not last forever, and the darkness is not infinite.

ACKNOWLEDGEMENTS

Writing this book is the single most mind-numbing, time-consuming, emotionally draining and tiring thing that I have ever done.

It is also the best thing I have ever done.

And I could not have done it on my own.

clears throat dramatically

Thank you to my mum, to whom this book is dedicated, and who was always excited about this book even though you were always wary that I could actually stick with something long enough to finish it. Five years is the longest I've ever spent on something.

Thank you to Laura, Moria, Ellie, Ruby, Alana and Kris, for being the best friends I could have asked for and for showing this book nothing but the utmost enthusiasm. Moria, your desperation to read this is probably one of the only things that kept me motivated for so long. Love you all <3. Ellie, you better not have skipped the whole book to come and read this—I'm watching you. Laura, I've known you for six years and never once have you wavered in being an incredible friend, and the most supportive person I know (I know this is probably the nicest thing I've ever said to you—but thank you). Ruby, my wife ;), you're hilarious, I love you. Alana, I adore you completely, and I adore your enthusiasm for this book, and your excitement for its release. Kris, you're never going to read this book (and that's okay, kind of), but if you ever read the acknowledgements, then hi *waves*, love you lots.

To my sister, Jess, for not once doubting that this was going to be a decent piece of literature.

To my dad, for being sceptical that this was going to be anything but a flaming mess—you made me want it to be absolutely incredible just to prove you wrong.

A world of thanks for my closest online writing friends—there aren't many of you, but you're incredible. Mya, Sylvia, Jay, Diya ofc (don't let your ego get too big but you're in this acknowledgments twice xoxo). It was an honour to have you by my side in this whole thing. Even if we never really had proper conversations, you popping in every now and again to throw support at me means the world.

Thank you, finally and mostly, to my incredible beta readers. You are the best people I could have possibly asked for to read my book and help me bring it to its full potential, in no particular order: Rosie, Amaya Crawford, Tankuare, Emilie E, Karma Alexandria, Diya (fetus I love you for being such an incredible writing friend from day one), Emma, Freya L, Madeline B, Rihalya Sivakumar, Mya and Olivia Rebhun.

Every single one of you are amazing and I could not thank you enough <3

It takes one person to write a book, but it takes an army to finish one.